DR. LEONARD COLDWELL
INSTINCT BASED MEDICINE®

CW00819187

THE ONLY ANSWER TO™ SUCCESS

YOU WERE BORN TO BE A CHAMPION

21C PUBLISHERS
READING YOU LOUD AND CLEAR

THE ONLY ANSWER TO™ SUCCESS

Copyright © 2012
Church of Inner Healing
Second Edition

ISBN 978-0-9824428-6-9
Cover: Lee Fredrickson
Book Design: Lee Fredrickson

21 PUBLISHERS
READING YOU LOUD AND CLEAR

DEDICATION

To the spirit of America! To the true heroes of Freedom, the inventors of the right to pursue Happiness!

This book is dedicated to AMERICA, the greatest Nation in the world. This wonderful country I love so much. This book is dedicated to the American people that with their big hearts and love freed and saved my family. To the American soldier that gave my family freedom, hope and a future.

This book is dedicated to the unbreakable spirit of my fellow Americans that will never saddle for anything less than what they can be, have or achieve.

This book is dedicated to the seeker of the truth—the truth for the secret to Happiness, Health and unlimited success, but most of all Freedom!

This book is dedicated to the men and women that are willing to do whatever it takes to turn their live's into the masterpiece it is suppose to be, and that are willing to stand up one more time than life throws them down.

This book is mostly dedicated to the Champion that knows that he or she were born for success, created for greatness and designed for the best life a human being can experience.

Welcome to the Winner's Circle—welcome to the successful side of life—Welcome to the true YOU!

This book is dedicated to: YOU!

Hello Champion—Welcome to the life you deserve...

With Love Dr. C. (Dr. Leonard Coldwell)

CONTENTS

TESTIMONIES

WHAT INTERNATIONAL LEADERS ARE SAYING ABOUT THE AUTHOR

D r. Coldwell's books have always had an immediate and positive impact on my doctors and their patients. They successfully move us to confront the truths behind our challenges, and how to take effective action. They are a must read for all.

—Fred Van Liew, Author *Adrenal Exhaustion & Chronic Fatigue: How To Stop The Nightmare!*

The Only Answer to Cancer and *The Only Answer to Stress, Anxiety and Depression* and this book, *The Only Answer to Success* are three of those rare books which can save your life or someone else's life and give you success on the way. Natural Cancer treatment is very dear to my heart since I was diagnosed with terminal cancer in 1994 but, through totally natural means, lost the cancer and gained optimal health through its treatment. You can, too, following the deep wisdom in this book.

The cancer establishment doesn't want you to know that you have safe, effective and inexpensive natural options since cancer is the single most profitable disease ever encountered by mankind. Brave leaders like Dr. Coldwell are dangerous to the industry that depends on your illness and your ignorance: nowhere is that more true than the multi-trillion dollar cancer industry.

Dr. Coldwell is a gifted doctor whose special gifts are curing people and telling the truth about disease—and the industry that wants to keep you as sick as possible as long as possible. His pioneering work has brought him the success and reputation to back up what he says. I believe in his new books, *The Only Answer to Cancer* and *The Only Answer to Stress, Anxiety and Depression* and this book, *The Only Answer to Success*, because I know that Dr. Coldwell's work has helped huge numbers of patients with cancer and other terminal diseases. I am proud to have Dr. Coldwell as my fellow health freedom fighter.

—Maj. Gen. Albert N. Stubblebine III (US Army, Ret.)
President Natural Solutions Foundation
www.GlobalHealthFreedom.org

"It was an honor to be able to work with Dr. Coldwell for all these years and to witness the daily miracles that seem for Dr. Coldwell just simple "normal." I have seen patients that have been on their deathbed recovering from cancer or patients with no hope. I have known Dr. Coldwell's main miracle his own mother that Dr. Coldwell cured from liver cancer in a terminal state over 3 decades ago, for many years and I have researched all of her files and data and the more I read about how sick she was with her Hepatitis C, liver cirrhoses and terminal liver cancer, and the more I read the more impressive her total healing became to me.

I have seen many patients that Dr. Coldwell cured from cancer and other diseases like Multiple Sclerosis and Lupus and Parkinson's and even muscular dystrophy and many, many more and I am still in constant awe of Dr. Coldwell's talent and results. I am so glad I could study with him personally and to learn his IBMS™ directly from him. When he left Europe, he left a huge hole, a massive empty space, in the world of cancer treatment behind. I am honored and excited about the possibilities that Dr. Coldwell opened up for me as his Master student and that he has the trust in me and my talents, that he picked me as his successor when he retired from his work with patients. "

—Dr. Thomas Hohn MD NMD Licensed IBMS Therapist™
www.goodlifefoundation.com

Research in the USA and Australia reveals the 5 year survival benefit to chemotherapy patients is 2%, that's a single week, for living in hell for 5 years! Orthodox medicine butchers, burns and poisons patient-victims and frequently shortens their lives, meanwhile their life savings are transferred to the medical establishment. Dr. Coldwell is a heroic pioneer who has delivered thousands from this fatal ordeal. This humanitarian's vital book may save you or a loved one from a world of pain. Step "out of the box" and study it carefully for your own sake.

—Dr. Betty Martini, D.Hum, Founder
Mission Possible International
www.mpwhi.com

My son is my hero and the hero of countless other people that he touched with his outstanding greatness. God gave him the special talent and power to heal. I was his secretary when he had his first office when he was just 14 years old and I saw so many miracles happen every single day. I always believed in my son and his abilities to help other people to overcome their life's challenges and when he simply cured them in the shortest amounts of time.

I know what it means to get a death sentence. When the doctor told me that I had liver cancer in the terminal state and only had 2 months to a maximum of 2 years to live, I locked myself in my bedroom and cried for 3 days. It was my own son that gave me the reason and motivation to fight and to live. It was my own son that cured me from a terminal disease with no hope of healing or survival 38 years ago. Now I am 74 years old and in the best shape, health and vitality of my life. I owe this to my wonderful son, Dr. Leonard Coldwell, the greatest healer of our time.

Even if he always says: "It isn't me that has cured my patients, they have cured themselves" I still know and insist that it was him and the powers God gave him that cured me and all the other patients. Without him we would not exist anymore!

Son, you gave us the strength to fight, to hang in and to survive. You gave us your love, trust, honesty, and your knowledge, but most of all your inner strength. In turn, this gave us the strength to believe in ourselves and our future. It was always you that motivated your patients, readers and seminar attendees to get up and fight and to get up and walk and to never, ever accept any other outcome but total health, success and happiness. It was, is and always will be for me: Always YOU!

Your loving Mother,
—Mama Coldwell, summer 2009

Dr. Leonard's books are packed with the most advanced health information to back up the fact that God heals! In over 15 years in the natural health field I've never met anyone who has worked as hard as Dr. Coldwell has, to bring the health message to the masses. I am glad to, because his message is so needed. It is no surprise to hear that stress leads to disease, but what is a surprise is not too many people talk about it on the level Dr. Coldwell addresses it in this book. If you want to lose weight, gain energy and avoid or heal disease, the suggestions in this book will bring you right on track to achieving you goals. This is very informative information in this book and anyone serious about maintaining his or her health should read it. I think it belongs in ever home! Let's face it, stress is the root cause of all disease and dr. Coldwell does an excellent job in destroying the root.

—Paul Nison-Raw Food Chef and Author

www.PaulNison.com

This book has an energy—an energy that can change your life for the better! Dr. Coldwell provides the simplest and most practical steps, complete with exercises, that you can use to eliminate the primary cause of all disease from your life. Stress leads to energy loss which inevitably results in illness. Should you implement the practical steps revealed within this book, you will inevitable suffer from great joy, vitality and a love for all life!

If you want to live a long and healthy life, open this book, follow the guidelines, do the exercises—and you will do so. Not because you get lucky —but because you are now aligning yourself AND living principles that result in optimal health and longevity! Health reveals itself to all those who are ready to live according to the natural laws Dr. C so clearly writes about in *The Only Answer to Stress, Anxiety & Depression.*

—Robert Scott Bell, D.A. Hom.

Homeopathic practitioner and nationally syndicated radio host also known as "The voice of health freedom and liberty!"

THE COLDWELL PROMISE

Dear Reader,

I promise that if you read and practice this program your life will never be as it was before. You will learn how to take charge of your feelings, your behavior and your energy so you will finally be able to take control over every part of your life.

Your future will no longer be a fearful, unaccountable and uncontrollable occurrence, lacking conscious design, but the logical result of conscious planning.

This book you hold in your hands is a powerful manual that can change every area of your life. It will help you to turn your life and the lives of those around you into an adventure, an experience, a pleasure, and above all it will offer you the opportunity to be free of the influence and manipulation of others.

With the information contained in these pages you will at last have the opportunity to use your unlimited potential every day, so you can make your life continuously more successful, harmonious, content and happy. In short, you now have the opportunity to change your life forever and to shape it into the masterpiece it should be.

Your new friend
—Dr. Leonard Coldwell

THE SCIENCE
OF SUCCESS

IBMS™—Instinct - Based - Medicine® - System™
(All rights reserved)

I have written this book with the latest information pertaining to the science of success, success training and conditioning, and with the information made available in personal motivational conditioning. Stress is simply the response to a threat, real or imagined, and the more we feel our life is threatened (whether it's financially, physically, mentally or a relationship, a job situation, or simply the need for life's recognition from our peers etc.) the better the chance that this stress will either trigger a flight or fight response. Stress is triggered when we feel we cannot fight or run away from a dead-end job or relationship and we feel we are stuck with it. The more we hate our situation or cannot stand it anymore, the more mental and emotional stress we create—feeling of helplessness—causing depression or/and anxiety. Mental and emotional stress is the main cause—86% to 95%—of all illness. Illnesses are usually caused by living in constant fears, worries doubts, lack of self love and self esteem, hopelessness and most of all lack of success in all parts of life. Anxiety is simply the reaction to stress, causing you to feel overwhelmed by life

13

itself or certain parts of life or tasks, goals etc. Depression is nothing less then the knowledge life could be better than it is right now—the feeling of losing, being out of control or simply having no hope! Depression and anxiety is always caused by not doing the right actions and not having a true foundation built on your own individual personality, your individual character traits, your common sense and instinct! Living with compromises against yourself on a regular basis is the guarantee for one or all: Stress, Anxiety or Depression. With this book I will help you to create a stress, anxiety and depression proof life! I will give you the educational tools and coaching you need to learn how to see and treat life's "problems" and how to turn them into "challenges," and I will give you the knowledge and action plans to take on this great opportunity—this great change that we call "LIFE" in a manner that will enable you to always have your individual: "Only Answer to Success."

Success comes with change

Never before have the numbers been as high as they are today for people in need of medical care due to chronic illness, or for those who have died a premature death. The death rate from cancer and heart disease is constantly rising. The reason for this is that our bodies have not yet learned to deal with the stress and demands that diminish our energy, and affect our health in a way that has neither been known nor seen before.

We must all be prepared to accept a greater responsibility for our own health and for the health of those we love. We can no longer depend on other people, including therapists and politicians.

It is only logical that there is a cause for every illness and every symptom. The causes lie in our environments, in the way we live, in what we eat and in the way we think and feel, including the compromises we make, etc. All of these factors can lead to dis-stress and dis-ease that can take energy away from us that we need in order to stay healthy. With a lack of energy our body doesn't have the necessary power that it needs to function, much less at an optimum level.

If too much energy is missing, or if energy is missing too long, the result is a logical malfunction in our biological system.

We must take responsibility for our own lives by taking charge of our health and creating a future full of vitality, strength, energy and enthusiasm.

This book is written to give you the opportunity to change your unhealthy behavioral patterns by using new information and techniques, some of which you know and have probably consciously or unconsciously already used. This book will help you to lay down the foundation for a long, healthy, happy and successful life. My **IBMS™**—Dr. Coldwell System™ is an amalgamation of the essence of all known, useful and result-producing systems with my thirty or more years of experience in health research and life coaching.

But let me warn you—this is not a book of positive thinking, it is a book of positive actions. This is a book that can help you to take charge of your life, your health and your fate, but only if you are willing to practice what you learn. Often laziness and/or ignorance are the reason that we get sick. The only way for us to recover and become healthy again is to take charge and make a positive change.

I assume that you are a winner, a doer, one of many who want to turn their dreams and goals into reality, even though you may not yet have reached that point at this time, but you will succeed because you are willing to do all that is necessary.

You would not have bought this book, if you were not one of ten percent of the people who take life in their own hands. You are not someone who counts on the government's dole, or waits for their ship to come in; you are not someone who waits to win the lottery, or waits for a sugar daddy to come take care of you. You are a doer and are willing to do what is necessary. I assume that this is not your first self-help book, and it won't be your last.

This book is written for people who are willing to put in the time, ideas, energy and perseverance needed, who are already using their skills and talents successfully, and who are ready to make a change to produce better health. You certainly deserve to remain fit and healthy so that you can become old enough to enjoy the pleasures you have earned from your hard life's work and you certainly deserve to see your grandchildren and your great-grandchildren grow up.

Successful people will not let other people, their surroundings or the weather influence their feelings or behavior; they create and develop their own rules for life, and they are willing to do whatever it takes to ensure their good health, happiness, and success.

To be successful means that you set goals in every area of your life whether you have already reached a goal or not, and you are following a path by which you can reach and fulfill your wishes and dreams.

We can excuse our failures for as long as we want; we can blame others for our bad luck and for all the negative situations in our lives, but no matter who gets the blame, it does not change the final result. Looking for someone to blame will not help in any way.

Before you waste time looking for faults or excuses, it is better to quit vacillating. Draw a line over your past and previous mistakes, over the past mistakes and misdeeds of others, over your own pattern of hesitation, laziness, and omissions. Start over, take charge and take the responsibility for your future—it is truly in your own hands. Remove the whining and self-pity from your life, it will not move you forward—it only holds you back.

In this book, I offer you a complete, understandable, easy to learn health concept that will rapidly bring you positive results. In just a short amount of time you will be able to start laying the first stone towards a long, fulfilled and healthy life.

We often hear that someone who was only thirty or thirty-five years old died of a heart attack while running or playing tennis, or we learn that businessmen or women in their fifties have a nervous breakdowns or simply crash from exhaustion. These situations beg the question, "What are we doing wrong, what do we need to do to live a healthy life, and what should we do so that we can enjoy finally the success for which we have worked so hard?"

Only when you are completely healthy can you fully enjoy life and aspire to achieve optimum success. Don't settle for somewhat healthy!

Health means the complete function of all mechanisms in an emotionally, mentally and physically successful person. Illness is an imbalance of these elements, caused by lack of energy. This shortness of energy can be triggered by environmental stress, negative behavior or thought patterns, or from deficiencies in almost any area of life.

Fitness is not the same as health; fitness is the ability to perform athletically, which does not necessarily mean that a person is healthy. People need to strive for complete health as a permanent condition, and that means a holistic sense of health, not just fitness.

Health has nothing to do with luck or misfortune, nor does it have to do with genes or inheritance. It is not a punishment to become ill, nor is health a favor. Health is the logical result of our personal conduct, the natural response of our bodies to nutrition, movement and breathing habits, including the way we cope with emotional, mental and physical stress, fear, worry and anxiety.

If we cannot handle our stress it will eventually affect our health. These factors and many others play an essential role in the developmental process of our health. If you are sick, you need to do, 100 percent, the right thing to get mentally, physically and emotionally healthy or you will stay sick. Being healthy is like being pregnant, you can't be a little pregnant—either you are or you aren't pregnant. The same is true with your health, you are either healthy or you are not!

Through modern research, we know that headaches, circulatory problems and intestinal difficulties, including other physical, emotional and mental problems, are only symptoms of illness or disease. It is not enough to treat the symptoms, you have to simultaneously look for the cause of the symptoms. If you eliminate the cause of illness, the symptoms disappear on their own.

For example, if you spend more money than you have, you must get rid of what is causing you to spend in order to stop the spending; you must find ways to prevent further spending—only then will the symptoms of the monetary shortage be removed. Therefore, you must find the cause for your illness or limited health, and get rid of the cause before you are able to enjoy optimum health.

If somebody has a headache, he can of course take one of the many headache pills on the market and hope that the headache goes away. But headaches can be the result of different causes, negative emotions such as anxiety or anger, muscle tension, poison by unhealthy food, a shortage of oxygen, poor circulation, blocked nerve passages, dehydration, and much more.

If a nerve passage is blocked and you suffer continuously from pain in your neck and shoulders, you may find that your spinal column has been drawn out of its normal alignment. Stress from your work may even be the cause of a slipped disk. In these instances, you can swallow a ton of pills without the slightest chance that the disease will disappear. In other words, you can numb the pain for a limited time, but you will not achieve any long-term change without fixing the cause of the pain.

If your finger is caught in the door, it would be foolish to take pain pills while your finger is still caught in a door. Just as you must open the door and free your finger, so it is that you must remove the cause of every illness. You are responsible for your complete cure and continued health. Only you can make the necessary changes in your physical and emotional condition. Only you can relieve the symptoms by taking away the cause.

Dear reader, this book is not going to tell you that you can become healthy with positive thinking. This book is written for doers, for those who act. In the psychology of success, we distinguish between the two different types of people—those who act and those who simply talk about acting.

This book is written for positive doers. Your health does not just happen, just as money does not fall from the sky. You put extra effort into your work and your career, so you must strive for a healthy mind and body. This is the only sure way to produce and enjoy perfect health. You have to create and keep your health!

Could you imagine yourself as successful if you were suffering from pain and in need of nursing and medical attention? I don't think so!

My definition of success encompasses total all-around success. Success must be built in every area of our life—this means health, financial success, partnerships, contentment, happiness and love. We must recognize that for emotional and physical health, we need the same basic components for happiness and success.

Success is a feeling, not something tangible. We all have a different understanding of what success means to us. To be successful and healthy, you have to feel successful! Every individual has their own frame of reference for what will make them feel successful. Only you know what success means for you.

I am giving you a set of instructions to enable you to be completely independent from that of other people, circumstances, genetic makeup, the full moon, bio-rhythms or even your horoscope. I am also giving you a possibility to take full charge of your physiological, emotional and mental health. You will never be the victim of circumstances or fate; rather you will be the creator of your own future, if you apply what you learn. You will be responsible for your own life, your level of health, and your success.

To avoid areas of conflict or the causes of unwanted behavior, limitations and undesired results, we must first recognize, define and understand them. Only then can we find solutions to cope with these challenges. Living in denial or delusions will not make anything better. You have to adjust to problems, limitations, etc. in order to change them.

I have written down all the information you need. I will be your health and stress reduction coach, so that you can become completely healthy and fully successful in life. I hope that this book will make it possible for you to use more of your unlimited potential, so that you can help yourself and others to recognize your talents, so that, together, you will not only reach the summit, but also stay there, and proclaim your own personal success in life and in health.

Our health is a lifelong gift that we can only experience and enjoy when we are happy, content, well balanced and satisfied in every area of our life. Most people know what they must do to change and how they should go about it—but they do nothing. It is not enough to know what to do, but you must act on your knowledge. This is the difference between health and illness, success and failure. It is not always the complex or the difficult that makes the difference between health and illness. Often a thousand little things, obvious facts, laziness, comfort, cowardice or ignorance are what make the difference, whether we live and enjoy our life on the highest level—or not.

People often believe that easy or pleasant things cannot be good. If medicine tastes good, it will probably not work. This is usually not true. It is, however, true that there are no isolated tricks or secrets that promise lifelong health, vitality and the expectation of longevity. There are no magic pills that can cure the common cold; five-day miracle diets do not work, nor do promises to be fit, slim and beautiful in three days. Health, like illness, is a slow process, the logical consequence of correct or poor behavior in many areas of life.

As your personal wellness and health coach, I want to show you how to quickly and successfully improve the quality of your life. If you are willing to practice a few basic essential elements, which are necessary, easily applied and executed, your quality of life will rapidly improve.

Solutions are always simple, until someone needlessly complicates them to sell you an expensive solution!

After many years of researching and testing people who work in stressful environments, it is now possible to identify and define the causes of chronic and even death-threatening illnesses. Only decades ago, we were convinced that health problems resulted from our genetic makeup, fate or bad luck. Today this has changed as we now are aware that every person has the possibility to live a healthy life, no matter what their genetic makeup.

If you do not reach your lifespan potential of 140-160 years, it is only due to emotional, mental and physiological stress, inferior nutrition, lack of exercise, poor breathing, and/or immune system breakdowns. You can avoid many of these health problems simply by learning how to cope with fear, worry and doubt.

You may have heard news about genetics and gene therapy, but I have these words of advice for you, *"Do not believe that genes predetermine whether or not you will get sick in your lifetime."* Studies of identical twins have proven, this is not so! Genetic predisposition does not mean that you will or will not get a disease. You are in control of your health; now is the time to take action and do something about it.

Notebook Essential for Reference

Before you start though, you should have a notebook handy so you can write down all of the information I give you, as well as answers to questions I'll be asking. By keeping a record of your thoughts and reactions, it will help you to develop a more perfect you. You'll be able to go over your notes and witness, in your own writing, how you truly think and feel, what is holding you back, and how you are changing over time.

Be sure to keep this notebook for future reference. Months, or years from now, you can read these old notes, and your thoughts at this time, and use them to understand your cycles of development, along with the lows and the difficulties you've faced. You will see how much you've grown, how much you've accomplished, and if you ever find yourself slipping back into the old you, you'll have a solid road map of just how far you've come—and you'll never want to go

)ack! But most of all, you have your own manual for how to control your own life and future. Be aware of the fact you cannot save someone that sinks into quicksand by jumping in after that person! You need to have stable ground under your own feet first, and then you can easily help the other person out of his or her misery! The same is true for life: you cannot help someone else to overcome stress, anxiety, depression, lack of self love, or even self hatred, hopelessness, if you have not first developed stable ground under your foundation of who you really are! So, if you want to help your spouse, children or friends, you have to start with your own life, your own foundation first! Your children, spouse and friends deserve the best: parent, spouse or friend you can be!

Answer all questions completely, even though they seem similar to answers you gave before. Also, write down all repetitions, because that is part of the IBMS™ technique procedure. It will not only help you to recognize your current programming, but also to condition the desired mental, emotional and physiological behavior patterns you're seeking. Everything you desire in your life will soon become a natural part of your thinking, feeling and way of acting.

Treat yourself and buy a nice, hardcover journal and write on both sides of the pages. This way you're mentally preparing yourself for something special, and you also won't be tempted to rip out any pages if you need to make your grocery list or write down a phone number.

Your personal success journal can help you many years down the road. By going back over your notes and seeing how you dealt with a similar problem before, you'll be able to eliminate other conflicts easier and more effectively. This success journal can also become a valuable reference aid for your children and others that are important to you.

IBMS™ Defined

To understand it well, I will again give you my definition of IBMS™ (The Instinct Based Medicine® System™.) IBMS™ is a method that will help you achieve your highest personal goals and unlimited success in every area of life, while sustaining the best possible health and vitality.

I have developed and perfected this system with knowledge gained from extensive research, as well as observation and experience gained in my practice with patients. It is a system created for personal motivation, self-healing and self-help for every area of life.

My friend, I offer you this self-help philosophy for your personal and individual use.

If you have any questions or suggestions please write to
instinctbasedmedicine@gmail.com
or go to
www.instinctbasedmedicine.com
You may also visit
www.drleonardcoldwell.com

YOU WERE BORN TO BE SUCCESSFUL

Hello Champion!

You may wonder why I call you a champion. Because you are a champion! You were born to be a winner and to be successful, healthy and happy! If you are not successful, healthy and happy today, you just lost your way along your path through life. I have never seen a born loser, but I have seen millions of born champions that simply got derailed from their path of success. Believe me, there is nothing like a born failure and there are no permanent failures. There are only results that we produce that are the way we like them to be or not. That's it, there are just results, and if we don't like the results we produced or are producing right now, we can simply make the decision to change our way of thinking, decision making and action and we will produce different results!

Failure is an event not a person. Why we so often think we may be failing in our life and are not able to live up to our true potential can be easily explained by the fact that we all have heard on average over 184,000 times up to our 18th year of age: " No! You cannot do it! Nobody can do it!" Etc. etc. etc.

Harvard University conducted a study that concluded these numbers. Which mean we were conditioned to believe we are incompetent, a loser or unable to achieve anything of meaning.

But that, ladies and gentlemen is not the truth; it is simple brain washing and negative conditioning of the worst kind. Because the very opposite is true! You, and I truly mean YOU, are born to be a winner, a true champion, an achiever of your goals and dreams and desires! Yes, and I know what I am talking about because I have seen over 2.3 million people in my life seminars and over 34 million people via telephone seminars, video or internet seminars etc. and I found the truth when I got the comments and success stories from my millions of readers, listeners, students or patients. And the truth showed to me that each and every obstacle can be overcome, every goal can be achieved and every success can be produced. The only condition to do so is to make a commitment to your own greatness and that you are willing to pay the price.

Many people think they need some kind of luck or specific circumstances or other people to create the life they desire and that is absolutely not true. All you need is you! All you need is yourself! You have carried the seed of greatness within you since you were born. You are natures or the universes or Gods masterpiece however you want to call it, it is the same energy. Name it as you like. You were created after the likeness of God, you were born to be a champion. The mathematical chance that another person will be born and be exactly the same way that you are is 1 in 55 billion. That mean you are unique with your unique talents, character traits, possibilities, dreams and desires. You are the only one that is capable of accessing and using your uniqueness to produce the unique results and success you desire.

You already survived the most dangerous time in a human's life, the nine months in your mother's body. And when you were born, billions of microbes, bacteria, fungi, and viruses attacked your little new born body and your own immune system just dealt with it without any major problems. Basically simply because you are alive you are proven to be a winner or you simply would not be here!

I have never seen a born loser or failure—but I have seen a lot of people that did let their past experience and the opinions of other people hinder their own greatness and success. Often people simply are so derailed from their true self and their own personality and character that they do not have the belief system or self esteem, self love or confidence to believe that they can have, be and achieve anything they desire. So they don't even try anymore to create the life of their dreams the life that would really fulfill all of their life's desires.

But let me tell you the truth! I know that you can be, do and achieve anything you really want. If you are willing to let the negative programming, the brainwashing, the social hypnosis and the misinterpretation of past events (so called failures or mistakes) go! We all make mistakes—that is how we learn. The only way to grow and develop ourselves and to learn what works in life and what doesn't is to try something new! Now we produce a result—good or bad—wanted or unwanted—so what it has no meaning it is just a part of life, a part of learning, a part of becoming stronger, better, more confident and successful in life. If you know what does not work you will learn from this result and you will change your approach next time—and if necessary again and again until you produce the result you wanted to achieve at the first place. You will achieve success the same way as Thomas Edison after 10,000 failures to produce the light bulb or 25,000 failures to produce the battery. An unwanted result is just a step on the ladder to success!

When we simply recognize that there are no mistakes, no failures as long as we learn from unwanted results we did succeed and as long as we are not willing to give up to work on the realization of our goals and dreams and are willing to do whatever it take to succeed we will end up being the champion we were born to be!

Honestly we are the only obstacle in our life that can stop us for good. We simply need to get out of our own way to be able to walk the path of success that was always there for us. We need to simply let go of the past and negative experiences in our mind that keep us from using our own excellence. Yes, you can whine and complain all the time and have self pity parties with yourself as long as you want to and look for experiences why you have an excuse to be allowed to fail or how bad your past and your childhood has been and that you had such a bad start and so many things in life working against you—but what does that do for you? Nothing, except keeping you where you are—living a life that has nothing to do with your true potential and what and who you truly are.

I don't want to offend you. You may have had a rough start or a rough life but, my dear friend, WHO hasn't?

So stop the whining and complaining and let go of the past. The only form of psychotherapy you will ever need to overcome the horrors of your past is to simply make the decision to:

"Let go of the past— and move on!"

Nothing is gained by looking back or looking for excuses why you have all the reasons to fail in your life. That does not help you in any way. So, since it does not do you any good—recognize that every morning is a new birth, a new beginning, a new start, a new opportunity to produce different, better, more effective results.

Every morning brings with it the opportunity to live only in the present and produce the future you desire. So why would you even want to waste time and energy on negative events in your past?

The only formula for success is: to be yourself; the true you and to use the unique and unlimited potential that you were born with and to get up one more time when life throws you down and simply be willing to do whatever it takes to achieve the results you desire. That's how simple the only answer to success is. Just be yourself, follow your instincts, use common sense and learn from your unwanted results and keep on trying until you arrive at the destination of your life as a true champion.

You do not need anything from the outside. You only need to use what God, the universe or nature gave you. You are already successful. Everything you desire, every goal you have, every dream you ever imagined is already true in a different world on a different frequency and you simply need to tune into the right frequency to make everything a reality in your own life.

It is like wanting to listen to a radio show on 99.9 FM but you are dialed into 69.9 AM. The other show is still there you simply have turned on the wrong station the wrong frequency. All you really need is to become one with your true self, your own champion station or frequency, and the success you already are, and then use your instinct and common sense to make your own decisions free of manipulation of the past or your environment.

If you understand the absolute truth that you were born to be a champion, born for success, for the best of the best and you stop making compromises against yourself and simply let the winner potential come out of you, that is ingrained into your existence, then the dirt, the ballast of the past will simply disappear. You don't need to deal with the past, you don't need to be held back by the past in any way shape or form because in your inside you are already a true champion. So feed the winner potential in you let the champion grow—believe in yourself, let go of the past, love yourself and do what you feel is right, do what you instantly know is the right thing to do, follow your instinct, use common sense and all the obstacles of the past will simply fall off and the true champion in you will emerge like a bird that is pushing the eggshells off when it is born, you will push away the past and all the elements that stopped you until now. And you are free, truly free—for the first time when you make the true decision to be yourself, to let go of the past and to never make a compromise against yourself, the true you, ever again, and you make the true decision to do whatever it takes to be successful and to stand up one more time than life throws you down—then my dear friend here is the only thing I have to say:

You are now the champion you were born to be! It may take some time to realize in your life's entirety all the potential and dreams that are representing the true you, but I know something about you that you may not have realized right now:

I will see you in the winner circle—I will celebrate with you in the brother or sisterhood of champions your life's successes, I welcome you to your true life, the life and future of a true Champion. Welcome to the world of happiness, health and success—now I know you will turn your life into the masterpiece it is suppose to be! Hello Champion! Welcome to life! Be yourself and all is good!

Conditioned Repeat and Desired Disorder

The IBMS™—technology I developed, in which the brain directs the teaching and learning, is based on the knowledge that the mind functions most effectively in analogies, visual images and by constantly expanding its area of knowledge.

In teaching the IBMS™—technology, I will first show you the whole picture and then take a step back to explain to you each separate segment of this image.

Indirect repeat is a part of the programming and conditioning, and of the disorder; the jumping back and forth between separate parts is a desired measure that facilitates learning. So when you run into a repeat, just say to yourself: Ah, another conditioning! If you run into the repeat of a theme we discussed before, just think: Good, now I can expand my knowledge and skills in this area again.

I have drafted my books, videos and cd's in such a way that they are easily understood, converted and applied by everyone, no matter the level of education and experience. Solutions are simple, until someone makes them complicated and uses them for his or her own profit. Therefore do not look for complicated, complex or expensive solutions. Always look for simple, natural solutions, because the best answer is frequently the most simple and effective measure.

Do not let other people convince you that you need their help, their system, their dogmas or even drugs to turn your life into the masterpiece you desire. When you were born you brought everything that you needed for great personal achievements and success with you. You, dear reader, were created for success!

No one has the right to manipulate you and tell you what is good or bad for you and what you can and cannot do. You are the only person on earth who knows what makes you happy, satisfied, contend and successful, and why you should do or not do something.

After you have worked through this book and applied the material, you will no longer depend on the weather, other people, circumstances, the past or anything else. This book will help you to develop the awareness that you were born to be successful and deserve the very best. It would be absurd to be satisfied with the average or a shortage. IBMS™ will teach you that it makes absolutely no sense to be satisfied with less than you can be, own or achieve.

Why should you be content with less enjoyment, poor health, little happiness or lack of love, if you can have it all by using your true potential to fulfill your dreams, desires and goals? Believe in yourself, trust yourself and discover in your peers the same greatness that they can find in you. Get ready to make the very best use of the one element that is needed to find the greatest success, happiness, contentment, love and satisfaction: the ability to become a real team player.

If you have any questions or suggestions please write to
instinctbasedmedicine@gmail.com
or go to
www.instinctbasedmedicine.com

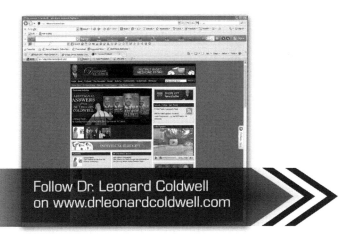

Follow Dr. Leonard Coldwell
on www.drleonardcoldwell.com

WAKE UP THE WINNER IN YOU

How do you develop a positive self-image?

It is not important what other people think of you or what they think of your accomplishments. The only thing that is important for your personal success is that you believe in your own accomplishments.

The image you have of yourself determines whether you see yourself as a success or failure. The way you see yourself, whether you are overweight or slim, healthy or sickly, a success or failure, will be all that remains in the long run.

Your life is a reflection of the constant thoughts and programming which you have anchored in your mind. This means that the previous knowledge about yourself has become a fixture, a concrete misconception of your talents and of you as a person.

If you have, due to remarks from others in the past, developed a self-image clouded with failure, if you believe that everything you touch will break or that all you try to do will go wrong, then you have developed this image through outside influence and it has nothing to do with reality.

Fortunately, you now have the opportunity to change your self-image, and you can enjoy all the intuitive physical and emotional results that come with it. To produce other results than you have up till now, it is important that you get the information of this book, so that you can change your image, your behavior, skills and possibilities.

Generally speaking, if you want to have the same results you had up until now, then you can do things exactly as you have done them before. On the other hand, if you want different results, you must do things differently.

All information and knowledge is created in the brain through neurons connecting with the aid of dendrites. This is a kind of micro build-up in the brain that looks like a spider web.

There have certainly been instances in your life when you have tried to understand a concept or problem and just could not figure it out. After spending some time with the problem something suddenly clicks, because the brain has been given the possibility to put things together and grasp the solution. When you read the problem again it is hard to understand why you did not understand it before, because the solution now seems quite simple.

The reason that you could not figure it out earlier is that certain dendrites in our brain were not yet available and only originated during the learning process.

This is just a small example for better understanding, because I want to let you know that I do not want to impress you with the two or three foreign words I know.

I am making a special effort to give you an easy to use, effective, user friendly, practical and sensible work manual, not a literary and technical manuscript in hard to understand scientific jargon. I hope you like it.

People are analogous. Simply put this means that we learn most easily when we study material in the right context. For instance, school children have an easier time remembering certain facts and figures if the information is presented in a movie, than if they have to read them in a book. You will also find it easier to absorb new information if someone tells you a story and the material is in context.

To think and understand analogously, the brain must continuously create images that offer instruction by comparing the new information it receives.

If you are repeatedly told by your parents and grandparents that you will be overweight when you are older, because everyone in the family is obese, you will develop a self-image in your mind that tells you: I will be fat.

In my experience, and from information gathered by research from IBMS™ in Canada and the USA, I have learned that the image we develop in our mind leads to a self-fulfilling prophesy. This means that if, year after year, you program and condition a certain image in your mind it will become reality.

This realization of the image we have in our mind is very evident in the ability of athletes. As you may know, I have had considerable success in the training of world renowned professional athletes. I assisted in the training of the German medal-winner Uwe Buchtmann for the world championship bicycle race in Japan in 1992. He did not train for the single sprint instead he trained for tandem competition. He had to enter the race, because several of the other riders were ill. Without training, he set a new record and won a medal.

Together, before the race, we worked to change his self-image until he was completely convinced that he had all the skills, strength and possibilities needed—as related to cycling—to produce the desired result. He entered the race with this irrevocable self-image and with total self-confidence, self-esteem, determined concentration and intense focus on the desired result, instead of on the many things that could go wrong. In the end, this new self-image propelled him to win the medal.

Several times I have observed karate experts suddenly unable to break the stones that they could break two weeks earlier with their bare hands. Ask them why they could not do it and they will tell you: "This time I could not picture the break in my mind."

So, if you are not able to picture future success in your mind, if you can't see yourself using the necessary talents and skills, then you will program yourself negatively—the exact opposite of the way Uwe Buchmann programmed himself positively for his self-fulfilling prophecy.

When I treat cancer patients, I start the therapy by first changing the patient's self-image and the image of their illness before we enter the phase of healing and training. After that we start with the conscious activation and put the self-healing and regeneration powers to work.

The many completely healed people who suffered from illnesses that were considered incurable and whose life expectancy was, according to their physicians, extremely low are the best proof that nothing is impossible if a person is willing to do everything necessary to reach the desired result.

What I am trying to say is that people can only get better and heal themselves when they no longer feel like the helpless victims of cancer, muscular dystrophy, rheumatism or gout. Instead they will start to produce images in their mind that influence their physical development, stimulating the activation of their immune system.

If you want to learn more about this subject, please read my book, "Finally, Say Goodbye to your Illness!"

Once you recognize the enormous influence a change in self-image has on the physical condition of chronically ill people, you will understand that it is even easier to bring about positive changes in a healthy person.

People who are overweight try one diet after another often gaining weight after each one and never change their self-image. They do not see themselves as slim, vital and fit. They carry the image of a fat person within and this image forges realization.

If you want to lose weight and become healthy and successful you must first do this in your mind. The success of positive thinking is also based on this premise. The changes are not the result of positive thinking but of a change in self-esteem.

If someone is concerned about his weight, and pictures himself slim, healthy and fit, he will become dissatisfied, because of this inner programming with the present situation. The desire to get and keep a beautiful body, vitality and energy becomes stronger along with the need to change, eat less and work out.

When you do not make enough money to feel financially independent and free, if your profession is not your calling and you do not enjoy it, if your relationships are not what you want them to be, you have consciously or subconsciously conditioned patterns of behavior, such as laziness, indecision and carelessness for a long time.

Of course no one wants to be sick, lonely, unloved, weak, washed out, to fail or to be a financial failure. Nevertheless, many people have installed strange images of themselves along the way.

My statements can easily be summarized. To be successful you must learn to think and see yourself as a success. Whether this success becomes a physical, emotional, or material reality is not important.

In the New-Age Movement the enormous positive influence of mental training, hypnosis (The Ericson-Programming), positive thinking, visual concentration, etc. on the development of people's destiny has been discussed. The foundation for these functions does not lie in the physical or paranormal but is found in normal neurological functions.

You develop a positive self-image by changing the images you carry in your mind. With continuous reinforcement you must make sure that the new, desired programming is correct. You must not forget that it is not enough to imagine those mental pictures once or twice. You **must program those pictures permanently; we call this conditioning.**

As soon as you see yourself in the state of both behavior of desire, when you think about a certain situation or a certain skill, you can consider this behavior pattern as conditioned. But it is wise to condition it over and over again, so that you will not lose the conditioning.

Now create a positive self-image

You must be able to see yourself as a winner before you can live a life of success.

Because the idea of "winner" is frequently misunderstood, I would like to give you my personal definition. In my opinion, a winner is someone who does not try to beat somebody else, but who tries to overcome their own inner beast. A winner combats his own worries, doubts, fears, weaknesses, laziness and all the other elements that keep him from turning his life into a masterpiece.

A winner is someone who can overcome himself and the inner voice that tells him to procrastinate and do it later. A winner is someone who can master his foolish pride, take the first step and make up after an argument, even when he know he was right. A winner can cope emotionally and physically with the difficulties of every day. He can take responsibility and therefore be in control of his life. He determines and shapes his future without being waylaid by doubt, fear and false programming.

Success will start if you believe in yourself, your skills, possibilities and talents. Please, don't forget: You can change who you are and what happens in your life if you change and take charge of the pictures you allow in your mind. If you are occupied with deficiencies and failures, those images will rule your conscious and failure, illness, fear and lack of success will soon become a reality.

Foolish remarks, like: "I knew all along that I could not do that," or "I could have told you that it would not work," always verify preceding negative programming. I am convinced that 95% of all people who live in the Western world don't have a clue of the achievements they are capable of because they have been told from an early age what they cannot do; no one has told them what they can do. Those people do not know what they want to achieve in their lives, because they do not know of what they are capable.

Let us start by putting down the basics, so that you can develop a self-image that tells, no not just tells you, but screams to you: "I can do it!"

Taking stock of your personality

I am sure that you have heard the stories about soccer stars who insure their legs and movie stars who insure their unblemished skin. I read one story about an athlete who insured his legs for 15 million dollars. I ask you: Would you like to see a pair of legs that is worth 15 million? If you do, look down at your own legs. I am convinced that your legs are as valuable as those of an athlete.

I am sure that your skin is worth as much as that of a movie star, and I ask you seriously; would you be willing to give up your sight for 15 million dollars, an arm for 10 million or perhaps spend the rest of your life in a wheelchair in exchange for a hundred million?

You will say: Coldwell what do you mean? Of course I won't! And that is the point I am trying to make.

You were born with a body that is worth billions. Think about the prize your kidneys, your liver and your heart are worth. If you add it all up, you will conclude that you have a billion dollar body! You entered this world with the most perfect tool that nature created.

Your eyes can distinguish 10 million different shades of color. Your heart pumps 6000 liters of blood daily. If we could build a building to store the capacity of your brain it would need a space twice as large as the Worlds Trade Center offered. If we used the most modern technology in the building of microchips with the same capacity of a brain, it would cost billions of dollars; need the cooling capacity of the Mississippi River and the electricity used by an average size city. Even then it would not be able to come up with an idea of its own.

But there is something even more important than your billion dollar body and that is your billion dollar personality, which can understand and forgive, have empathy and love.

When you become aware of this, you will quickly decide that

you entered this world as an unbelievably rich person with a unique personality.

You are the only person who can use this unique and valuable potential.

Why should you be satisfied with less than you can be, own or achieve? You possess a billion dollar personality, a billion dollar body and you were born for success.

It is time to become dissatisfied. If you ask yourself seriously whether your life reflects the optimum you can reach, you will conclude, just like me, that there are always new opportunities for success.

You will decide that you are not experiencing and enjoying life to the fullest and do not have all you could have. We are all falling too quickly into a mode of contentment, hesitation and procrastination; we look for excuses to postpone and because of that, we program the average and the inferior.

We must stop the slide into the trap of contentment where we say: "Oh, I am doing quite well. Others are worse off. It could be worse and I should be satisfied." Those statements make us satisfied with less than we could experience and enjoy.

If we orient ourselves downward, we head for the catastrophe of the average and the inferior. If you orient downward, you are directed downward, it becomes a habit that we approach and on which we focus our attention.

Once we allow our mind to be satisfied with less than we can be, own or achieve, we program less for our future.

The greater the goals we aspire to, the greater our dreams and the greater our lives will become. If we strive for the realization of big dreams and goals, the quality of our lives will inevitably improve. We can therefore only win and never lose, when we have great dreams and goals.

No more fear of failure

Most people have had poor experiences with the setting of their goals. They set goals they did not reach. They suffered failures, became a laughing-stock, suffered humiliation and developed an inferiority complex. This resulted in certain neuron-association in the brain. A neuron-association is a complicated word for a simple situation: a stimulus or certain information is received by one of the senses and this leads to a certain action.

If people connect in their nervous system the setting of goals with painful memories, then they will avoid the setting of goals in the future, so that they can avoid those negative feelings.

But, dear reader, only someone who gives it a try will produce results. Result follows action and only by learning from our experiences can we grow and finally reach our goal.

There are only two ways to fail:

• Giving up, by not finishing or by abandoning the action we need to reach a goal.

• Not even starting to realize the reaching of a goal

These are the only possibilities of failure, because when you do something you produce results. Statistics show that the first five trials out of six do not offer the desired results. This does not mean that we have failed rather we have created a situation that needs improvement and gives us an opportunity for further action.

Every action creates a certain result and if you do not like it, you learn from it. You know what you have done so far and now you can change and improve your work, so that you can reach a more effective result.

If you keep at it, look and work for better results then you will reach your desired goal.

When Thomas Edison was asked whether he felt like a failure after he failed 25,000 times in his attempt to create a battery, he answered: "Why should I feel like a failure? Now I know 25,000 ways how it does not work."

When Edison worked for two years fruitlessly in his search for electricity his friends left him and the banks announced that they would no longer pay his employees. A reporter asked him whether he was finally willing to give up. Edison answered, "I cannot possibly give up, and I have to succeed." When they asked him why he had to succeed he responded, "I do not believe in failure."

Develop dissatisfaction as a starting tool

When people speak about successful managers the name Lee Iacocca pops up all over the world. This successful manager of Chrysler took over when the company went into chapter eleven and the prospects of Chrysler were less than grim.

He recalls coming home one day and saying to his wife, "I don't think that I can bring the company back into making a profit." She reacted by saying, "Mr. Ford and his company, who let you go for lack of talent, will be delighted to hear that."

She put her finger on his sore spot, his vanity, and his self-confidence was stimulated with his desire to fight and win. In turn, he coined the phrase: "Welcome frustration." From then on he no longer focused on what could go wrong and might not work, but only on what he was determined to reach. He focused his attention on the solution, not the problem.

When you look today at the economic success of Chrysler, you will see what I mean.

Learn to become dissatisfied with yourself if you can put your finger on areas that are not outstanding or exceptional and do not correspond with your potential.

Now please do the first exercise.

Exercise 1:

Write down every area in your life (finance, profession, career, relationships with your children, partnerships, health, etc.) that you have taken for granted and commented, "It could be better or worse." Write down why you are dissatisfied, especially the things that annoy you.

Exercise 2:

Write down precisely how, in the above mentioned areas, you would like things to change. Write down your life as it corresponds with your wishes, dreams, talents and skills. What could be your level and how great you could be? Be as specific and exact as possible. Visualize and write down the advantages of these changes.

Learn to generate dissatisfaction and frustration, in order to drive yourself to action. If you are not dissatisfied, you become comfortable and lazy and put change off until later. You may wait until tomorrow or the day after tomorrow or next week. You will always have an excuse to do it some other time.

You do not need to be satisfied with being average or living with a shortage. Therefore, please begin here and now to take control of your life and determine your destiny by deciding how your life will be in the future.

Don't forget: you were born to succeed!

A vivid example and meaningful analogy is the story of a man who visited a friend and found him on his porch in a rocking chair enjoying a beautiful day. Beside him lay a dog, which kept whimpering, whining and growling. The man asked his friend, "What is bothering your dog?" His friend answered, "The dog is lying on a nail." Amazed the man asked, "Why does he not get up?" "Because the pain does not bother him enough," was the answer.

How many people do you know in your environment who whine, whimper, growl and complaining their difficult lives? They lament over how few opportunities and possibilities they have had, how their parents did not leave them a penny and nobody ever offered them a chance.

Sometimes we catch ourselves with similar thoughts and comments, but from now on we must work together and realize on such occasions to realize that if the pain is not bad enough to make a change and do something about it, then I must increase the pain, focus my attention and finally do something about it. Do not wait until fate might drop something in your lap.

Instead of waiting at sunset for a prince on a white horse who will save you from all the small and big disasters in life, search for a prince, buy him a white horse, send him in the right direction and tell him to take off at sunset. Otherwise, you may wait your entire life and never meet him.

And to those of you who are waiting to win the lottery—don't count on it. The chance is about the same as being hit by lightning. Those who build their future on such a hope and do nothing about their own development would not even know what to do with the money if they did win, because they would know as little as they did before. Therefore, decide now to create your own success by using your billion dollar body and your billion dollar personality. Employ your own talents, skills and possibilities with your intuition and your actions.

Either you will create success yourself or you will not have it. Luck is nothing but the meeting of preparation with opportunity. If you are not willing and prepared to accept and invest in an opportunity that is handed to you, all opportunities will be useless as far as you are concerned.

A popular expression says, "Everyone makes his own luck." That is the way it is, you don't get luck, you make it.

Start by telling yourself today: "From now on I will no longer wait for a stroke of luck or a lucky break. Instead I will take my life in my own hands and create a quality of life I deserve for myself and those I love.

Stay away from losers

Most people have no faith in themselves; therefore, they cannot realize their dreams and visions in correspondence with their natural gifts. Unfortunately, their skills, talents, possibilities, inspiration and sentiments are buried.

One of the main causes of this problem is the fear of failure. It is difficult to overcome the conditioning we have received since childhood. Furthermore, energy robbing people often stand in the way and prevent us form reaching and increasing our success.

I ask you to please separate yourself from discouraging energy robbers. These are the people who discourage you and tell you over and over: "Don't even try that. It's not going to work" or "Let it be. If it could be done somebody else would have done it already. Why do you think you could?" Those people nurse doubt and feed our insecurities with their skepticism. Their fear is caused by poor self-esteem and little self-confidence.

I divide people into two categories: appraisers and exploiters. The first group is made up of evaluators. The appraisers know how to do everything better, but never try anything. They will judge, criticize and decide, in hind sight, whether something was good or bad. They will tell you what is wrong with your marriage, even though they may be divorced five times and live a lonely life.

If you write a book, an appraiser will criticize it and tell you that "you should have done it differently" or "I could have done a better job." Even though he has not written a single sentence and sits in an easy chair he will still tell you that he could have done it better. He will gripe about the accomplishments of others. He will try to pull others down to his own lower level. He is afraid to try to do something, because he is afraid that he will fail. So that others will not notice his lack of success, he talks about everything he could do and could do even better than others, but act he will not.

Energy robbers will wake you up at three in the morning, whine for hours, rob you of your energy and strength, and when you try to do everything you can to help them they will tell you, "I think you are wrong. I think it will go better if I do it my way." If you cannot get rid of those people, you will find that they keep annoying you at any odd time and keep complaining how bad things are, how tough life is and how everyone is against them.

Remember, nobody has ever built a monument for a critic and

nobody ever will. To criticize the achievements, dreams, goals and performances of somebody else is, in my opinion, one of the ugliest things a person can inflict on someone because nobody knows the circumstances, opportunities and inner conflicts of another human being.

I am convinced that nobody has the right to criticize other people. This, of course, does not include constructive and helpful criticism. Instead I am speaking of destructive, offensive and disparaging remarks about someone's achievement, behavior or personality.

Watch out for the energy robbers who want to talk you out of your dreams, inventions, and visions of life improvements. They plant doubts in your dreams because they no longer believe in the realization of their own. You are meant to be successful and if others no longer believe in themselves it is their problem, not yours.

Therefore, do not listen when someone say, "My grades were better than yours when we were in school. If I can't do it, you certainly can't." Get used to a new pattern of behavior, and say:

"Right makes might!"

Live by this motto and make it a part of your pattern of behavior. When someone tells you: "If that were possible, somebody else would have done it already." Just say:

"Right makes might!"

When someone tells you: "I know people who are far more competent than you. If anybody can do it, it will be one of them— certainly not you." Just say:

"Right makes might!"

When somebody tells you: "You have worked on that for such a long time without getting anywhere. Why don't you just give up?" Just say:

"Right makes might!"

When somebody tells you that you won't be able to steer your partnership back on the right course, just say:

"Right makes might!"

When somebody tells you: "Your kids are not doing well in school. They will not complete their education and succeed in their chosen professions." Just say:

"Right makes might!"

Use all your strength and possibilities to accomplish your plans. All your dreams and everything you really want—your visions, the goals you imagine and the plans you harbor can only be fulfilled because you already have the possibility to realize them. Your mind will only give you the suggested desires and goals because the dreams and plans are already planted in your subconscious.

You can reach and possess everything you cherish in your dreams if you only start to use and put your billion dollar body and your billion dollar personality to work.

"Right makes might!" (or *Now is the time)*

The danger of positive thinking

Positive thinking has caused a great catastrophe in the Western world. Many people have become convinced that they only have to think positive to get positive results. This idea, of course, is nonsense.

If you want to achieve something, you must do it and not hope and wait for somebody else to do it for you. You cannot expect destiny to drop the fulfillment of your life's task, your development and opportunities, in your lap.

Just try it out. Sit down at your desk, close your eyes and visualize yourself reading your mail, paying bills and making necessary phone calls. Will your work be done when you open your eyes?

After this pitiful attempt at positive thinking and positive suggesting you will conclude that none of your work is done and that your workload may actually have increased in the time you did nothing. Your work certainly did not diminish and you did not improve personally. If you wait long enough, nobody will remember you or have something to do with you.

Positive thinking alone will not change or improve your life. Only when **positive thinking** leads to **positive action** will you have the opportunity to shape your life in the desired direction.

If you want to reach or accomplish something, you must take action. Do not wait for someone to do your dishes, clean your car or answer your mail.

Do it immediately

One way to increase your dissatisfaction in certain areas and to keep yourself from doing things is the foolish expression: I will take care of it tomorrow. You weaken yourself by promising yourself that it will be done and the result is that you get used to procrastination. You can install and condition a bad behavior pattern in a short time with hesitation and procrastination. At first you will put things off, but soon after you will not do anything at all; therefore, nothing will get accomplished.

The question is, if not now, when? Anything you don't do now may be done much later or, more likely, not at all. At the moment you should tackle or cope with an affair your chance to succeed is the greatest, because the area of responsibility is filled with emotion. It may no longer be possible to do things if we put them off to a later time.

I understand that the first step is always the most difficult one. But even the longest trip, the farthest voyage, starts with the first step. Once you have started to tackle a job and devote yourself to the work it will be only a matter of time until you experience small and large successes. The distance to reach your goal will decrease while your enthusiasm and energy to realize your goal will increase.

Program yourself to be a doer! Tell yourself over and over, "The best time to do something is now." Stop looking for excuses! Losers always have excuses for not doing something. It may be the weather—too hot, too cold, rain or the wrong time of the year, the wrong place, wrong clothes or maybe you just don't know the right people.

Everything you can do today you should do right now. Tomorrow you cannot earn interest on the dollar you do not make today. The healthy food that you do not eat today cannot help you to detoxify tomorrow, so that you will feel better and have more energy. Everything that you do not do, when it could have been done, will either not get done at all or will have a lesser result. In the worst case scenario, you might put it off to the wrong moment when action could be catastrophic. If you must meet with a person you really do not like and you keep putting it off, you may build up negative energy that explodes at the wrong time.

Therefore learn that the right time to act is now.

Let go of the past

To take charge of your life you must, here and now, be willing to let go of the past. Live in the now! Make plans for the future and start working on the realization of your plans and dreams.

Nobody benefits from complaining about the past. It makes absolutely no sense to look backward and cry about former mistakes and "what-ifs". No matter how much we regret the past we cannot change it. We cannot compensate for a missed opportunity.

We can only act in the present, so the present is where we must focus. If we were not kind and understanding in the past with our spouse or partner, if we could not talk with confidence with our boss about an increase in salary or if we could not be confident with a client, it does not mean that we must fail in the future. Every day is the start of a whole new life. Every second of the day offers new opportunities to start over.

You must stop looking back and living in the past because then you will move unavoidably into a catastrophic future. If you are driving forward in your car but keep looking back into the rearview mirror or on the floor, you will quickly cause an accident. Only when you look ahead can you steer, turn and adjust your direction when necessary.

How to program

Our subconscious cannot distinguish between what is real and what happens in our imagination. That is why you feel good when you tell a friend about a great party or how well you did on an exam.

Feelings are caused by stimulation of the nervous system. To our brain it makes no difference whether this stimulation comes from the inside or is provoked from the outside.

If you, for instance, envision yourself as giving a great toast at a wedding, being an outstanding leader at a seminar, or as wonderful teacher or chef, your subconscious stores this behavior as if it really happened.

The more frequently you envision or experience yourself as successful, confident and self-assured in a desired situation, the stronger you program this certain behavior pattern. As soon as you can see and experience yourself in your mind as extremely successful, the effectiveness of the programming will increase and will play a greater emotional part.

Not only the effect, but also the speed of the programming is determined by the intensity of your feelings; therefore, it is important to think about desired, future situations with joy, passion and enthusiasm, so that you can program them faster, more efficiently and with greater intensity.

Unfortunately, for this same reason you will also program a situation you fear much more easily, because the angst will be enforced when you have negative thoughts about it.

If you give this idea some serious thought you will come to the conclusion that you have nothing to lose, even if you do not immediately succeed 100%. For instance, if you are giving a speech no one minds if you get stuck for a moment or have to read a few lines to get back on track. No one will hold it against you if you do not sound like Dr. Martin Luther King, Jr. or Ghandi.

We all know that this can happen or may have already happened to us. We must learn to accept ourselves and others. When we have enough heart to accept that we are not perfect and that it is those small mistakes and weaknesses that make us human and endearing, we can enjoy our lives with joy and freedom in contentment and harmony. The anxiety and the pressure to be successful will diminish.

It is tragic that many of those close to us actually hold us back, even though they mean well and do not want to hurt us. They may say, "Why don't you keep your secure job on the assembly line and avoid the trials of independence? Now you know what you have, you have no idea what may happen if you take chances and rock the boat." They will paint everything in the bleakest colors and you will lose the courage to try for your desired and intended changes.

Tell your parents, family members and friends who are discouraging you: "You are important to me, and I respect you. I do not want to distance myself from you, but you force me to do so. You put a damper on my enthusiasm and hold me back from reaching my goals and realizing my dream. It is my life. I must live it as I see fit and if I want to be happy, I must do what I think is right and be the architect of my own experience. What was right and wrong for you is not necessarily right and wrong for me, so please let me make my own decisions, because I am the one who must live with the consequences."

I want to remind you here that you are the one who must determine your future. You are responsible, whether you like it or not, for the path of your life. Accept this responsibility, take control and, from now on, determine your own destiny.

You must begin to build and expand your own self-image in a positive direction. When you think or talk about your skills and talents you must do it in a positive and desired way and not with an image of failure, loss or mediocrity. Certainly you must not listen to the negative influences others!

The basic tenet of my IBMS™-Technology is that **the past does not determine the future**. When you are no longer willing to let

the past cast a shadow over your future this will become your tenet as well. Therefore, make this decision right now: From now on I take control of my future. I take the responsibility to be fully aware of all my actions and I will accept the consequences that this newfound responsibility entails.

You were born to be successful and you do not need to harbor a negative self-image. Don't forget that it is up to you, whether or not you let the meaning of other people influence you negatively or whether you remove the energy robbers from your life.

Exercise 3:
Write down the names of the people who have a negative influence on your life. Include how and why they have a negative effect.

Exercise 4:
Now write down the names of all people, groups of people, organizations, etc. that have had or will have a positive influence on your future development. Write down how you can have more meaningful and more frequent contact with them?

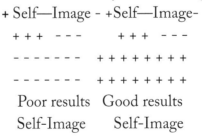

The foundation for your self-image

+ Self—Image - +Self—Image-

+ + + - - -	+ + + - - -
- - - - - -	+ + + + + + +
- - - - - -	+ + + + + + +

Poor results   Good results
Self-Image   Self-Image

These drawings represent how everyone has a bank account of sorts in which pluses and minuses are deposited.

If we have a certain success, a large or small plus is entered. A growing collection of pluses means that we are developing a stronger self-image in this area. Too many minuses mean that we have acquired a poor self-image.

If, for instance, you are asked to give a toast at a wedding and you feel rather uneasy, as we often do in such situations, and you knock over your glass of wine which runs on the white tablecloth and then onto the bride's wedding gown who runs crying from the reception, then you will enter a huge minus for public speaking.

If then, at another speech for your colleagues you burp loudly while you are holding the microphone, you turn red and can't utter a word you will enter an even bigger minus.

Now, say you had to give a little talk to say thank you for receiving an award, but you forgot your notes, stuttered and stumbled with the microphone. By this time you have entered so many minuses in the area of "public speaking" that just thinking about speaking in public makes you shiver. It might even lead to a panic attack.

You can regain the desired effect by making use of the fact that the brain cannot differentiate between reality and imagination.

You can convince your mind that you can give a speech by adding some mental pictures to the previous occasions. You can imagine enthusiastic applause and some affirmative remarks by your spouse, children and friend who tap you on your shoulder and say, "You did a wonderful job."

Or, following the example of gestalt-therapy, you can go in a room by yourself and recite, over and over again, a perfect, strong emotional speech filled with enthusiasm until you have entered enough pluses to surmount the minuses.

You are the only person who determines the images your head produces and what is allowed in your mind and what is not. The voice and sound you hear and the images and sentences you form in your mind when you think or talk to yourself have a lasting influence on your conscience and, therefore, on your energy and behavior.

If you say loudly with conviction, "I absolutely cannot do that," it has a catastrophic influence on your self-image. Develop an attitude that says, "I can do that—of course I can." You will find that such an expression has an unbelievably positive influence on your self-confidence and thus on your self-image.

Of course, you could let the words "I can't do that," sound sexy to make it irrational and silly. Your mind will reject everything that is silly and irrational and refuse to program it.

You can dismember the sentence by giving it a false accent. Maybe say it softly with a funny Mickey Mouse voice. Turn the volume softer and softer, as if you turned down a radio, until you final clicked it off completely to silence.

To avoid a vacuum you must, if you use the turn-off technique, immediately replace the message with a positive message. For instance, immediately repeat, "I can definitely do that!"

In the beginning this may not be easy and you may feel a bit funny. With practice you will find that you can install a new pattern of behavior and thinking after repeating this about 21 times. You will begin and complete a desired change in this way.

Know where to focus your attention

If you look at a play and focus on all the actor's mistakes or flaws in the set design, you will leave the theater saying, "That was awful."

Instead, you can choose to watch the same play and concentrate on everything that is beautiful and the effort of the actors to give a wonderful performance for your enjoyment. When you leave the theater this time you will feel good saying, "This was a lovely evening."

The play, the location and your companions for the night were exactly the same, but from the moment you start to evaluate a situation and focus your attention on a certain aspect, your focus and attitude will determine the outcome.

Everything in your life depends on you. You can focus on a problem and let it make you sad, frustrated, angry, depressed, and afraid, or focus on a solution and develop a feeling of control because you are in charge of your life.

The focus determines whether you feel sad and sorry for yourself or whether you get gather your strength and energy to tackle and overcome the problem.

At any rate, don't ignore conflicts or problem situations. Professor Bernhard Siegel from Yale University, a physician and best selling author, reminds us repeatedly that cancer patients influenced by the false belief of positive thinking alone who say, "I am doing okay, my health is good," will die because they give their subconscious a false sense of security. By telling themselves that everything is fine they do not take any action or responsibility for their health. Instead of activating their immune system at the time they need it most, they turn it off.

According to Dr. Siegel and Dr. Carl Simonton's, a successful oncologist in Texas, the patients who have the greatest chance to overcome cancer are those who make their bodies fully aware of the catastrophic illness that has taken hold of them. Their bodies respond to this knowledge by gathering all their strength to activate their immune system and repair the damage caused by the illness.

Learn to face the facts, define them and work on desired positive changes.

The power of believing

Believing, and not necessarily a belief system based on religion, has the strongest influence on our behavior and on the results we will produce. Our self-image and self-confidence are nothing but the reflection of our talents, skills and belief in the ability to use them.

Modern psychology teaches us that whether you believe you **can do** something or if you believe you **cannot do** something—you are always right.

The foundation for this truth lies in the structure of the brain because a belief system is merely a key that turns certain areas of the brain on or off.

If you believe that you can do something, your belief system turns on those regions of the brain that are specific for the necessary skill. If, thanks to a poor image, you cannot tackle a certain job or find the solution to a problem, you will indeed not be able to do it because you have switched off the necessary areas of the brain.

(Maybe add definition) Believing means that you are absolutely certain how or what something is. If you believe that you are an attractive, valuable human being, you will act totally different than when you believe yourself to be unattractive and inferior. Both may be wrong, nevertheless you will produce results which directly or indirectly reflect what you believe.

Belief is the result of confirmation in intellectual, emotional and physical areas. If you receive, as in the above mentioned example of public speaking, too many negative reactions, you will program the belief that you are a bad speaker. If you, on the other hand, program positive images in the manner I taught you, you will develop the belief that you are a good speaker. Both may differ from reality, but the influence on your life will be enormous.

We must learn to identify our poor and negative beliefs, remove them from our conscious and replace them with helpful and positive beliefs. In that way we can avoid being controlled by an existing inner power of which we are not even aware.

Exercise 5:

Identify the belief systems that you harbor which negatively influence your performance.

Write down those false belief systems. For example:

I am too old to start over.

I am too young, nobody will accept me.

I can't do that, because I am a woman, or, because I am a man.

I am a poor speaker

I will never succeed in any job, because I do not know enough, I lack the talent, I am too dumb, etc.

1.

2.

3.

4.

5.

6.

Exercise 6:

Now, re-evaluate every false belief system that you have recorded and, in this exercise, record why it is false. For example, if you have written: "I can't do that because I am too young" replace it with the words, "Youth means strength, vitality, power." Replace every negative belief system with a positive one.

    1.

    2.

    3.

    4.

Exercise 7:

Write down why the negative believe system is absurd and makes no sense. For example, it is absurd to believe that being too young can stand in my way, because especially for young people, all doors are open. Young people receive all the opportunities to change life continuously in many new and different ways.

    1.

    2.

    3.

    4.

Learn to believe in yourself by concentrating on your skills, talents and success.

Exercise 8:

Write down everything of which you can be proud of now and in the past. Write down the many little triumphs that you hardly remember, such as passing an exam, solving a problem with a friend, helping your children with some difficulty—anything you have done for yourself and others.

Exercise 9:

Make a list of all your advantages, benefits and talents, even those you may not have cultivated quite yet. Write down everything that makes you a valuable person. For example, maybe you are a good friend, a good listener, a wonderful painter or are a gifted musician, etc.

Exercise 10:

Now think about all that you want to accomplish in your life. Write down the talents and skills you want to acquire, build up or expand.

Exercise 11:

Now that I have focused your awareness on your positive attributes, I would like to go one step further and ask you to write a speech that someone will give on your ninetieth birthday in recognition of your countless achievements.

Even if that speech appears absurd to you, don't criticize it. Make use of it, try it out, act on it and then decide to make it happen!

Never again evaluate your own life (is that really what you mean to say? I think there may be a better way of saying this). Don't judge or criticize something you have not tried; try things out first. Try everything on your plate and then decide how it tasted, whether you liked it or not.

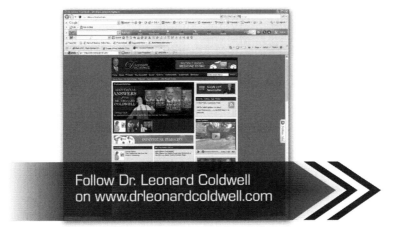

Follow Dr. Leonard Coldwell
on www.drleonardcoldwell.com

CREATE UNLIMITED FAITH IN YOURSELF AND OPTIMUM SELF-WORTH

Elements of a successful personality

Dear reader, you already recognize that failure, as well as success, is not just the luck of the draw. Both failure and success are the result of continuous thoughts, actions and feelings.

Because your willingness to work, your energy and your capacity to take risks depends on your feelings, it is absolutely necessary that you don't let others negatively affect your self-image or self-confidence.

If someone makes a remark about your skills and achievements such as, "You are not smart enough," "you lack the skills," or "you won't finish it anyway," they are really asking:

- "Is this person competent enough to achieve something in this area?

- Does this person have the right education, the specific knowledge and enough proven success to qualify for this task?"

- Does the person who asks these questions do you any good with this criticism or does their criticism harm you?

- Does this person have the information, specific skills and success in this field that makes them qualified to speak to you like this?

Is their criticism constructive or are they out to hurt you?

Is this a happy person—successful, content, well balanced, or is he or she envious, dissatisfied and frustrated?

You will quickly realize that most people who are smug and aloof and who feel that they can judge you, lack the qualifications to do so.

As soon as you recognize this, the foolish, unqualified and often nasty remarks of this person will no longer influence you emotionally.

Start a club in which you encourage and inspire each other.

When you start to enjoy the exchange of wonderful ideas and success, others will also begin to enjoy your success and help you to achieve even greater triumphs. If you want to have friends, you must first be a friend. Don't say, "I will do this for you, but then you must do something for me in return." Show others that you are really interested in them and want to share in their destiny. You enjoy their good luck, but you will also be there to give help, advice and comfort when they need it.

You will soon find that your life has become richer and more fulfilling. You will be surrounded by encouraging, positive and successful people with whom you share real team-play, and that you can help and encourage each other along the way.

You can reach everything you desire in your life, when you help and support others to fulfill their wishes.

Develop a healthy feeling of self-worth

As you have read before, I am convinced that you have a multi-million dollar body and a multi-million dollar personality. Now please do the next exercise.

Exercise 1:

Write down in which ways you are endearing and admirable. Perhaps you are honest and reliable, helpful and a good listener. Perhaps you help others with words and deeds. Maybe you have a beautiful smile and make others laugh. Be specific and write a full page.

I am an endearing and admirable person because:

Take charge of your physical appearance

Dear reader, did you ever realize the magical influence a new hairstyle has on the behavior and self-confidence of your wife? Does her behavior not change with \a new style or color she really enjoys? Does she not move more gracefully when she returns from the salon? And dear ladies, does your husband not behave differently when he is all dressed up in a new suit, shoes and tie?

You can see from those small examples how a different appearance can change your feelings and behavior; therefore, it is important to take deliberate charge of your appearance. Even at home, dress in a way that makes you feel good about yourself. When you look in the mirror you must feel uplifted, confident and improved.

Exercise 2:

Write down what you need to do to create your multi-million dollar appearance. What is your ideal weight? What are the best clothes for your life in private and at work? How do you want your hair to look?

Exercise 3:

Now write down how you look today.

Exercise 4:

Write down as clearly and completely as possible, why you want to make changes in your appearance. Don't forget: When the reasons to act and persevere are big enough, it is worth the cost.

Exercise 5:

Make use of the principle of (was this mentioned before, by this name?) pleasure and pain. Write down the consequences of not persevering. Next, what will the results be if you do make these changes? What benefits will you enjoy?

Learn to put pressure on yourself, so that you will act and persevere instead of waiting for bad luck to pressure you into making the necessary changes.

Exercise 6:

Write down exactly how you will realize these necessary changes.

At the end of this section I would like to draw your attention to the fact that many people dress well for work, but walk around sloppily in their free time. They should dress even better for their partner, who is the most important person in their life. Think about it; is it not important to dress well for your spouse?

Learn to inspire yourself

The best opportunity to destroy and break through negative belief systems is to get a hold of the unusual success stories of others.

If your brain has been given enough information about successful people at every level of society, who, despite incredible obstacles, made the impossible possible; you can also look for solutions instead of looking for excuses or perhaps not even trying.

You will develop a new belief system with positive thoughts such as: Everything is possible if I am determined enough. Everything is possible if you really want to arrive at a certain goal.

Perseverance is the foundation of all success

Chinese people have been known to water, fertilize and tend the seedlings of bamboo plants for five years without detecting any growth. They nurse a plant for five years without seeing any progress, and then in only six weeks the plant grows to a height of ninety feet.

You should keep this unbelievable feat constantly in your mind, because you can do everything right, do things better than others and still not immediately succeed. Just as the seedling that develops by growing a root system in the soil and suddenly growing into a big tree, so success can develop in a human life.

Napoleon Hill, one of the ground breakers in the science of success, tells in his work that the most successful people in the world often went through very difficult times before they achieved success. Several contemplated giving up or had already done so, but were willing to try once more when, suddenly, the unexpected and well deserved success happened.

We often hear people speak about "overnight success." For example, when hear people talk about Tina Turner and her successful breakthrough solo album "Private Dancer," nobody bothers to remember the eight years of perseverance in which she worked, gained experience, and developed and honed her skills and talents.

There is no such thing as an overnight success. In the same way, there is no such thing as an overnight failure. There are also no self-made millionaires, because all lasting success is the logical consequence of continuous thought, action, and feelings. Financial success is the result of team-play. The road upwards is not climbed alone. Many other people contribute, help and work together; they struggle and share their sorrow, because no one can produce that kind of success entirely by himself.

We can't do anything by ourselves, but if we work together everything is possible.

Learn to become a good team-player

The best and most valuable element in the building of optimal self-image, and for creating a feeling of self-worth and self-confidence, is the willingness to be a team-player. If we enjoy helping people to reach success, others will find joy in helping us and in the realization of our dreams and goals; together we can achieve far more than what we could reach on our own.

Look at the flight formation of wild geese. They fly in an angle with the leading position continuously rotating from one goose to another. Because of this mutual support the geese can fly from 70 to 90% farther than a single goose could fly on its own. The leading goose breaks the wind resistance and the other geese fly in the draft. By changing the lead no one goose becomes so tired that he can not take the burden for a while.

"Upwards together" is the motto from my IBMS™-Technology and the motto of my own personal thinking and behavior. You must seriously consider who the people are with whom you would like to share, conquer and enjoy your successful future. If, at this time, you do not know such people, you must give some careful thought as to where to find them. Think about the organizations, lectures or seminars and other opportunities that may be available to meet these people. If you do not go after the life you deserve, you will not find it.

In a TV interview I was asked, "Dr. Coldwell, in your opinion, what is the secret to success?" I answered truthfully without hesitation, "You must learn to love people."

Learn from people who have courage

Read the stories from those people, who have overcome incurable diseases, or who have overcome apparent insurmountable problems and conflicts. Read the books from Norman Cousins, Dale Carnegie or Napoleon Hill and let yourself be inspired by people, who shout at you: "Yes, you can do it." Leave the people, who tell you: "NO, you can't do that," simply behind you—with the already learned behavior pattern: **"Right makes Might."**

Stay away from those influences that destroy your self-image, such as time consuming, foolish TV programs. In those shows the hero is either in trouble or gets out of trouble, only to get in hot water again. The problem is that we are a product of our environment. Our view of the world is embossed by the images we allow to enter our mind along with the thoughts we carry, ponder and relate.

I am convinced that nobody is bad by nature, but some people became bad and mean by bad inner direction or bad influences from their environment because they had no other plans of action available.

Criminals or people who are indifferent to their fellow human beings will change their thinking and behavior completely if they are brought together with law abiding and inspiring people. After a short conditioning time they no longer desire to go back to crime, malice and violence. The original need in nature is team-play, honesty, fairness, harmony and happiness.

It is incredibly bad for your self-esteem if you believe that your destiny is determined by the stars, a full moon or the weather. Of course you will feel helpless, manipulated and no longer in control of your life.

It is the same if you believe in your horoscope. I have worked out an applicable horoscope for you, so that you never have to read another one again.

Your IBMS™-Horoscope for today:

Today is an unbelievably good day to get great results!

Your destiny offers you great opportunities! Your life will change for the best.

Because today is such a special day you have the outstanding opportunity to let go of the past for ever, so that it will never determine your future again.

This day offers a new opportunity to achieve greatness, to start something new and to perfect or let go of the old.

Now, today you have an excellent chance to start all over and turn your life into an exiting experience. Turn your life into the adventure and masterpiece that you deserve.

Today is an ideal day to fulfill your greatest personal ambitions. Today there is a great configuration of the stars, and your skills and talents are at an absolute high!

Your energy level is enormous today and your enthusiasm is un-limited. Today is the very best day to start with the realization of your dreams, goals and desires.

Today is an especially good day to exile the inner beast that holds you back.

Today is the best day to get rid of bad habits and replace them with good ones!

Everything points in the direction that you should start today with the full use of your potential. Today it would be wise to do two things that will improve the quality of your life!

Today is the very best day to take control of your life and to determine your destiny!

From today on you will no longer be influenced by others when you have to make a decision!

Today is an especially good day to banish negative people from your life, those men and women who think they know better, the ones that will exploit you, the inconsiderate and pompous people!

You will make no more compromises, starting today!

This horoscope is good for every day in the year 2007 and will work every day!

Do not waste time

Losers live as though they have a thousand years. They will do it tomorrow or put things off until the day after tomorrow and spend hours on crossword puzzles instead of working on their development and improvement. Those people often value TV as their favorite past time and spend half their lives looking at senseless, ridiculous shows.

In the future, plan out what you really believe is worth viewing. Go through the TV guide in the beginning of the week and deter-mine what news, programs and films you would like to see. Then, make it a habit to turn off the TV the rest of the time.

Winners have no time to waste

Life is too short to waste even a second of the time you could use or enjoy—time in which you could make friends or make plans with other winners.

Exercise 7:

Think of new ideas that will help you to use your time more effectively in the future.

Take one step at a time

In my seminars and medical practice I repeatedly meet people who quickly realize how many things they must change in their lives. They despair and want to give up when they become aware of the mountain of work that lies in front of them.

But all this work does not have to be done immediately; that just is not possible and would overwhelm you and undermine your strength. If you undertake too heavy a task, overload and ask too much of yourself, you will lose your motivation to act and persevere.

After you have clearly defined the great tasks in your life, you must divide them in workable stages and tell yourself to take things "one step at the time."

Don't forget: if you make just a 1% positive change every day, it will make 365% in a year.

Exercise 8:

Pick a large task you have set for yourself and divide it into small, workable tasks.

Goals for different stages:

1.
2.

A cheerful smile enhances your self-image

Enter the club of friendly, smiling and encouraging people.

It is hard to imagine the positive influence of a friendly smile on your self-image and, of course, also on your environment. When you have learned to shake hands and look the other person smiling in the eyes, you will see that the world smiles back at you. As we all know, life is a reflection of our every day behavior.

Most people do not shake hands very well. Some reach out with a hand like a dead fish; the reaction is rejection, and that has of an immediate influence on their self-image.

Meet the other person with the respect he deserves, smile and give him a strong hand-shake without overdoing it and you will find that it will change the reaction of those around you and improve your self-image.

A cheerful smile has never caused a catastrophe, an angry stare all too often.

If a person cannot smile at you, he is a grouch. He is broken in the smile department and needs to borrow yours. And never forget: a smile is a gift to others, but an even greater gift to you.

Pretend that the person you meet and whose hand you are going to shake is one of the most important people you will ever meet, and that this person will become very influential in your future development. Be pleasant, nice and genuine as if the future of both of you depends on his attitude towards you. You will soon find that this person will take an important place in your life.

Exercise 9:

Write down how you, in the future, will approach people pleasantly with a smile. Visualize and record this future interaction.

Learn to finish a job

Losers do not mow their yard completely; read a book through to the last page, or finish a job. They have such poor self-esteem that they think that they cannot be successful and complete a task.

Laziness, lethargy and hesitation play a part in everyone's life and, of course, we seldom feel like starting or finishing a tedious job. But every time we fail to start, or quit halfway, it becomes a part of our self-image because we begin to see ourselves as people who cannot bring a task to a rational end.

Therefore, you must condition yourself to finish a job and to become a finisher.

Of course, we must not forget that flexibility is an undeniable part of success. If you are doing something and have come to the conclusion that it makes no sense, you must stop and replace your work with something that does make sense.

Exercise 10:

Write down all of the worthwhile jobs you have started, but not finished.

Now finish them.

Marvelous pluses for your self-image!

The best thing you can do for a positive self-image is to do something for others. When you help an elderly person cross the street or read a book for someone who is blind your self-image increases enormously because you have done something to help someone. Winners know the joy they experience when they make someone happy.

Exercise 11:

Think of something you can do for other people. It does not matter whether what you do is large or small; it is only important that you make them happy or enrich their lives.

Nobody's efforts are futile, if they lighten the lives of others.

Know how to quit

You probably realize that it is bad when you say that you are a smoker, a drinker or a poor spouse. You may not say this consciously, but your subconscious stores the pictures of this negative behavior and these customs. This, of course, has a disastrous impact on your feelings of self-worth and self-confidence. You must put an end to this type of behavior; it will threaten your future, your health, your success and your self-image.

Exercise 12:

Write down the bad habits and behaviors you want to end. These may include lack of exercise, poor nutrition, smoking, or, perhaps, a hot temper.

Exercise 13:

Please think about the consequences this behavior could cause in the future. Allow yourself to think of the worst that could happen if you do not change this behavior.

Exercise 14:

Now picture in the most wonderful, vivid colors the benefits and advantages you will enjoy if you make the necessary changes.

Exercise 15:

Write down the reasons. For example, "I want to make and stick to those changes, because…" Become aware of the necessity of those changes.

You know, dear reader: **"You were born to be successful."** Why would you want to hold on to the behavior patterns of a loser?

The right time is now

People who attend my seminars, my clients and patients tell me repeatedly: "I will do it later, next week, next year or some time." When I ask them, "When, exactly, will you do it?" they twist and turn until they see no way out and are finally willing to give an exact date. Unfortunately, 80% will not stick to that date even though they have set the time.

Our brain functions only in the present, in the now, in a ready to act position. Everything I want to do I must do now, today because "tomorrow" has no meaning. Tomorrow means that you have wasted today—given the time away and life, as we have already learned, is too short to squander even one minute.

Exercise 16:

What can you do right now to improve the quality of your life?

Get rid of your enemies

This provocative expression means that you must learn to turn your enemies into your friends. Most people who are argumentative and vengeful are lonely, bitter and disappointed. They have low self-esteem and little self-confidence. They avoid getting hurt by surrounding themselves with a hard exterior, a rough approach, and they hurl criticism and insults. These people have usually been deeply hurt in the past, so their neuron-associations tell them: don't let others get close; it will only lead to more pain.

Learn to see everyone as a perfect human being who may display behavior patterns different from his real personality. Be willing to take the first step. Do not wait for excuses or for the person to approach you first. Why waste time and energy? Why squander a day at being angry at someone when a discussion can clear up a misunderstanding?

When the Romans occupied Jewish territory, wise Jewish teachers told their people not to fight with the Roman soldiers, hate and annoy them, but rather to befriend them, get along, do their work better than expected, ask questions about their children and their home country, friends, interests and hobbies. Soon the Roman soldiers could no longer treat and torture their Jewish slaves as animals.

You probably know the foundation of the philosophy of success: Be willing to go the extra mile.

If you want to be very successful, you must be willing to realize special achievements. You must finish everything to the highest perfection. If you clean a plate, clean the plate as if your future depended on just that job.

Life gives us nothing for free, but it will give us everything we work for. Be willing to go the extra mile, starting today.

Exercise 17:

Which of your enemies can you turn into a friend and whom could you tolerate again, even though you know you were right?

Know who your partners really are.

We all know that we are influenced by our environment. We are usually attracted to people who are similar to ourselves. But there is certainly a process of adaptation if people want to be accepted and try to adjust to the behavior of others.

If you surround yourself with people who take drugs or behave criminally, it will be only a matter of time before the risk of following this type of behavior becomes acute for you, too.

Surround yourself with positive people who have the same goals. You will notice that you will also become more positive.

When Jews came together in Israel from all parts of the world after the Second World War, the Jews from African nations had a lower intelligence quotient than Jews from the western world. After living together for five years the intelligence quotient was on the same level amongst them all. This illustrates that our development is determined by our environment.

It does not matter if you do not like yourself. If you change what you allow to enter your mind, who you hang out with and what you do, then you can change.

Exercise 18:

Which people are bad for your development and the development of your family?

Exercise 19:

Why is the influence of these people bad? How bad could this influence become in the worst possible situation?

Get in shape

You must develop your own personal aerobic fitness program because energy, vitality, health and physical strength contribute to the shaping of a positive self-image. Do not overdo it though—a heavy load is not bad, but an overload is catastrophic; therefore, you must learn to train correctly. It is not difficult to do.

Get a hold of a cardiac monitor to measure your heartbeat. Train, after a fifteen minute warm-up, for about 15 to 30 minutes at your ideal heart rate: 180 minus your age. Subtract another 10 if you are recuperating from a severe illness. Work out at 180 minus your age plus 10 if you are relatively fit.

Now slow down to cool off for another 10 to 15 minutes. You will feel strong and fit because your body burned oxygen and fat for energy instead of the vitally important blood sugar, which is the case in anaerobic physical activity that is bad for you.

Consult a physician when you are in doubt.

Your body is your most important possession and it must last to the end of your life. You will damage your organs and suffer the consequences when you don't exercise enough, eat and breathe poorly, and do not get enough sleep.

It is easy to maintain your vitality and fitness or to get back in shape, if you do not damage your health. Just follow some simple basic rules.

Remember that your body consists of 70% water and it will collect many toxic elements if you do not eat healthily and drink enough fluids. These toxins can seriously damage your health. It is important that you eat fiber and water-rich fruit, vegetables and legumes. Fruit should not be mixed with other foods and should only be eaten on an empty stomach. You can eat other food thirty minutes after you eat fruit because fruit is digested and leaves the stomach in about half an hour.

I'm sure you are all too familiar with the so-called afternoon fatigue, the unpleasant feeling of lethargy and sluggishness after a heavy, poorly combined meal. You strain your digestive system when carbohydrates and proteins are eaten at the same time. If you are unfamiliar with this problem, please read my book *Finally Say Goodbye to Illness*. For even more information on this theme, read the book *Fit for Life* by the Diamonds.

If you eat food that contains 70% water, such as vegetables, it will help your digestive track and your energy capacity. You must make sure that your body has enough fluids for digestion and detoxification.

I would like to teach you an exercise that will stimulate your immune system positively without too much effort on your part.

Our lymph system and our immune system depend directly on deep breathing and movement. Lymph fluid can only move well when we inhale deeply in our lower abdomen or have sufficient movement from exercise. If you have no breathing problems, you should do the following exercises three times each day.

Inhale for four seconds through your nose, hold the air for sixteen seconds then exhale the air slowly for eight seconds through your mouth. If you feel comfortable, repeat this exercise ten times. Do not strain yourself. If this feels uncomfortable, slowly train yourself to get used to this rhythm.

I know from experience how difficult it can be to get up out of your chair at the office to move freely, or how difficult it is to eat wisely and focus on good nutrition during a business dinner. But it is up to you to deal with the inner beast, the laziness, hesitation, procrastination and indolence and say to yourself, "Today I will eat healthy, so that I will enjoy greater vitality. There is absolutely no excuse for neglecting my multi-million dollar body. I must keep it in excellent shape."

Exercise 20:

Now please write down what you will do for your body in the future, so that you can enjoy and experience a quality of life that results from having a healthy and vital body.

Improve your behavior.

We would all like to be surrounded by correct, honest, clean and cultivated people. Many consider it absolutely bad manners if someone shows up to a lunch meeting in crumpled jeans, sneakers and a t-shirt. Although it sounds rather tacky, it happens often enough.

If you work independently or in sales, proper attire is crucial to your success. The way you approach the world is the way the world will approach you.

It is important for your self-image that you behave correctly and with integrity. Avoid gossip and the behavior that is typical for young people who are still in a stage of development.

There is no shame in reading books about manners and good behavior, or to ask how you should act in a certain situation. It is better than putting your foot in your mouth.

There is no excuse for incorrect, dishonest or unclean behavior toward others.

Take heed: We all know how we should behave, but do we always do what we know we should?

Exercise 21:

Write down how you can improve your behavior in certain areas. For instance, you may want to speak more clearly and articulately or listen to others without interrupting, etc.

WE WERE BORN TO BE CHAMPIONS!

TAKE CONTROL OF YOUR LIFE

Guard yourself against manipulators

The worst thing you can do for your self-image is to become dependent on techniques, other people, medicine or drugs.

Dependence, in any shape or form, is a sign of inferiority and has a disastrous impact on your self-esteem and thus, your self-image.

As a former hypno-therapist, I have come to realize that hypnosis is a violation against humanity. It makes people unstable and dependent. It prescribes rules and regulations and tells people how to live their lives without independent thought. Furthermore, completely strange behavior and thought processes are installed that are alien to our personalities. This process can be disastrous, because all faulty behavior has a cause. It can only be removed if we recognize this cause and acknowledge the symptoms, not by deprogramming from the outside.

Be careful, when someone says they can solve your problems, help you and cure your illness—believe me they can't do it, and you will be the loser.

You were born to be successful and the only person who can have a lasting positive influence on your life is you!

Take all the support, education, books, training, information and advice that you can use. Test it to determine if it is right for you. Then utilize what works and use it according to your own understanding, so that you can reach your personal goals.

You can achieve everything that you imagine. If you cannot see yourself slim, no diet will have lasting success. If you cannot picture yourself successful in your mind, you will have no lasting success.

Look for positive results.

Nothing is better for a healthy self-image than personal achievements, gaining specific success and great results.

An important statement of IBMS™:

Everything worth doing is worth doing to the best of your ability
To put it differently:
Either do something intelligently and well, or don't do it at all; because you will do it indifferently.

If you produce a good self-image with your success, it will be easier to cope with dismissal, failure, setbacks and mishaps. It will also be easier to turn negative energy into a positive force.

Learn to do everything you do as well as possible.

Your self-esteem and self-confidence will grow, if you do your work with enthusiasm which, in return, will produce better results.

If you have increased your self-image by working on your highest possible level and by avoiding average work and results, you have conditioned yourself to gain greater achievements and unlimited personal results.

I call my IBMS™ a success-conditioning system because programming for one single achievement does not necessarily lead to lasting results.

If someone practices somersaults and succeeds only once doing it one hundred percent perfectly, it does not mean that he can stop with his training. He must condition the skill of doing this somersault, so that he can perform at the highest level at any time he desires.

I would like to mention once more that success and failure are not overnight phenomena and are never the result of a one time effort, whether good or bad.

Programming must be repeated regularly in order to become conditioned. Neither motivation nor success will last without active involvement. You must have a shower or take a bath daily to stay clean.

Learn to communicate
Most misunderstandings and disappointments arise out of poor communication.

Few people know that only 7% of communication is actual talk; we communicate 38% just by the tone of our voice and 55% with our physiology.

If we want to communicate well, we must learn to breathe deeply and avoid speaking with a nasal or raspy sound. We must learn to make the right gestures or, as I like to say, you must learn to "walk your talk."

We must learn the skill to really open our mouths, so that the words do not stick in our mouth and can be really understood by others.

The emphasis must conform to the language of the listener, but don't overdo it when you speak with someone who has less education. Also, avoid using slang or clichés with a person who is very well educated. If the person you are talking to has a preference for certain words, use them. If you establish a good rapport, the person to whom you are talking will relax and be more willing to give you information; it does not matter whether the material is of a physical or intellectual nature.

People absorb and work through information in different ways. If somebody receives communicated material visually, he forms images in his mind. If you deal with a visually oriented person, accent the appearance of a product. For example, "Look at the great color of that car. Do you notice the chrome work? Isn't the interior fabulous? Wouldn't your wife/husband like to take a ride in the mountains with a great car like that?"

If you are to sell a product, you must use both internal and external features to get the interest of a potential buyer.

If you deal with a person who is more of an auditory learner, you must point out how quiet the engine sounds and how softly the doors close. Let him or her know that from the inside of the car you can hear the songs of the birds and also enjoy the beautiful sound of the stereo.

Some people relate to things in a more tactile manner. They are the kind of people who like to do things "hands on." They want to get the feel of the car. Let the buyer get sit in the seat, adjust it and feel the shape of the steering wheel. You should point out the comfort of the upholstery. Remind him of the joy his wife will experience when she drives that car and how she will hug him for making such a terrific choice.

With a little practice it is relatively easy to identify the group to which someone belongs. Visual people speak in pictures. They may say, "I see that differently" or "I have a clear picture of this situation." Visual people often speak quickly and, often, with a slight nasal sound. They are cheerful, burst with energy and they get right to the heart of the matter.

People who are auditory will say, "That sounds good" or "That rings a bell." Harmony and the sound of a voice are important. These people are often well-balanced and stable. They breathe from the center of their body—the upper area of their abdomen. Visual people, on the other hand, breathe from the upper area of the chest and the shoulders.

Tactile people will tell you how something feels. They experience either a good or bad feeling. They are calm and speak slowly to make themselves clearly understood. They breathe deeply and their bodies are relaxed. They use the lower part of their body and are often slow in their movements.

If you learn to communicate well and effectively, you will produce greater success on a higher level than you now believe possible.

Of course, one could write a book about effective communication alone. For more information, please look at the books we have published about this subject or attend one of our IBMS™-seminars.

Develop the wisdom to ask for help

Nobody climbs to the height of success by them self, but many people fear to ask others for help, while they see it as a weakness. This is of course nonsense; if you had a broken arm or appendicitis you would not hesitate to go to a doctor. Why would you not ask for help in other areas?

If you are willing to help, you should allow yourself to ask for the help of others; this does of course not mean that you should abuse the practice. You would pay the price and end up lonely, bitter, angry and friendless.

If there is something you do not know, go to somebody who does. If there is something you cannot do, ask somebody who can do it for you, or who will tell you how to do it. Learn early to become part of life. Develop the willingness to help others and to ask for help.

Exercise 1:

Who can you help to reach their potential, and who can you ask for help?

You will only have those boundaries that you set for yourself.

The only borders to your human potential are those you set yourself.

People sabotage themselves without realizing it, as soon as they threaten to surpass the example, which they tried to emulate for a long time. They can not pass the man in whose footsteps they follow.

Set your sights far enough, then you will not exceed your limits.

It is not important what others say about you; it is important what you think about your own skills and possibilities. If you believe that you can achieve something, you will be able to realize that.

Do not emulate a follower

Several success trainers and systems are spreading the message that you should pick an example and follow the actions and behavior of someone else, so that you can produce the same results.

This thought process is absurd from the start, because everyone deals with different situations and has a different starting point. You are unique and do not need to follow the life of somebody else.

The foundation of every achievement is the recognition that we must follow our own goals in correspondence with our own skills and talents in the development of our own path of success.

A man, who weighs 140 lbs. and dreams of becoming heavy-weight champion of the world and trains as enthusiastically and determinedly as possible, will probably be knocked out in a few seconds, if he enters the ring and tries to fight a heavy weight boxer.

A good trainer is usually not the pupil of a guru or dictator; a good teacher must find his own way and develop a system in which he must use what others have taught him in combination with his own thoughts, knowledge and experience. If someone merely takes a shortcut or uses a pseudonym, while using a system of someone else, he will never surpass the person in whose footsteps he is following. Therefore every student must, during his development, become his own teacher.

If someone wants to sell you on the only system he calls true and edifying, you would know immediately that this person does not accept and respect your personality, individual skills and possibilities. Every radical system or believe is basically wrong. Nature itself is never is never extreme, it does not offer only black and white, but it gives us a tremendous array of colors with many blending shades in between. It would be absurd to rely on only two colors or even worse, only on gray.

A system, that supposedly functions by itself, solves your problems and offers you success without your active participation, should be dismissed as nonsense.

There is only one system that will offer you success; it is your own system. I have learned to classify those people, who consider themselves as masters in their field and the greatest teachers of our time, as dangerous crackpots. They frequently try to use the fame and success of others, who may have already died, and ride on their coattails. They do not have enough self-esteem and self-confidence to develop their own concept; I do not believe that they would make a good example for others.

I would like to give a small example of the teaching we use in our IBMS™-Training to demonstrate what I mean. The people, who work as IBMS™-trainers are exclusively chosen and trained by me in the basics of IBMS™-training without any influence of other training or instruction. The personality of the future trainer is taken in account and I do everything to assure that he maintains, builds and expands, from the beginning of his training, the foundation of the IBMS™ for the conditioning and development of his success, motivation and health-training, so that he can continue his grows as a person and trainer in the future.

Dear reader, I would like to remind you once more of my books, tapes and videos, directions and tools; they will help you to produce personal achievements and unlimited success in every area of your life. But you must do it in your own way with the use of your own true potential, employing your skills, possibilities and strength.

Only you can dream your dreams, only you can treasure your wishes and goals, and work on their realization. But I promise you that your quality of life will improve continuously, if you are willing to take this path, if you are really willing to take your life in your hands and determine your own future. You will no longer be helpless, depressed, frustrated or sad, without knowing at the same time that you can work yourself out of this negative situation.

There will be setbacks and adversity in everyone's life; we have to learn to cope with them and put them behind us. Our grief cannot change the death of a loved one, all our moaning does not bring back the money we lost in the stock-market, and all the self-pity will not improve our life.

Allow yourself time to be sad and mourn, but set yourself a limited amount of time and don't persist in mourning; plan to live an active and positive life again.

You have the right to feel dispirited, sad, lazy or frustrated, but keep it within limits.

It is conspicuous that losers are always ready to blame others for their personal mishaps or failure. Winners on the other hand always make the best of a poor situation and try to get quickly back on a desirable track.

Frequently we behave in a certain way without asking ourselves why, we do it because others did and we are not aware of the sense and reason.

We must learn to remove our blinders and look objectively at our life. We must inspect our behavior critically and ask ourselves whether we live sensibly and effectively.

I would like to explain here how you can gain this objective in a simple manner.

Think about a situation that causes you much difficulty, you do not quite know how to cope; you feel insecure, fearful and helpless and you think that you are not up to the task.

Exercise 2:

Answer the following question: What would you advice your best friend or girlfriend to do, if they were in a similar situation?

With this exercise you distance yourself from the conflict; you can be more objective and it will be easier to solve the problem.

There is a second possibility to get an overview of your situation and find possible solutions relatively free of negative emotions and fear. Pretend that you are in a movie theater and look at your present live; you are the director and try out different variations and possibilities. Play the solutions you like best and play them 20 to 30 times on the screen. Now turn of "your movie" and use your eyes and ears while you "experience" the situation as it would be in real life.

In this way you condition and program a new behavior pattern. A situation can be conditioned by only thinking about it and seeing and experiencing yourself immediately in the desired behavior.

If somebody, for instance, conditions himself to quit smoking and sees himself in his mind still as a smoker, who is trying to quit, the program has not yet been conditioned. Only when he sees himself in his mind as a non-smoker has he reconditioned himself and now he no longer needs to cope with withdrawal symptoms and other problems of addiction.

Disastrous developments are the result of compromise

If you want to damage your sub-conscious you only need to engage in compromise. You will of course object and say: "But life is nothing but compromise, we have no choice."

My answer: "No, do not make compromises, life does not demand compromise.

The definition of IBMS™ (Instinct Based Medicine System) says: "A compromise is something you do not want to do, but somehow you feel forced to do anyway." If you have a job and you do not enjoy it, there is little promise for the future. But if you keep hanging on, because you believe that you can't find something else and that you should be happy that you have a job at all in this bad market, you compromise.

With such behavior you give your sub-conscious the unadulterated message that you are not good enough to go your own way and find a job you can enjoy as much as if it were a hobby. Through innumerable small compromises, when you are annoyed with your boss, your co-workers, and the arguments you had with clients over a certain product, you surrender so much of yourself-esteem and self-confidence that your life has become one huge compromise. The result is that you will make compromises with your spouse, in your friendships, your health, the education of your children, your clothes, and finally in the quality of your life

You can of course condition the negative, destructive behavior of a loser as well as the positive, intelligent behavior of a winner.

About seventy to eighty percent of the people suffer chronic illnesses as a result of compromise.

On the basis of my research in health issues, my work for IBMS™—Research International, and with Coldwell Productions and Research in Canada, I have become convinced that cancer is a result of compromise.

Other factors play, of course, also an important part, such as thoughts of self-destruction, resignation or fatalism after some serious set-backs.

I want to clarify this. Many people think that they have made a compromise, when they have decided to work an hour longer every day, because they want to earn extra money to buy something special for a child's birthday, or because they want to send a child to private school. That is of course no compromise. If you make voluntarily a clear decision and when it is up to you whether to do something or not, it may be a sacrifice but it is not a compromise.

If you want to take your spouse to an Italian restaurant, even though you would rather eat Chinese, it is not a compromise. You know that your spouse would gladly go to a Chinese restaurant to please you.

Exercise 3:
Write down all the compromises you make in your every day life and become aware of the many things you do and have done, because it was expected by others. Recognize that you do those things, because other people did it or made you do them, even though you prefer not to do those things and do them anyway.

Exercise 4:
Now decide whether the things you wrote down are indeed compromises or voluntary commitments you gladly do for others.

Exercise 5:
Write down the worst that could happen, if you continued to make these compromises. Compile the frustration and pain, so that you can generate the pressure to do something about it and thereby realize a better quality of life.

Exercise 6:
Write down how much lighter and freer you already feel and how

much more energetic, healthy, happy and vital your life will be, if you no longer compromise.

Dear reader, this is your life and you must take care that it will really be yours from now on.

Perhaps you may want to use my philosophy:
Never let someone blackmail you.
Never sell yourself.
Never compromise at your own cost.

This is how we are manipulated

Did you ever pay attention to the manipulation of advertising? Did you ever feel really thirsty after a commercial about drinks?

The more you are aware of the danger, the easier it will be to resist. The better you know how manipulation works, the easier it will be to recognize and avoid.

Think about a typical commercial of cold drinks. It is hot, the people around you are perspiring and suddenly you remember the last time you were so unbelievably hot, and how incredibly thirsty you were. You begin to associate with the people in the commercial, because you have been there before. You hear the lively music and look at the lovely beach with happy, athletic, healthy people, who are drinking the stuff they are trying to sell you from ice-cold bottles that will deliver you from all evil.

First they show you a suffering with which, drawn automatically from your sub-conscious, you identify easily, then they show you how you will be fit, healthy and fresh, with all discomfort forgotten, if you only drink their elixir.

In this way they install in your sub-conscious the neuron-association: when I am thirsty, am hot and perspire, my salvation lies in that drink

To avoid this type of manipulation, you only need to evaluate the information in a different way the advertisers intended.

If you see a chocolate commercial, look at it ooze and imagine an awful, repugnant smell.

You can, when you look at people happily licking an ice-cream cone, imagine them getting fat and unsightly.

The most important statement you can make is the following:

Nobody can influence my behavior, feelings and programming if I don't let them.

We are who we are by what we allow in our mind

Nobody has power over us, if we do not give them the power.

Realize that it is the same power implied by sorcerers in countries where people believe in Voodoo.

Certain peoples have, during their cultural development, acquired a belief in the magical powers of shamans, witch doctors, voodoo priests and sorcerers.

Because this believe-system is fully installed in the minds of the people, the voodoo priests can use it in the way they want.

The voodoo practitioner will clearly state and install ahead of time the suggestion of the intended pain, medical decline or even death in the victim, and in this way determine his fate. The methods used in giving this information with voodoo dolls and other signs are well-known by the patient.

We of course recognize the absurdity of believing in the negative influence of magical powers on someone's life. But there are plenty of people who do believe, because they are early in life conditioned to believe such nonsense.

If you have a good self-esteem, you won't become a victim of such nonsense, because you'll know that you alone can have a lasting influence on your life, your body, your health and your abilities.

Hypnosis functions in a similar way. It works by focusing the mind on self fulfilling prophesies without giving the person an opportunity to develop and realize his self-image. Those so-called prophesies are then programmed and conditioned.

I want to mention again: You do not need other people for the programming and conditioning for what you think is right in your life.

Relaxation techniques, breathing exercises, and other measures to unwind usually make sense, but everyone must find out for himself what is good for him.

We have created the IBMS™-programming condition to help those people, who come to us for separate training, so that they will have an easier time to program and condition effectively. We help them to relax completely in only a few seconds. The more a body relaxes the freer and clearer the mind becomes, so that all the available energy that is otherwise used by unneeded physical functions is now available and the person can concentrate at the highest possible level to find the answers to certain questions.

An IBMS™-trainer will never answer the question: "What would you do in my place?"

He will not answer, because it would entail a form of manipulation, and every form of manipulation is strictly forbidden in IBMS™-training.

Exercise 7:
Portray how you will deal in the future with manipulative attempts from your surroundings, advertising, etc.

Learn from successful failures
If you really practice and put everything you have read and learned in this book into action, the quality of your life will continue to improve. As a result some people, who are envious or critical, will appear. They will try to ignore your success or ruin your pleasure.

Remember:
The world laughed at the Wright brothers, when they maintained that they could build a machine that could fly. But the world applauded when the Kitty Hawk lifted up into the air.

Small minds laughed when Thomas Edison told them that he would make a light bulb, but great minds applauded when the flick of a switch lighted up a town.

People laughed as Alexander Bell worked to make a cable through which he could send his voice, but everyone applauded when he made his first telephone call and gave the gift of communication to the entire world.

Remember:

Small minds may laugh, if you dare to go your way, but the people will applaud at the finish line when you arrive as a winner.

Therefore I dare say:

We will meet at the summit!

DETERMINE YOUR OWN DESTINY

The psychology of success

I have developed a three part seminar for this theme, because many people find it difficult to use these ever so simple functions and activities.

Years ago we believed that people's breathing, gestures, expressions and muscle tension were more or less in agreement with the way they felt. But we now know that just the opposite, a person's feelings result from his or her behavior. To feel really miserable, depressed, frustrated, inferior, weak or helpless you only need take on the corresponding behavior: speak slowly, slump your shoulders, let your head hang, look down and breathe shallowly. If you hold such a posture for a while, there is a good chance that your thoughts turn to bad things that either happened in the past or may be happening now, or could even happen in the future. You will begin to feel utterly miserable, and if you stay much longer in this psychological situation, the feelings of depression, helplessness, frustration and depression will increase.

Now every time you fear a certain task you will let yourself fall quickly into a physical condition that demands sympathy or you will show helplessness and weakness; others will avoid you and you now have an excuse for not functioning at this point in time.

Whenever you let your body go, you will quickly feel that way, because there is a so-called cybernetic exchange, through which physiological use and the emotional conscious influence one-another.

If anyone has conditioned themselves to give up in certain difficult situations, or carry a sign that says: "I can't do it," this pattern of behavior will soon become an automatic conditioned pattern that will quickly run its course. I am convinced that 98% of all depressed patients—those who do not suffer from an organic brain dysfunction—did nothing more than take a flight inward and have lost control of their direction.

There are, moreover, many people, who consider their helplessness as something positive and feel quite comfortable with their illness and lack of competence. They are getting attention, do not have to work or take care of others and they get the love and consideration they crave.

I hear all too often from patients, who are on the way to recovery that no body cares anymore and that they preferred the time when everything seemed nicer and easier.

At Irvine University in California they did the following research with depressed people:

The patients were told to sit upright, breathe deeply and forcefully, relax their body and lift their head and eyes while they focused on an object slightly higher; they furthermore had to put a broad smile on their face.

They concluded that none of the patients could feel depressed after twenty minutes in that posture. Nobody could feel depressed about a situation that had seemed so bad, if they kept an upright posture, continued to smile and breathe forcefully.

This teaches us that we are not tired, frustrated, and depressed because we feel bad, but that we feel bad because we ask for it with our physical behavior.

Therefore we must learn to live our life as a winner, to live it to the fullest and to enjoy it.

In my **"You were born to win"** seminars I ask the participants to sit up straight, smile, make fists and hold them up in the stance of a winner in the ring who just knocked out his opponent, they may even want to jump up and yell: "Yes" or "Hurrah!" Every participant is surprised that within three minutes they are no longer tired, frustrated or depressed, but instead feel strong, enthusiastic, energetic and full of vitality.

To enforce the effectiveness and to imprint the experience in their sub-conscious, I ask every participant to stay in this posture, keep smiling and look at the others attending the seminar and say in a loud and friendly voice: "My life will definitely be successful."

We must learn to live our lives in the psychology of a winner, experience and enjoy it.

By doing this, the people attending the seminar are made aware of their words by doing those rather ridiculous things, and the next time they feel like complaining by telling others that they just can't do something, they are reminded of their silly behavior at the seminar and will remember that they were born to be successful.

In my seminar, "The Behavior-Patterns of Success." the highly qualified participants, such as top-managers and business leaders walk grinning through the seminar hall as if they were royal musketeers on parade.

It is, of course, difficult for the participants to do what I ask them to do in the first ten minutes, but after a little while everyone has found out, simply by trying it out, that they can take control of their feelings, their thinking and behavior, the use of their energy, vitality and strength, if they are willing to try out what I propose.

In that way we move along aware and assured of victory, and every participant becomes stronger and more confidant, feeling better and assured, while they walk through the hall.

When we all sit down, feeling as if we own the world, as if we could achieve everything we have planned and want to do, we all feel that from now on we are in control of our life, our feelings, thoughts and behavior and therefore over the results we produce in our lives.

When the participants of a 6 to 18 hours seminar have learned to put themselves in the psychological condition and movements of a winner, they will take the attitude of a winner and begin to tackle their work with enthusiasm, passion, joy and energy and they will summon all the perseverance they need to fulfill their tasks.

Many of the fellows, who attend my seminars, are amazed, fascinated and intrigued how simple it becomes to solve problems and how easy it is to get terrific results. They have done it all before, but they either did not know exactly, use, or perhaps even forgot to make perfect use of the tools, possibilities, skills and talents nature gave them.

The IBMS™ does not really give you something new, because everything you need to be successful and happy in your personal achievements, you already possess since birth.

You were born to be successful and you are meant to make your life the masterpiece it deserves to be. You must have the attitude of a winner, you must behave, move and breathe as a person who knows that they can pursue their dreams and achieve what they want.

Be big enough to do the following exercise and experience how easy it is to gain control of your energy and your feelings—even at the risk of making a fool of yourself, if others are watching you.

Take a chair and sit upright. Breathe strongly and deeply into your lower abdomen and up under your shoulders. Tense your muscles pleasantly, perhaps open and close your fist, bring a winning smile to your face, look forward and perhaps slightly upward, now stand up forcefully, and while smiling take a step forward and say loudly: "Yes, I am alive, I can do it, I can succeed." Hold up your fist like a winner in the Olympics and call out, "Yes, I am born to be successful." If you really do this exercise, dear reader, you have your destiny in your hands. From now on nobody and nothing can stop you and take control of your feelings and your behavior.

You will feel as you behave. The word "Yes" triggers positive reactions in the immune-system that can be chemically measured. Be big enough to say "Yes" to life. "Yes" to success. "Yes" to your future. "Yes" to team-play. "Yes" to happiness. "Yes" to love. "Yes" to harmony. "Yes" to financial freedom and "Yes" to health.

Now put your book aside for a while, strut through the room as a hero, an adventurer or a winner in the Olympics. Lift up your arms, clench your fists, stop a second and shout, "Yes" while you tense up slightly, breathe deeply and shout "Yes" again. If you do this three or four times, you will feel your energy increase drastically, and if you do this twenty times in a row, you probably will need four hours of sleep less in the coming night, while you are completely enthused about yourself, your life and your possibilities.

You take control over your life, when you take control of your physiology. If you sit up straight, look confidently, and are sure that you can achieve what you attempt and know that nobody can stop, hurt or defeat you, you will feel in a short time a feeling of confidence and the strength to persevere.

If you have to make an important telephone call, sit down first in the right posture, and don't let others get to you with a negative influence. Don't slump in your chair, and don't let your facial expression become sad, helpless or frustrated, so that you will start to act as your feelings and expression suggest.

If you have not done the exercise as I suggested, you will think: This Dr. Coldwell guy is nuts. But if you did do the exercise, you will know that you had a remarkable influence on your energy, your feelings and, as a result, on your behavior. You know that nobody can take this away from you.

Be aware of your behavior, how you sit, stand, speak and breathe, whether there is somebody you fear, or whether you feel insecure. Make, in comparison, a picture in your mind of a situation in which you were very successful, won a competition or when you were completely confident; where did you sit or stand, what did you say, how did you move and breathe, how did you act? You now have a prescription for the use of your psychology.

Exercise 1:
Please write down what this exercise taught you and how you can use this information in the future.

Internal representation and communication

Internal representation and communication sounds quite complicated, but only demonstrates a rather simple and completely natural way of functioning. Whatever happens in our lives is neutral in value, and has little meaning, until we give it meaning; then our feelings give the situation a certain value. It all depends on the value we give something, whether we look at it positively or negatively, do we see it as a challenge or a blow, do we use it to develop and grow or do we let it destroy us.

If we are deserted by a spouse or partner, we can focus on everything we have done wrong; we can blame ourselves for our mistakes, for the things we should have done, and thereby get an inferiority complex. We can feel sorry for ourselves and become angry, feel helpless and frustrated. We may think that we were the guilty partner and become lonely as a result. We can also, as I advised one of my patients, stand at our front entrance, stretch out our arms and shout: "Next please!"

With that attitude we learn to place our attention on new opportunities. We can torment ourselves with destructive thinking or simply say: "Thank God, that makes room for another person."

Every situation has value or has a feeling of neutral, until you evaluate it in your mind.

It is the same with the tasks that lie before you. If you have to talk to someone and you consider this conversation in your mind as very difficult, you will allow a feeling of helplessness and you will fear that you do not know enough or that you might express yourself poorly. The results of your thinking will show themselves quickly.

If you evaluate, through your inner presentation, a situation as being positive and if you believe that this conversation will open up new opportunities, you will enjoy letting the other person know the ideas and possibilities that are open, and you will enjoy telling that person about your skills and talents.

My great colleague, Dr. Wayne Dyer said one time: "No matter how thin you slice it, you always have two sides." That is so true. There are always at least two possibilities and two ways to look and evaluate every situation.

You can look at the losses of your company as a challenge and grasp the opportunity for further development or obtain a better position; it will help you to work with enthusiasm on gaining a better future.

If you see the situation, on the other hand, as a hopeless disaster, you will approach the task as a thankless undertaking.

Does it make any sense to say when something happens that you cannot change: "If I only could have done something, or "What would it be like if it had worked out differently?"

It only makes sense to look back if you want to analyze what happened, so that you can learn from it and do it better the next time or not do it at all. Once you have filtered out all the information, do not waste another minute on what happened in the past.

Look ahead, it does make sense. Look in every situation for solutions and always ask yourself, "What is good, what do I see when I look hard enough?"

You can react to the waste at your place of work by responding: "I will be constantly challenged to change my life, to think, to organize and rearrange. I have new opportunities to be creative, make positive changes and realize my talents, skills and dreams."

Exercise 2:

Think about difficult situations in the past and present that caused you emotional problems. Write down which benefits could be drawn from it, if you wanted to see it that way.

The quality of our life depends on the quality of the communication we have with our self and our surroundings.

The power of flexibility

The difference between human beings and animals rests on free will, on the possibility to think things over before making a decision, and on flexibility.

Flexibility is the greatest strength we possess and it helps us to develop further continuously, so that we can reach our goals even after several failures, thanks to the experience we have gained.

We have all observed a fly that keeps hitting the window without learning that he can't go through the glass. The fly flies with full impact and strength against the class, without hitting on the idea to look for an open window or try it in a different way.

There are, of course, many people who behave like flies and repeat the same pattern of behavior, even though they do not reach their goals with the results they produce.

What it amounts to is this:

> If you want to keep achieving what you have so far achieved, you only have to do exactly what you did before. If you, on the other hand, want to improve your life and get better results, you must do things differently from the way you did them before.

What was good for the last ten or twenty years is not necessarily good for today—certainly not in every facet. Everything evolves, and so must we. We can no longer adhere to the fundamental principles of Napoleon Hill, Dale Carnegie or Earl Nightingale, even though they were, twenty to thirty years ago, the gurus of success-training.

I do not want to diminish the excellent principles of their fundamental research. The personalities and achievements of these men were remarkable, and I fully endorse them. But new developments have been made by Og Mandino, Dr. Wayne Dyer, Zig Ziglar and many others.

Nobody wants to undergo heart-surgery with the methods that were the newest and the best fifteen years ago. For the same reason, we should not lean exclusively on the information and technique that was the newest and the best twenty years ago.

We recognize losers by their extreme inflexibility; they refuse to accept change, because they feel they cannot handle and control change.

The more foolish someone is, the less flexible that person will be. They will repeat for the rest of their life, mercilessly and in the truest sense of the word, what they have learned before—without considering their losses.

If we focus our attention on the possibility that we have the power to change our decisions at any time, we develop the ability to change our inner representation and communication, thereby improving our self-confidence and self-esteem, our willingness to act and persevere.

Always ask yourself, "What can I do to profit from this situation?" "What can I do to reach my goal?" "What are the better elements in this situation?"

Exercise 3:
Think about what seemed a negative situation in your past or present and think what might have been good in this case? What can I learn from this? Write it down.

Conversations with yourself
The person with whom you communicate most frequently is you—you do it with your thoughts, with images, but also by what you say and do with your body.

If you want to make changes in your feelings and behavior, you must make changes in what you allow to enter your mind. The most important elements are your thoughts and the conversations you have with yourself.

The brain is by nature a machine of questions and answers. It asks in every situation: "What is the meaning of this? "What should I do? "What does this do for me: Will it bring me joy or pain; will it be good or bad? How should I react?"

To react intelligently, the brain searches for analogies and similarities. If you, for instance, made the right moves with your car, when you were in a dangerous situation, you can now do it again as you did before.

If you have learned to react by putting your hands over your eyes, you will most likely do the same.

It is therefore important to live with self communication that says:

"Yes, I can do that!"
"Of course, I can do that!"

If you find yourself in a new, difficult situation and say to yourself: "I know, I can't do that, I can't possibly complete this job," you have pre-programmed yourself with this art of self-communication to feel and behave negatively. Your actions, or even the lack thereof, will be average or nil.

You have nothing to lose when you tell yourself: **"Yes, I can do that, yes I can."** The worst that can happen is that you become a failure in your own eyes, but even then you would have produced better results, than if you had told yourself: "Of course, I can't do that," and then did nothing.

With positive self-communication and confidence you have absolutely nothing to lose; you can only win.

Learn to say in the future: "Yes I can. Right makes might!" Look yourself in the eyes in a mirror, point at yourself and say confidently with a determined expression:

"You were born to be successful!"

Let the negative thoughts that keep plaguing you explode, or play those negative sayings you have in your mind backwards like a record; you can also play them fast forward making them sound sillier and sillier, until they disappear. Then you will be ready to replace them with a positive expression: "Of course I can do it!"

If you give your very best, you will achieve the best. You can't give more than the best you can do.

There is no reason to pre-program poverty, to picture yourself as inferior or to communicate with yourself on an inferior level.

If you had a little dog that was absolutely afraid of a new easy chair, you would not push it out of the room and say; "You dumb dog, get out, you will never get over your fear, anyway." You would pet the little thing and say: "Come little puppy, don't be afraid, this chair is nice; it won't hurt you." You would naturally encourage and help the dog to overcome its fear.

Why would you treat yourself worse than your dog?

One more question.

Do you perhaps own a million dollar horse?

If not, just pretend that you have a million dollar race-horse. If you had such a horse, would you take it from one party to another without giving it enough sleep and good food, but give it unhealthy fluids, alcohol, coffee and cola and, instead of fresh air and exercise, let it smoke and put it in a room with nothing but frustrating noise?

When you get my analogy you will most likely say, "No, of course not."

If you would not do it to a horse, why would you do it to yourself? Are you less valuable than a dog and a horse?

We are often willing to treat other people and our animals better than we treat ourselves.

But dear reader, don't forget: You are the most important person in your life and you must treat yourself that way, otherwise the consequences could be disastrous.

If you do not treat yourself well enough, you could fall apart from giving too much to others before you can reach your goals. — That will be nobody's gain.

You cannot get somebody out of quicksand by jumping after them. You must get yourself on solid footing first, before you can pull them out.

Many people try to help other people from a position of weakness and do only harm, because in destroying themselves, they give others a feeling of guilt, leading to a worse frame of mind.

But when you help sick people from a feeling of confidence, because you are full of vitality and strength, and they can with your help take their lives in their own hands again, than you will probably be successful, because you will have the strength to convince them.

It is just as foolish to contemplate helping someone financially, when you are not solvent yourself—you will both end up in trouble.

The right way would be to either encourage the other person to get himself on a more solid footing, or to get your own life in order, so that you can help the other person from a position of strength.

Those examples depend of course on certain corresponding situations, as with everything in life, you can't make sweeping judgments.

I want to give you information, tools and work-manuals to use with my IBMS™-training-technique, but I will not tell you how to act, or make your decisions for you.

I only want to point out and explain certain things, so that you can give it some serious thought and decide for yourself what you can do with this information and those techniques; you can choose the right path and the right actions to reach your goal.

Losers, those who frequently fail and those who rob the energy of others, are always looking for possibilities to diminish the intensity and quality of success of others thereby pulling them down to a lower level. In that way they will have an easier time coping with their own situation. (If you are giving a lecture or leading a seminar point out those weaknesses, so that you do not have to listen to their criticism and be pulled down to their level.)

Especially foolish people, the real losers, will always be talking when they should be listening, and they will cackle and snicker when it is time to be serious. They will react violently and hysterically to criticism, even when it is constructive.

Losers don't think about constructive criticism, proposals for improvement, up to date information or recommended changes; they try to hang on to the old ways, so that they can defend their old way of thinking and doing things by thrusting aside as bad, unbelievable and unacceptable, everything that is new.

Dear reader, by reading my book this far, you have already proven that you are not a loser. Therefore I want to emphasize the following once more:

Life is too short to waste your time on energy-robbers, losers, killjoys and quitters, even if you became 140 years old. You must therefore ban those people, whose behavior patterns constantly show the pattern I have described, for good from your life.

Don't forget one rotten apple can spoil a whole basket, and one person, who is not good for you, can be responsible for destroying your chance to enjoy the quality of life you deserve.

A life full of passion, enthusiasm, joy, adventure and achievements lies ahead of you, because you were born to be successful. Why should you let a loser, who has no self-confidence turn your life into something inferior and below average?

You deserve success, go after it.

If it seems that I speak so often about losers and failures, it is, because I want to encourage you to ban those energy-robbers, negative people, killjoys and discouraging critics for good from your life. Because:

We are, what we are, through what we allow to enter and feed into our minds—and this happens in the immediate environments in which we travel.

Even a strong believe-system can be so shaken by the continuous doubts of people that we deal with on a daily basis that it becomes hard to believe in the realization of our dreams, goals and possibilities.

The quality of the materials that we use to build our house determines the quality of the house in which we live. The emotional influence of our surroundings and our own internal communication determine the quality of the house we build and the aspects of our destiny.

Exercise 4:
Write down how you can improve and inspire the way you communicate with yourself.

Association and Dissociation

A direct influence on our feelings and on our emotional state of mind gives our brain the ability to disassociate if we look from the outside as observer, or the ability to associate as if we were in the middle of something, as if it were really happening.

Pretend that you are sitting in the first seat of a roller-coaster. You see the peak of the roller-coaster in front of you; you hold on tight to the rail in front of you, and you feel how you are slowly pulled upwards; when you are on top you shoot suddenly straight down, shooting past the rails, faster and faster, you make a strong right curve and rush back up, you make a fast left and shoot down again. If you really associated with this trip you just played in your mind, even listened to the noise as if you were really in the roller-coaster, you developed a real feeling of such an experience.

If you now experience the ride dissociated, see yourself on the outside looking at a roller-coaster, following a ride and stand back, do not hear the noise and are just an observer; you will conclude that your feelings are totally different.

If you must think about a threatening or negative situation, do it in a dissociative manner, as if you were looking at the screen in a movie-theater.

You can do an interesting exercise with an emotional shift. Remember something that happened earlier, today or yesterday, and you still remember it well. See the picture in your mind, close your eyes, and let the picture move further and further into the distance until it becomes very small, now cover it with a black dot. You will now get the feeling that the event never took place, or at least very long ago.

You can use this ability of your mind every time you would like to distance yourself from negative feelings and memories.

Overcoming fear

Fear, dear reader, is not a negative emotion, in the contrary; it is a challenge, something good to protect you. Without fear we would take unnecessary risks that are senseless and foolish and may have already been conquered by others.

Fear should not control our life, thinking and behavior; rather we should control our fears. It is important that we pay attention to the warning signals, accept the message and prepare ourselves to cope with it.

Being prepared takes care of the real fear

I have proven with a video camera that you can be cured in minutes from life-long fears and phobias without recurrence, if you are willing to use the tools given to you so that you can free yourself of the fear you want to shed.

We have succeeded over and over again to program a smoker into a non-smoker in 22 minutes—usually without falling back or suffering from withdrawal symptoms. Fear, phobias and depression can be removed forever—in at least 99% of all cases—with 12 IBMS™—training sessions.

People, who have been treated for 10, 20 or 30 years by psychiatrists, can frequently be helped, if they accept the help IBMS™ offers to free themselves from their circle of depression, frustration, fear, hopelessness and futility.

Please, never forget that there are no insoluble problems, just problems you have not solved yet, or problems that you have not tried hard enough to solve. I have come to the conclusion in my work as therapist that there are no incurable illnesses, only incurable patients, who like being the center of attention. They are not willing to do what is needed to get rid of their cancer, gout, muscular atrophy, or rheumatism. Everyone of our patients, who was willing to take his life in his own hands and determine his own medical development, could bring about drastic changes with the help of his physician and his own determination.

Improvements in the quality of life is reached when you make a distinct decision to no longer tolerate and accept the difficulties with which you are coping and decide that you are willing to go the extra mile to be who you can be and reach what you can reach. It means that you will do all that is necessary to reach your goal by doing what you in combination with an effective team-play can achieve.

Knowledge is not strength.

Do you know people, who know exactly what and how they should change their lives—who know how to do it, but still don't?

And that is just the point: knowing is only the potential for power, only in the use of the knowledge lays the actual strength.

You can have all the skills, talents, possibilities and qualifica-tions—if you can't change these with your actions into results, they are useless.

Many people know that they can achieve more than they are doing at this time; it gives them a sense of security, so they do noth-ing to improve their behavior, and the result is failure.

Instead of talking about what we can do, we must start doing it. The more often we actually do something, the more normal it becomes for our nervous system to program action into place.

It is sad, if we at the end of a situation must say: "I am sorry I did not do that." It is better to say: "I am so glad I did it."

Neuron-associations that determine your life

As mentioned before, a neuron association is an anchor that oc-curs in our nervous-system when a stimulus triggers one of our five senses; this leads to certain emotional or physical reactions in our behavior. It does not matter whether this stimulus comes from the inside or the outside, whether it happens in reality or is just a part of our thought process.

We must learn to make complete use of the possibilities that we possess thanks to the power of our neuron-associations, so that we do not do the wrong thing in certain situations, either unconsciously or unwillingly.

If we react over and over in ways that are similar and incorrect in certain situations, it is the result of a type of digital recording in our nervous-system; this message is replayed automatically in corresponding situations.

We have recorded an unbelievably large amount of messages over the years without realizing that this was happening.

If you suffered, for instance, a serious disappointment in a relationship with a partner, it is possible that you anchored a neuron-association in your nervous-system that close relationships will cause you pain. This neuron-association will necessarily give your brain a message to withdraw from future entanglement and pain,—and the brain will continuously give you this same message when similar situations arise.

You try, for instance, to accumulate money and become financially independent, but every time you have saved some you sabotage your success, consciously or unconsciously, with messages from negative neuron-associations that you have installed over time. For instance, many of us have programmed information that wealth is bad; with messages that we received from our environment.

Nonsense and foolish expressions that entrepreneurs exploit people, that rich people are lonely and unhappy, and warnings from our parents that you must sweat for your money or that your boss is going to exploit you so that he can get rich, have programmed many people with negative emotions about wealth and riches. Those people carry neuron-associations that sabotage their work with negative programming.

Ivan Pavlov did his famous experiments with dogs before 1940. Every time he fed his dogs and just before he put down their food he would ring a bell. After a while he could measure the saliva and digestive fluids of the dogs any time he chose to ring a bell.

He gave us the proof that it is possible that just a sound, a message from outside, could stimulate a neuron-chemical process, such as a release of hormones, the activation of glands and the functions of organs.

This is called a provoked reaction through an outside stimulation; it is a neuron-association.

We have discussed, how we can bring about an intense positive condition through an effective and optimal use of our physiology, and if we use an optimal internal representation and communication to do this, we emphasize the high intensity of these positive feelings drastically. This awareness is far more effective and helps us to do everything we want to do with greater enthusiasm and success than any other emotional condition. We can store a gesture, a sound or word and recall these feelings in a second.

We know today that every human feeling is registered in our bodies through bio-electrical and neuro-chemical processes. Those processes can be measured.

Today a scientist can determine the condition of a person at any time by withdrawing some blood without having any prior information.

It is also possible to measure and organically screen good and bad feelings in the body.

It is therefore very important that we support our immune systems with positive and helpful chemical stimulation. We can do this by shouting loud and clear: "Yes, I can do it!"

Put yourself in an emotional and physical "Yes" condition by no longer allowing yourself to program and condition, consciously or unconsciously, the negative use of your emotional and physical possibilities.

Exercise 5:

I have the greatest successes in my seminars: "The revolution of the mind," "You were born for success," "An appointment with your destiny," "Strategies for success," or "Successful behavior," if I can convey the message that it is easy to take charge of our feelings, our energy and our actions, and how simple it is to store those skills (with neuron-associations), and how necessary it is to recall them with a favorite form of recollection.

I want to make this skill available to you.

Please have the courage to completely do the following exercise

Stand up straight. Take a strong and deep breath with your whole body; put a strong expression on your face, relax your muscles and clap your hands while you shout enthusiastically: "Yes," and smile brightly, as if you just won the lottery. Now think about a very positive and real situation; think about your greatest success—if you can't think of one, make one up. Clap your hands again and shout one more time: "Yes."

Now walk through the room as we have learned before, with your spine and head straight, proud and victorious, full of enthusiasm and self reliance; know that your are vigorous and strong. Clap your hands again and shout full of enthusiasm: "Yes." Now stand still, lift your fist like a winner while you shout: "Yes." Shout "Yes" to yourself, "Yes," to success, "Yes," to a promising future. Walk back and forth as a tiger in a cage, strong, confident and deliberate. Imagine that nobody can stop you, that you are guaranteed to achieve absolutely everything you want and that you will fulfill your every dream. Now, while you see yourself fulfilling every wish and dream, snap the finger of your right hand confidently and shout: "Yes." Bring your arm way back and shoot it forward and upward, while you keep snapping your fingers. Keep thinking about the great successes and achievements you will produce; now repeat this at least from six to ten more times.

Bring your arms up one more time, with your fist balled,

victorious like a winner and shout: "Yes," one more time, while your body and mind express the confidence of success, clap your hands and shout: "Yes," joyfully.

After snapping the fingers of your right hand about thirty times while you were in the positive emotional state, you have installed a recall mechanism; you can use, and even improve, this mechanism at any time.

If you find yourself, in the future, in a difficult discussion, snap your fingers and think simply: "Yes." The brain does not see the difference between the real and the imaginary.

It makes, basically, no difference which movement you make to trigger a neuron-association. Pavlov gave us some simple rules for the installation and recall of neuron-associations:

- A trigger should always be employed at the absolute height of an emotional situation. (Otherwise the wrong feelings or a dysfunctional trigger could exert itself.)

- The trigger should be unusual or something we usually do not use.

- The trigger should always be employed in exactly the same way.

- The trigger must repeatedly be reinstalled or renewed, and we must do so at least 25 to 30 times repeating the reconditioning exercise.

- We can set the trigger with one of our five senses that we prefer, but it should be set every time and recalled in exactly the same manner.

- We can test whether we set a well functioning neuron-association by putting ourselves in a negative, weak, frustrated or sad mood; by using the trigger we can observe an immediate change in our feelings and body.

- Again, the trigger must be used exactly in the same way as we installed it.

It is often necessary to reprogram and anchor the stored neuron-association that we have used for one or ten years. But you have now learned how you, in seconds and, in a pleasant way can take control of your life, your feelings and your behavior by taking control of your neuron-associations.

Exercise 6:
To remove a bad neuron-association you must first write down why this association is wrong and causes you trouble. Consider whether you have any negative associations in partnerships or earnings and write them down.

Exercise 7:
Write down why certain statements and thought processes are wrong and make no sense.

Exercise 8:
Write down the difficulties those neuron-associations have already caused you and how they may do so in the future.

Exercise 9:
Write down why it would be foolish to hold on to those bad neuron-associations.

Exercise 10:
Write down the advantages you would enjoy if those associations would be changed for the better.

Exercise 11:
Write down the combined reasons why you should and are going to change those neuron-associations.

Exercise 12:
Write down the changes you decide to make with this technique.

Decisions determine your destiny

Dear reader, the time to determine your life and shape your destiny, has arrived. If you ask me how, my answer is:

You decide!

Our decisions determine whether we act or not, whether we persevere or not, because our decisions focus our attention in a certain direction and therefore our decisions tell us how to use our physiology and whether we use our potential or not. Our decisions determine our entire life and the successes and failures we produce.

Think back five or ten years and consider whether your life has improved and become much nicer in certain areas since you made a certain decision and followed the plans you made. The decision you make today will also influence your destiny and determine your future, because every decision is a cause for development—positive as well as negative.

If, dear reader, you do not start to make your own decisions, others will do it for you—for their benefit and not yours. Most people find it difficult to make a decision, because they do not like to accept the responsibility for a failure or for unforeseen results. Just because of this, dictators and gurus can take authority.

I ask you now: please make the following decision that is in my opinion the most important one of your life:

"From now on I will never be satisfied again with less than I can be, own or achieve, because I know that I am born to be successful!"

A real decision means that the possibility of acting differently or allowing a different outcome of a situation will not enter your mind. If you allow a possibility of acting or not acting at the same time, you do not make a decision, instead you are deceiving yourself.

Exercise 13:

Write down three decisions you made in the past but did not follow through with to the end, decisions that would have changed your life for the better, if you had completed the task or if you were still working on them now.

For instance, how you could have exercised more, ate healthier, gave up smoking or were a better life-partner.

Exercise 14:

Write down the long and short-term price you are paying, the pain it caused you and the agony it still may cause in the future.

Exercise 15:

Write down the benefits you may have when you complete the work on those decisions now. (Short term, middle, and long term.)

Exercise 16:

Write down in what way you could still realize these decisions. Develop a written plan and strategy.

Exercise 17:

Summarize and explain why you would like to work on those decisions and follow them through to the end.

"I want to follow through on these decisions, because..."

Exercise 18:

Every decision needs a short description. Write down at least three ways in which you could start working either today or at the latest tomorrow.

Life is neither fair nor unfair

Dear reader, we all too often complain that life is not fair and that we are getting a rough deal.

Life is neither fair nor unfair, life is not for or against you, life just is. And your destiny is what you make of it, or are going to make of it.

A hailstorm destroys the crop of a hard working farmer in the same way it destroys the crop of a lazy one, but the hard worker will plant again and may harvest an even better crop than before.

The lazy farmer gives up, grumbles, complains and cries; he will gripe how hard life is treating him and finally goes bankrupt.

When something happens, don't take it personally, because anything that happens is value neutral until you evaluate it. It is easier to deal with the tasks, blows and challenges, if we accept the demands and work on a quick and effective change.

Nothing that happens is either for or against us; life is as it is, and therefore we must make the best of it.

Learn to be enthusiastic about yourself, your life and your goals
To reach your goals and achieve what you really want, you must build up a high degree of motivation.

The level of motivational intensity you can build up for a task that you must do determines what you will or will not get out of life.

I will tell you a little story to show what I mean:

A rich oil baron from Texas had a beautiful daughter whose name was Maxima. He did not quite know how many millions he had, because the wells kept giving while he was asleep. Maxima was an only child and she would celebrate her 21st birthday in a month. The baron thought that the time had come to find a husband for his daughter. He threw Maxima a birthday party and invited all the eligible young men he knew.

While the guests gathered around the Olympic size pool, they saw that the water was enjoyed by Piranhas and Alligators. The baron gave a toast to the beautiful Maxima and ended with inviting the young men to dive in the pool. He told them: If one of you has the courage to dive in and swim across the pool he can make a choice out of three offers. He can choose $5,000.000 in gold, he can take a thousand acres of my best oil containing land, or he may take the hand of my beautiful Maxima, who is my only heir.

He had hardly finished speaking when a young man splashed in the water and swam with record breaking speed across the pool and pulled himself up the other side.

Everyone clapped with enthusiasm and the baron walked up to the dripping young man. He said to the fellow: "That was a remarkable performance. I admire your courage. Tell me what you want. Would you like to have the $5,000.000 in gold? "No," answered the young man, "I don't want your $5,000.000."

"Alright," said the baron, would you rather have the 1.000 acres of oil-rich land?" "No," said the young man, "Keep your land, I don't want it."

"Ah," said the Rich Texan, "You want to marry my beautiful daughter."

"No," said the wet, shivering young man," I do not want to marry your daughter."

The amazed oil baron asked the fellow: "Then what the heck do you want?"

"I want to know the name of the idiot, who pushed me in the pool." Was the answer.

This little story shows you how motivated and determined you must be to get what you really want, if you do not want to be side tracked by temptation. The analogy of this little anecdote shows that without motivation, enthusiasm and determination great goals cannot be reached.

There is only one form of real motivation, and that is self-motivation. And as we have seen before, we can motivate ourselves with the joy-and-pain principle. The only form of motivation we can receive from others is the help to strengthen our own, because all other motivation coming from the outside is really de-motivation; it will produce results that are different from the results that we really want.

Every outside motivation is, in the long run, a form of manipulation. No matter how well it is meant; it becomes a negative influence.

Some people have an easier time motivating themselves when they think of the negative results they will have to face, if they do not reach their goal. Others motivate themselves by looking at the happy results of fulfilling their dreams.

Exercise 19:
Write down how you want to motivate yourself in the future.

I like you, because...
A great form of team-play, motivation and mutual respect is the small cart of the Ziglar corporation: "I like you, because..."

I will tell you how it came about.

When the Zigler corporation had developed and made a logo that said: "I like you, because...," they went, happy with their result, to an expensive restaurant where they wanted to celebrate the making of their first emblem. They took the emblem with them.

They had an outstanding waiter, who anticipated their slightest needs; he was unobtrusive and deferential, polite, pleasant and courteous.

The service had been so great that they left a 25% tip, which was, even in this restaurant, a very generous gratuity, They moreover decided to leave a little note with their new slogan: "I like you, because..."

Just after they left the restaurant they heard someone calling: "Ladies and gentlemen, just one moment please."

It was the waiter, who was wiping the tears from his eyes, holding their little note in his hand:

I have been a waiter for twenty five years and have received plenty of tips, but never before has anyone been so great to do something so personal, thank you with all my heart for this lovely gift."

I want to show you with this story how easy it is to make others happy, and thereby to motivate them to perform better continuously. Wouldn't you have liked to be the next guest of this waiter?

Because you know how well this waiter would have served his next patrons.

It does cost little to give joy to others by giving them recognition. Let people know how significant they are, that you like and appreciate them. Write down what they deserve to hear:

I like you, Mr. (Ms.)

Because....

Signature

The most important story I ever heard

I want to tell you the story of Bernie Leftschick, who, at the birth of his son, was convinced that now all his dreams were fulfilled. He had two lovely daughters and a wonderful wife, now he also had a son.

After a while he realized that something was not quite the way it should be. The little boy's head drooped strangely to the left. When the pediatrician checked the child he did not consider it something serious, after some time the baby would have the strength to lift his head and everything would be alright.

But Bernie was not persuaded and decided, when he observed the baby, that something was wrong. They took the child to a specialist, who diagnosed a slight disturbance in coordination and treated the baby accordingly.

The situation did alas not improve and Bernie took the boy to the best known nerve-specialist in Canada.

The child was examined again; the diagnosis was that the child was a *Spastiker* and that he would never be able to talk, learn to talk or count to ten. The physician advised the Leftschicks to put the child in a home where they could take care of him; it would be the best thing for the child and the family.

But Bernie said: "I am a salesman not a buyer. I don't buy your advice and I refuse to believe that my child must spend his life as a vegetable." They went from doctor to doctor, but each specialist told him the same thing. He visited at least thirty specialists, but they all told him: Your child is a *Spastiker*, he will never be able to swim, ride a bicycle or speak a full sentence.

Then they heard about a Dr. Perlstein in Chicago; he achieved amazing results, but was booked years in advance. They called Dr. Perlstein's secretary and asked for an appointment. She told them that they may have to wait for two years, but to leave their phone-number, just in case somebody would cancel.

After eleven days they received a call, the parents of a child from Australia had to cancel their appointment, if they could be in Chicago on that day Dr. Perlstein would see their son.

The doctor gave the child an examination as he had never had before. But after the examination the message was the same: "Your child is a *Spastiker;* he will never walk or talk..."

But Dr. Perlstein said that he did not believe in giving up, in incurable diseases, or in unsolvable problems. He told them that they could try one way, but only if they were willing to give it everything they had.

The Leftschicks asked the doctor what they could do.

"First you have to encourage the child and make demands. "You have to take him to the edge of his possibilities, whether it is moral or immoral, and whether you have the right to do it or not. "Keep encouraging him and keep on driving, put him on his feet, and when he falls down do it again, and if he falls again put him again back on his feet, even when he whines and cries and begs you to stop and it tears your heart out. You must keep it up, day after day, hour after hour and minute after minute, and you can never stop training, encouraging and pushing; if you let up for a minute you will lose everything you have gained up till that point."

"You have to keep it up for months, perhaps even years before you may see any improvement, but you must continue on the path you chose. "And one of the most important things, 'Never teach or train him in the presence of other *Spastik* children, because as soon as he sees them he will copy their movements.' Don't forget we all become a part of the environment in which we move."

"You must know, whether it is moral or immoral, good or bad, you must persevere. Even if it tears your heart out, and takes your last ounce of strength; you must persevere."

The Leftschicks flew home and arranged a training area in their basement; they hired an athletic trainer to work every day with the boy.

It took months before the child could move his limbs even a little—the slightest movement.

It was not until a few years that the physical therapist called them and said: "Come on home, I think we have won." Bernie drove home as fast as possible, filled with expectation. When he came home little David was laying on his stomach on his training pad ready to do his first push-up, the first one in his life. The little boy, who had never been able to use the left part of his body, was ready to push himself up with both arms.

While he tried to push himself up he did not have a dry inch on his body, the sweat ran in streams, but slowly, trembling, he pushed himself up, while his mother, father, his sisters and the trainer burst out in tears. They all knew: happiness is not joy, happiness is victory.

Happiness is victory over restrictions and limitations, over statements like: "That is not possible, you won't be able to do that, it is impossible."

David Leftschick was examined in the foremost medical institutions in the United States; they all stated that he had no nerve ending connections to the left-half of his body and had absolutely no balance. They all confirmed: "This boy cannot stand and walk on his own, he will never be able to swim, ski or drive; he will never ride a bicycle, speak or count to ten."

In October, 1971 a friend visited the Leftschick family in Canada and what he saw was so unbelievable that he wished all the TV cameras in the world could film it. A confident young man came up to him; he had a strong, athletic and healthy body and he said smiling: "Welcome to Canada, I am David Leftschick."

David does 1100 push-ups each day and runs 6 miles; he is now one of the best golfers in Canada. He has also won many tennis championships in Winnipeg.

This fellow, who was supposedly not able to count till ten, graduated with honors in technical mathematics from Raven High school.

In 1974 David took a life insurance policy for $100,000, and is, so far as I know, the only person with this disability to receive this.

When the insurance company had given him a thorough medical examination they were convinced that they were not taking a risk by insuring this healthy, strong and vital young man.

When he was a little boy he had to wear leg-braces every night, so that his legs would not waste away, and every night he cried: "Please mommy, not tonight, they hurt, please no braces tonight; please daddy, not so tight please!" Every parent knows what it means when their child cries: "Please one night no braces and please not so tight."

It was because they loved the child so much that they could refuse to see the tears running over his face and tighten the braces, so that some day the tears from today would turn into the laughter of tomorrow, the laughter that would last his entire life.

I told you this story, because it is a beautiful example that many people were willing to follow a dream —the nurses, physical therapists, physicians, his sisters and family, friends and above all his parents. This enormous and unbelievable result was the result of team work; it was only possible to achieve this result by people working together as a team.

It is a story of cooperation, team spirit and solidarity. It is a story of great life long goals; it is a story of perseverance even when there was often no visible proof of improvement.

When the boy was too little to carry a tape-recorder, there was always one close to him and he could hear his father's voice: "You can do it, my boy!"

His mind was continuously filled with positive statements and encouraging information.

When we get enough encouraging influence from our surroundings and hold on to enough positive information, all success is possible.

It is easy to make use of the power that comes from good decisions
If you must make a decision, ask yourself:

If I make this decision will it bring me closer or take me further away from my goal?

If I realize this goal will it bring me closer to reaching my target?

It is difficult to make a decision—therefore do it fast.

Once you have made the decision everything else becomes easier.

Make many decisions. The more decisions you make, the more successful you will become, and the more affluent you will be. Just as your muscles become stronger when you use them often, so do your decision muscles get a work-out. Enjoy the strength you receive from making decisions.

Every decision you make offers new opportunities. A good decision often brings a positive change to your entire life. My life has really been changed by the seminars and lectures I attended, the books I have read and the tapes I heard. You can never know how your life will change, therefore live with positive expectations and use your opportunities.

How will you spend the next ten years? What will happen in the next ten years? Your life will not be determined by your possibilities, but by your decisions.

Use the unlimited strength of making your own decisions, if you want to live successfully in the years to come being happy, content, comfortable and successful.

Exercise 20:

What decisions do you want to make, so that you can turn your life into the masterpiece you deserve? Which are the decisions you have made and did not realize, but will start realizing now?

The Niagara Syndrome

When you decide to take your life in your own hand, so that you can be in charge of your own success and happiness, you must:

Decide on the standard of living you want to have this year and every year thereafter. Take a sheet of paper and write down where you want to be this year. How do you want to live? With whom do you want to share your life? You can find out what you want by knowing what you do not want.

Make a plan or take a sheet with directions! You will be lost without a plan the very first time the going gets rough. So get a map! It's simple—just find somebody, who is already following his or her path and who is successful.

Learn also from your own experiences. It will save you time and agony and it can protect you from the waterfalls in life.

One part of your plan must be a correct division of your task into stages; this will keep you going and will lead to forward progress.

Begin now!

People, who have failed in the stream of life and who have no faith in themselves are already out of the game.

Personal Rules

Parts of our belief system are the personal rules we have developed for special situations.

These rules are usually if-then statements, such as: if my partner is not friendly to me all the time, then he or she must not love me anymore.

If I want to be successful, then I have to keep on working as hard and as much as I can. (Complete nonsense.)

Rules are really not based in reality, but are a part of a belief system that was imprinted on our minds in the past.

If your father, for instance, believed that he could only become successful if he worked long hard hours, then it is possible that you accepted this foolish way of thinking and worked strenuously to become financially successful.

If you have installed the rule: "If my husband loves me he will not raise his voice at me," but if your husband has installed: "If I shout at her, she knows I am serious," the opposing personal rules can lead to serious conflicts. Therefore, you must get to know your own rules and the rules of those around you.

You can get to know the rules by asking a few simple questions:

What must happen, so that I feel okay? And, what do I have to do, so that you feel loved, respected and accepted by me?

You can also formulate the questions in the following way:

"How do you know that you are successful? What must I do, so that you know that I respect you? Etc.

Exercise 21:

What should happen, so that I can feel successful?

How do you know that I respect and love you?

What should I do to make you feel loved?

Personal Value Systems

You can know your personal values by asking yourself: "What is to me the most important in the area of......"

The answers to this question may be:

Team-play

Independence

Unlimited possibilities to make money

Creativity

New challenges

Working with people

Exercise 22:

Write down ten things that are very important to you in your profession.

Exercise 23:

Establish your own personal value-system. Write in order the importance and correctness of each issue.

There are, of course, also negative values, such as feelings, situations, and other things that you would want to avoid.

Exercise 24:

Write about those feelings you experience in your work. What would you rather never to do again? Put those feelings also in order of importance.

You can, of course, write in order the values for different areas in your life. You could ask your partner what is important to him or her in your personal relationship.

Exercise 25:

What are the feelings you would like to have more frequently? Write them again down in order of importance.

Our behavior is often determined by our belief system and the rules that have become part of our personal values. Take charge of it and you will be in control of your life. Please, go over those lists every four or six weeks, so that you can change the goals and rules according to your cycle of development.

Exercise 26:

Write down the three most positive and the three most negative feelings you have in your life.

Uncover all your destructive behavior patterns

In what situations do you always react differently than you would like to react?

After what situations are you always sorry that you did or did not do something?

In what situations do you repeatedly destroy successes you had earlier achieved?

This negative behavior is either caused by false programming, negative neuron-associations, or unconscious self-sabotage resulting from false programming.

If you behave differently from the way you like to behave, it stems from false neuron-associations.

Exercise 27:

Write down in which situations you repeatedly sabotage your own success (unconsciously, of course) and in which situations you behave differently from the way you would like to behave.

Exercise 28:

How would you like to behave in those situations in the future?

Exercise 29:

Why should your foolish, dumb and silly behavior up to now stop immediately?

Exercise 30:

What were the drawbacks of this behavior in the past and what could you expect in the future?

Exercise 31:

What would the advantages be if you changed your behavior?

Exercise 32:

Write down how you want to change your behavior, include your goals. Write down the reasons for those changes.

You have already learned how you can install a mechanism to recall a new association for positive feelings.

Please stand up and look at the old unwanted behavior pattern and consider why it is so dumb and absurd.

Pretend, that while you are looking at the behavior pattern that you erase it with a huge eraser, let it become lighter and lighter until you cannot see it anymore. Now take your magical eraser, tap it on an imaginary linen cloth on which appears a picture of the wished for behavior. This picture shows your future behavior. Snap your finger and shout: "Yes!" Repeat this 25 to 30 times and let the picture become clearer, colorful, more beautiful and shining, until it shows the behavior pattern you want it to be.

Goals—your pathway to success

Goals are the basic requirement for success, because when we do not know where we are going we will be blown like a leaf by the winds of destiny.

We will easily get lost if we are on unknown territory without a map. Clear goals, chartered pathways and strategies form a so-called map for the territory on which we function.

You certainly know who the escape artist Houdini was; he was famous for escaping out of jail, from a straight jacket, hand cuffs and safes.

He was challenged by a small town in England; they told him they had built a jail cell that was absolutely escape-proof. Houdini accepted the challenge. He told them that if they let him in the cell in his everyday suit after searching him and then left him alone, he would escape from the cell.

The great Houdini was taken into the cell in the presence of reporters, jail-guards and spectators; he was then left alone. He took a thin but strong thread from his waistband and started to work on the door-lock. But no matter how hard he tried he could not force the lock. After working for an hour he felt exhausted against the door, which fell open. In all the excitement, they had forgotten to lock the door.

The moral of my story: the door seemed closed for the greatest escape artist in the world, because in his mind the door was closed.

It is like that for many of us. In our mind many doors seem closed, and therefore we do not even try to open them.

Now let us pretend that the genie of fairy-tales appeared to you, and you could wish for everything you wanted, or it would be possible for you to reach your true potential with your multi-million dollar personality and your multi-million dollar body in a way that nothing was impossible; you could reach everything you wanted and realize all your dreams, nothing would be denied.

Exercise 33:
Please write down what you would like to change, if you knew that nothing could be denied.

Exercise 34:
Write down everything you would like the genie to give to you.

Exercise 35:
Write down all the goals you have in the area of changing and developing your personality.

After you have written down all your personal and social goals, write behind each one a number for the weeks, months or years it will take you to realize this goal.

Exercise 36:
Now please write down your material and financial wishes.

After you have done this, write down again in what time you would like to achieve this.

Exercise 37:
Now please write down your professional and career goals.

Exercise 38:
What are the crazy things you would like to do in your life and have

not done yet? Where do you find the motivation and fun to do those things that make life worth while?

Exercise 39:
What are your goals for immortality? What are the traces you would like to leave behind so that others will know that you have lived? What would you like to do, so that you can leave the world a little better behind you?

Exercise 40:
Now take the three short term goals from every category, and write them here under each other.

Exercise 41:
Ask for every goal: "Is that really my wish or is it just the influence of my environment?"

Exercise 42:
Is this goal morally acceptable and can I live with the consequences? If not scratch it.

Exercise 43:
Are you willing to do everything that is necessary to reach this goal? If not, scratch it.

Exercise 44:
Does this goal fit in with my other goals?

Exercise 45:
Can you mentally see yourself experiencing this goal? If not, scratch it.

Exercise 46:
If you cannot say "Yes" at least once to the following questions for each goal, scratch that goal.

- Will reaching this goal make me happier?
- Will reaching this goal make me healthier?
- Will reaching this goal give me joy and improve my quality of life?
- Will reaching this goal give me emotional peace and harmony?
- Will I feel better and more secure when I reach this goal?
- Will reaching this goal improve my relationship with my partner?
- Will reaching this goal strengthen my self-confidence?

Exercise 47:
Write down for every goal, which people, or groups of people, you need to reach this goal?

Exercise 48:
Write down the skills you have to learn or improve so that you can reach those goals.

Exercise 49:
Write down a plan of action.

Exercise 50:
Write down the disadvantages you will suffer, if you do not reach this goal.

Exercise 51:
Write down the draw-backs, hurdles, obstacles and conflicts you may meet on the way.

Exercise 52:
How would you react?
By setting a true goal you must write down exactly every detail that you must realize to reach your final goal. Only in that way you will know what you really want, and only then can you reach the greatest perfection.

THE WORLD IS A WIDE OPEN PLACE

Considerations

To begin this chapter, I would like to tell you an anecdote about an Indian-tribe in South America.

When people of this tribe become very old and a burden, one of the children or a young member of the tribe carries the older person through the rain forest and up to the mountain, where the elder is left to die.

A young man, who carried his mother up the mountain, noticed that she was using her arms and hands and seemed to be leaving things behind.

The frustrated young man, probably feeling guilty and sad, asked his mother: "What are you doing?" His mother answered lovingly: "My son, when you leave me up the mountain to die, you have to go back by yourself through the jungle; I am breaking off some twigs so that you can find your way back"

This little story shows you the power of love.

The Story of a great Man

The man, whose story I will tell, has probably helped more people to change their lives in a positive way than any other. In his books, which have sold 25 million copies in 18 different languages, he has told numerous people to take their lives in their own hands.

He was an advisor to presidents of the United States, heads of states, movie and rock stars, physicians, prisoners and just ordinary people. He helped drug-addicts, alcoholics, and he helped numerous athletes to become very successful. He appeared on radio and TV and, in the war against Korea, he received the highest distinctions that an American could earn in war time.

For twelve years he was the editor of an American success-journal and at the age of fifty two he withdrew from active journalism to devote his time to writing, speeches and lectures.

He became the first person to receive the Napoleon Hill gold medal that is given to people who help others in their development of personal success. He is one of 14 people, who have been accepted in the International Hall of Lecturers.

His book: *The best Salesman in the World* has been sold in many languages, and it has sold more copies than any other book dealing with the same subject.

Even now 100,000 copies of this book are sold every month.

He was the first caller in the wilderness. His call was: "Yes, you can, you can do it!"

The man I am speaking of is one of the most generous and greatest colleagues I have in the world. He is responsible for my fascination with the psychology of motivation, success and personality training. And I thank him for giving me the courage to choose the path of personal motivation.

His name is Og Mandino.

I want to tell you, parallel with Mandino's story, the tale of a 35-year-old bag-person from Ohio.

After the police chased the bag-man from his shelter under a bridge, the man tried to find protection against the rain and wind elsewhere, and while he did so he looked into a window.

He saw a hand-gun for 29 dollars. He searched in his pocket

and pulled out three ten-dollar bills and a hand full of cash–it was all he had. He thought: "With this I can buy the gun and some bullets, put the gun to my head, and my misery will be over. Never again will I have to look at that loser in the mirror. Never again will I have to suffer and start over again."

I am telling this story for those people, who are still living, but who are emotionally and mentally dead; they are ready to give up their future, hope and life. Those people are already dead at the age of thirty or thirty-five; they will have to wait to be buried until they are seventy or eighty years old.

Never before have so many people become addicted to drugs or alcohol. In our country alone 300,000 people commit suicide every year, and 5 million prescriptions are filled every month for tranquilizers and valium.

But life is a game and you can be a winner, if you know the rules.

The bag-man was still standing in front of the window and wondering whether he should put the gun to his head, but he decided against it.

The story of the bag-man would not have had an ending, had he pulled the trigger to end his life, because this bag-man was Og Mandino. He decided to go to the library and started to read out of sheer boredom. While reading, Mandino thought about laying a foundation. The foundation he laid out became the groundwork for the greatest motivational speaker of our time.

The problem with living is that nobody gave us the rules to play the game of life. Nobody has told us how to set the right goals, to build effective strategies or how to motivate ourselves and others. Nobody has told us how to plan our time as well as possible, and nobody has told us how to dig ourselves out of the hole in which we landed. Nobody has told us how to behave as well and as effectively as possible in our surroundings and how to deal with stress.

You, dear reader, have now learned the rules. You know how to set goals, build effective strategies and motivate others. You know that you have to pay the price for success: you must act, learn, persevere and act again until your goal has been reached. You have become a professional in the game of life—to be active and successful, while others are spectators and might even have to pay a fee to watch you do it.

You will belong to the people who will gain respect and applause, because you know the rules and how to play the game.

Invest in yourself. Whenever you have the time, learn something useful. Listen to an informational tape when you are driving. Don't waste time on silly sitcoms, about negative people with trouble, inferiority or other such negative elements that are not worth your time and talents. Start today to live your life on the highest level and to build your future, so that you can reach your highest potential.

Please God, forgive me when I whine

Today I saw in the streetcar a little girl with beautiful blond hair. I admired her from afar and was even a little envious. I wished I had beautiful blond hair like that. But when she got up, I saw that she was limping and needed to use a crutch. She was a cripple, but even so, she gave me a pleasant smile when she left the streetcar. When she passed me I could not help but think: I have two legs, I can go where I want, run and jump, please God, forgive me when I whine.

On my walk home I stopped at a chocolate vender and bought some bonbons. The man looked so cheerful that I enjoyed talking with him and spent more time than I usually do. His joy affected me and I went home cheerfully a little later. When I left, he told me: "Thank you, it was a pleasure talking to a gentleman like you, even though I could not see you; I am blind."

I have two eyes and can see all the beautiful colors, the rainbow and the smiles of the people I love. I can see the light, the stars in the eyes of my love, the world belongs to me. Please God, forgive me when I whine.

Further down the street I saw a child with beautiful blue eyes, she was looking at the children, who were playing in the street and she looked undecided. I stopped a moment and asked her; "Why are you not playing with the other children?" She did not react or turn or look at me, the child was deaf.

I have two ears and can hear the birds sing and the voices of the people I love. Please God, forgive me when I whine.

I have eyes to see the world, ears to hear the most beautiful sounds, feet to carry me wherever I want to go. Yes, life has blessed me, the world is my oyster. Oh God, forgive me, when I whine.

You see, dear reader, there are always two ways to look at the world and our destiny, and now and then we should concentrate on what we have, and appreciate how lucky and privileged we really are. Too often we are not willing to recognize and be grateful for what we have and own.

When you are depressed, sad and frustrated, do the following exercise: Take the morning paper, look at the obituaries and read the names of the people who died. You will find an endless list of people who would have gladly changed places with you, no matter how miserable you feel right now.

There are always people who are in worse shape than you, but do not concentrate on them. Focus on how wonderful and beautiful your life really is.

Mark Twain wrote about a cat that sprang on a hot oven and burned his feet badly. The cat never sprang on an oven again, not even a cold one. We are not like animals or like this cat. We are not inflexible like a cat, or like a fly that keeps bumping into the same window; we can be flexible. It is this ability that separates us from animals.

If you really want to be successful, you must learn to cope with failure, rejection and refusal, antipathy and dislike. You can't avoid producing results that you do not like, and you can't keep away from people who sometimes treat you differently than you deserve. If those failures do not encourage you to try harder, you will give up, or you may no longer believe in success and quit working on the realization of your dreams.

Don't let pain, refusal, a failure or negligence lure you into complacency, so that you will give up trying. Never forget: when successful people write a book about your life, will they write at least five chapters on your personal failures, suffering and lack of success.

The only people who never fail are the people who never try—they are the real losers.

Develop self-confidence and courage, rely on your multi-million dollar body, stand behind your multi-million dollar personality and develop the strength that was shown by Rosa Parks. Rosa Parks, a black woman, refused to give up her seat in the bus to a white person at the end of a tiring day, even though it was demanded by law. Rosa Parks decided that she was more important than that law. With her civil courage this mother sparked the civil rights fight against race discrimination that shook America.

Little Amy

Little Amy was a seriously, emotionally disturbed child, she behaved like an animal. She bit, spit and scratched anybody who came within arms reach. She was kept in a cage in a psychiatric institution. Everyone had given up on her until an older, mature and especially patient nurse spent years to get an entrance to little Amy. The miracle happened, one day she made a crack in Amy's façade and she found an opening to communicate with Amy.

Amy left the institution completely cured only to return years later as a nurse, so that she could give back the gift she had received from the elderly nurse. She became an exceptional nurse, who dedicated herself to the most difficult and hopeless cases.

Helen Keller, one of the greatest writers of our time, became deaf and blind at a very early age after suffering a bout of scarlet fever. She wrote outstanding works, and when she was asked how she could manage her life so well, she would answer, "If it were not for Annie Sullivan, who steadfastly and patiently, full of love and confidence worked with me; if it were not for this wonderful nurse and friend, nobody would ever have heard from Helen Keller." It was Annie Sullivan, an understanding nurse, who taught Helen Keller to communicate with the world around her.

If you want to enrich the lives of your fellow man; if you want to improve the quality of your own life and the lives of those around you, then do that, as if you had removed a dark cloud from your life and theirs.

If you knew that all the people you meet today would die at midnight, how much friendlier, kinder and with how much more compassion would you treat those people?

A valuable letter

Here I would like to show you a letter from an 82-year-old lady. Please read it well:

> If I could live my life over, I would try to make more mistakes. I would be more relaxed, have more confidence, and, above all, I would do crazy things this time. I would have more faith in myself and try all kind of things and not just dream about them.
>
> I would be less afraid, take more chances and use more opportunities; I would have fun and enjoy life. I would travel more, climb more mountains and swim in more rivers; I would watch the sun rise, eat more ice-cream and fewer beans. I would put more excitement in my life and not just think about it.
>
> I was always considerate and humble, was never daring, never spoke up loudly and never fought for my rights. I would rather give in than start a fight. I lived that way hour after hour, day after day, year after year.
>
> There were also beautiful moments in my life, but believe me, if I could do it again, there would be many more, and

really, when I think about it, I would try to have nothing but beautiful moments like that.

I would try to have one beautiful moment after another, instead of spending my life doing the things other people wanted me to do.

I am a person who never went anywhere without a thermometer, hot water bottle, raincoat and umbrella. But if I could do it again I would travel lighter, much lighter. I would start walking barefoot in the grass at the first sign of spring and keep on walking deep into the fall. I would smell the flowers and enjoy the sun on my face, Yes, I would enjoy life, every minute and every second.

I would have much more fun, realize my dreams, set more goals, be friendlier to others, smile more and be more engaging with others.

I would do it all, if I could relive my life, but you see, I can't.

But you, dear readers, you can. You can, at any time, make new decisions, start all over and produce new and better results.

I am a stranger to you and it is my dearest wish to be your friend, helper and advisor—a helper on your way to personal achievements, to personal success on your way to the top.

I would like to break some branches for you, as the old Indian woman did for her son, so that you can find your way back to greatness and pleasure. I would like to end by saying to you: "Do it! "You can fulfill your dreams. You can own and be what you want, if you are willing to take your life in your hands and determine your own destiny."

Never be satisfied with less than you can be, own or achieve, because you, and I really believe this: **You were born to be successful!**

THE TRUE SECRET OF
ULTIMATE SUCCESS

One of the best discoveries I've found in life is that we can only be happy, content, healthy and successful if we learn to accept ourselves and be ourselves. We need to live according to our own wishes, needs, and dreams, not somebody else's.

We are constantly conditioned to believe that we can't or shouldn't be, as we feel in our heart that we should be. Statements like, "You can't do that" or, "You should do it this way" have trained us to suppress our own needs and personality, replacing them with foreign characteristics, forced on us by others.

When we no longer live according to our own instincts, emotions and inner signals, we become restless and frustrated, which causes incredible stress. And, while we feel uncomfortable with being something we aren't, we simply don't have the strength or tools necessary to be the person we truly are. Many times we're afraid to be the "real us" for fear of what others will thing.

The truth is, we were all created differently; there is no real norm for the right or wrong behavior. (We aren't talking about criminal behavior!) It is impossible to set a standard for the "right" wishes, needs and dreams. Every person has the right to live as they want. They have the right to make mistakes, to develop, mature and develop their own ways of changing their behavior.

The most important requirement for real contentment and an optimal quality of life is the recognition that you are as you were meant to be, and therefore you are alright. You are empowered with unique, wonderful talents, possibilities and skills and there is no one like you on earth. It's this uniqueness that makes a future full of possibilities, opportunities, challenges and successes possible for everyone.

Not until you learn to accept yourself the way you are and use your potential to work toward your own goals, will you enjoy a life without compromises, tension and pressure, without self-deception and duplicity.

You are the only person with whom you have to deal with for the rest of your life, so you must learn how to get along with yourself. Every person must understand, accept, respect and love themselves. After all, how can you accept other people the way they are, if you have not accepted yourself the way you are?

If you really want to know yourself and find out your personal goals, values and rules, I urge you to thoroughly do the work I offer you in this program. Only when you really know yourself and your needs, can you give your life a direction that corresponds with your personality and true goals.

Positive Thinking—Positive Acting

Positive thinking alone will not change your life, because positive thinking is only a requirement for positive acting; while negative thinking is the prelude to acting negatively.

Your life will not produce positive results with positive thinking alone. All our wonderful dreams, those exciting goals, and inspirational mantras will be of no help in overcoming conflicts in your life—unless you take action!

The expression: "Everything will turn out positive if you think positive," has been the downfall for many people because *only positive behavior produces positive results.*

Positive thinking is an intention to perform a needed task to the best of your ability. It is the requirement for inner security. However, nothing will change in your life unless you start taking that first positive step on your chosen path.

True positive thinking means knowing exactly the chosen goal, including the calculated results, you want to produce, no matter the difficulties and obstacles that are in your way.

The Power of Change

As soon as you make some changes, not matter how small at first, you will notice something interesting taking place. Other people may react irritable, or even aggressive, if they are insecure, because they thoroughly dislike the unknown or unusual. Of course, those who are secure with themselves will be happy and congratulatory when they see you making progress.

However, you must be prepared for the strangest reactions to your changes, because some people may refuse to listen or even be hostile. Perhaps you've already experienced this when you've lost some weight or gotten a better job or a raise. Some of your closest friends or relatives may act disinterested, rude or even jealous.

The more people understand your new way of thinking and behavior, the more support you will receive when there is a crisis or when you are insecure or in doubt. As you do make positive changes in your life, be sure to include everyone in on it. Let them know what your plans are, the new methods you're trying, and any new information you've gathered. This way, they can adjust themselves to these new changes that may take place in your life and will be more willing to help you. People like to feel needed and included in your life, even in some small capacity. As I've mentioned before, you must be a team player to become really successful. Do not work on your goals in the secrecy of your room, let others play a part.

Hesitate No More

I think by now you understand the importance of recognizing which negative behavior patterns you have acquired, which you want to change, and a good idea on how to program these positive traits into your subconscious. No matter how eager we are to change at times though, there is very often one thing standing in the way: procrastination.

Procrastination and hesitation are nothing but typical patterns of learned behavior. There are people who delve into a task immediately, look for solutions, develop a plan of action and start on the task at hand. These people are not better than you or I, but they have learned to motivate themselves. They have conditioned themselves to take action so that it has become a natural way of behaving and is now part of their personality. When you realize that getting things done quickly and efficiently is simply learned behavior, it becomes easy to program yourself into solution-oriented thinking and acting.

Stress that could have been avoided results from procrastination. In other words, procrastination is thinking about work instead of doing it. How often have you put work aside that increased, adding more to it, putting it off for days, weeks or even months, only to find that all your headaches were for nothing, because once you started looking for an answer the problem was quickly solved? Or, once you started getting something done and sticking with it, you found that the task wasn't as time-consuming or as bad as you expected? Once you got those tasks completed you felt so relieved, but only after you ruined your quality of life and diminished your energy for quite some time.

Hesitation and procrastination are serious stress factors that can easily be overcome. When faced with a task, ask yourself, "Can I solve this problem? Is this something I need to do or should do?"

If the answer is yes, begin immediately.

Setting Goals

Goals give our lives direction; goals represent the perimeters of our territory so we can move confidently toward our unseen future. The future can be something strange, threatening and unknown, something over which we have no control, until we recognize that we can influence the direction of our lives with concrete goals and positive action. Once we realize this fact, fear of the unknown and the fear of "fate" will disappear because we know we are in charge of our future.

It's extremely important that you define the goals you want to reach in every area of your life. Having clear goals helps you to stick to your own interests, and makes it easier to get back on track if you stray a bit.

Ask yourself if your current life reflects your true aspirations. Does it show your achievements, skills and talent? No matter whether you answer this question with a yes or a no, ask yourself whether you know where your life is heading. Go deep inside and find the answer. What do you really want to reach in your professional and personal life? Do you have goals worth fighting for?

We are only content when we are growing, when we mature and develop. Personal growth and development are the true meaning of life. You will be really happy and content when you have grown as a human being, when you have explored your talents, possibilities and skills. On the other hand, you will be quite dissatisfied when you're at a standstill.

But how can you be proud of your development and success when your life has no direction, when you recognize no victories, and when you have not moved one step ahead? This is why it's so important to have goals in life. Besides larger goals, be sure to set smaller goals as well, so you can enjoy each small success on your way to your final achievement.

It's easy to plan short term goals if you know where you finally want to arrive. It's like taking a road trip. You plan each stage of your trip and look back on a well traveled day, then drive some more.

Whatever your dreams or desires, they can come true with continual goal setting and action. There are no limits on your road to success unless you set those limits yourself. In the philosophy of success we like to say, "Reach for the clouds and when you have arrived, go for the stars!"

Be aware that you are not in the world to survive, but to live. Live your life and enjoy it. You can do this only when you give and live 100% and refuse to live with compromises and limitations. Reach for the sky and set many intermediate goals so that you can measure your progress and celebrate small successes in between.

There is no such thing as good luck or bad luck. Your future lies in your own hands; you make your luck, which is simply the meeting of work and possibility. There will be many opportunities coming your way, so be prepared to make use of the possibilities that life offers you. In the long run it depends on your actions, what you make of your life, and how you use your full potential.

*Reasons

We always need good reasons to act and persevere, because sometimes our level of motivation is not strong enough. We need strong reasons to get up when life throws us down; to be successful we need to keep moving.

You need a good reason to continue on those days when everything goes wrong, your best friend lets you down and another one cheats you.

Exercise 1:

Because they are your very own reasons, your goals, your level of motivation, your willingness to act, I want you to define and write down, now, what motivates you. If everything goes wrong, when it rains on your parade, when your check bounces and the dog chews up your new shoes, what keeps you going?

Please write down, as well as you can, the real motivating reasons that encourage you to persevere in similar negative life situations. What motivates you to improve the quality of your life and lift it to the level you desire?

Do not sell yourself short, demand and expect the very best. There can be no more compromises, excuses, or even half tolerated results. Expect the very best for yourself and for your life and do everything possible to turn your life into the masterpiece it is meant to be. To be able to do this, you must find good reasons to encourage yourself to fight, to act and persevere.

Motivation

As I have mentioned before, if you want to act goal-oriented, you must set a goal, so that you can act goal-oriented. It sounds trite, but I will say it anyway: "Action without careful planning is irrational."

It is important that the energy we use agrees with our behavior, so that we can motivate ourselves and consider the odds of reaching our goal, because the intensity and perseverance while we do our work are, in the long run, determined by the sum of our reasons for reaching this goal.

To encourage ourselves to act and persevere, we must recognize and understand our winning strategies. There are people who can distance themselves from situations. Those people may say; "I do not want to be poor any more, I will no longer be sick." Those people motivate themselves to move away from negative situations.

Other people motivate themselves by looking for pleasant rewards. Those people will tell you that they would like to become wealthy or want to be healthy.

Once you recognize in which category you belong it becomes easier to motivate yourself.

I use the "Joy-Pain" principle, and I advice you to move in that direction. The method is simple, and when you apply it diligently it has a powerful effect, because your motivation depends entirely on your emotional adjustment.

Focus your mental vision on your desired goal, and imagine:

- what will this project cost you

- what will be the price you will have to pay

- what you will have to deny yourself

- what will be the pain you have to suffer when you do not make this decision

Then imagine the opposite:
- what will you gain

- what are the advantages when you do the work

- how much better and richer will your life be

- how will the quality of your life, your self-esteem and success improve?

- will non-action cause hardship and action produce pleasure?

If you are still not acting, it will probably be because you have not suffered enough pain. Imagine in your mind the pain, then create a great joy, both as intensive as you possibly can, and correlate them with non-action and action; you will recognize that you have no choice but to act. You will find that this method will be a strong force; it will help you to reach out and achieve your goal.

Strategies

You have now decided to act, and are strongly motivated to tackle your imagined goal. The next important step will be to make the right plan; what is the best strategy on your path to success?

It makes no sense to do something and expect it to go well by itself. Perhaps what you would like to do right now is the correct thing, but maybe it is not the right time, or it may just be wrong to take the first step right now.

This means that you must first consider which approach will be the best. If a task can be done with just one simple action, the question still remains whether there are other ways, and then it is up to you compare the pros and cons and decide on the best way to do so. If this way turns out unsuccessful, it was still not wrong, you did get results and by making some changes you can modify your approach as needed.

With greater assignments there are often "Several ways to get to Rome." It is absolutely necessary to plan carefully, so that you can act goal-oriented. Organize the chosen task into small steps you can control. This is not only important for the work, but also involves the allotted time, so that you can proceed with your plan and reach your final goal.

In this way you avoid pressure and stress, you can be content when you finish a step and become more motivated to make the next one. By dividing your task in small steps you will feel, moreover, more confident that you will be able to do the job. The first step is frequently the most difficult one, and once you master a job, the rest will go smoothly.

When you have decided to tackle a job, do not be tempted to put your work off until later.

Act swiftly, and if you have to put things off, renew your goal, so that your well planned strategy will not fall by the wayside.

Believe in your own creativity! If your intuition told you that you can reach a certain goal, your mind will develop the path to succeed.

This does not mean that you cannot follow the example of successful people, people who have already arrived at their chosen destination. This pattern of thinking, behavior and action of successful people I call molding. It is the pattern of selection in nature.

Perseverance

I have mentioned already several times that it is important that you persevere on your way to a goal, and not give up half way. I am not thinking of hanging on for dear life that only causes more stress and illness.

What I do mean is that once you have considered a goal attainable and worth fighting for, then this goal is worth your perseverance, even when you run in to seemingly insurmountable stumbling-blocks or must deal with envious and negative people, who try to defeat you.

Make my already often mentioned opinion your own: An obstacle standing in your way is not a problem; it's a challenge to help you grow!

You are on your way to success with great self-confidence, and by overcoming obstacles your confidence grows, because it increases with real life experience, including the compliments you receive in your work.

In conclusion I would like to say:

1. Concentrate only on success. Follow your intuition, and follow the positive image you have made of yourself. This does not mean that you should ignore your weaknesses, You should define your weaknesses and remove them. This means that you should think positive and solution-oriented about your actions and results, so that you program a strong self-image.

2. Learn to see failures as challenges, as opportunities and possibilities to grow, mature and develop. See failures as learning material in your further positive development.

3. Follow the example of those people, who live as you would like to live and who behave as you want to behave. Your subconscious will give you the information, so that your actions and behavior will produce the results you literally "have in mind." The subconscious is prepared to pass on your inner messages, as long as they are not absurd.

4. Surround yourself with positive people, because those in your immediate surroundings portray a lasting program for your subconscious. I am not speaking of the dreamers, who float through life, but of those people, who concentrate on solutions, search for answers and who are working actively on creating a successful life. Stay away from people who question everything, who condemn everything with a negative prognosis, who stop you from acting and discourage the realization of your dreams, wishes and goals. Surround yourself with people who make you feel good and who help you to be yourself; they will contribute to your enjoyment in being the person you really are.

5. Never fear the future, because we know from experience that from the hundreds of fears only a few will become true, and even those will become true in much weaker form than we anticipated. We usually have very little influence on future developments. Prepare yourself for eventual crisis and dangers, then let go. Unless a difficult situation becomes acute, it should have no importance in your life.

6. Look forward to your future with pleasure, because with this book you have learned to take control over your life and determine your own destiny.

Final Observation

Many outstanding scientists have proven that the impossible can become possible. Great inventors have been criticized and attacked, but they have something that sets them apart from other people, they have an inner dream, they carry a mental conception of their life, and from the results they can and want to produce.

At this point I would like you to create a picture of yourself, to fashion an image of your life and future that it is so fast and enormous that you are willing to do everything that is necessary, so that you can produce, build and obtain every success you desire.

I am absolutely convinced that we as human beings can produce with our mind, with inspiration and all other possibilities with which nature has endowed us, the ability to realize every dream we carry inside. I am convinced that there isn't a goal we can imagine that we cannot realize.

Our subconscious knows our possibilities exactly; it recognizes our skills and talents and therefore, after many years of research and experience, I dare to say: everybody, and I mean everybody, can reach the goal they creates in their mind; because once the wish is planted in the mind, the brain creates the possibility.

I am absolutely convinced that every human being can reach everything, really everything; they make up their mind to achieve. But do not forget that the foundation for success is the willingness to do everything that is needed to reach that desired success.

With the IBMS™ I developed, I put everything you need at your disposal, so that you can turn your life into the adventure and experience you always dreamed of, with all the success, harmony, contentment, health, happiness and peace you could desire.

When I developed my IBMS™-training system, I wanted, above all, that my system would be clear and easy, easy to use and reproduce. My argument was to develop a system that led to great personal achievement and success in every area of life, so that every person would have the possibility to turn his life into a masterpiece.

Therefore, I want to point out one more time that you are the only person who can fill your life with success, harmony and happiness. Nobody but you can take away the worries, fear and sorrow; you alone can remove the conflicts in your life.

Only when you fully recognize that you are the only person in the world who can have a permanent influence in your life; your life will become truly your own. In this book I have given you, not just scientific data and facts, not just methods and strategies, but real life strategies to achieve anything you want in life.

If you develop the willingness to act in correspondence with your own personality, if you keep working on the realization of your wishes and dreams, if you do every day two or three things to improve your life, so that you come closer to your goals, your life will become the experience and adventure that it can be.

I have tried to introduce you to a philosophy, which helped me personally. By refusing to use expressions such as, "That does not work" "That is not possible" "That will never do," so that I could prove to you that everyone can reach all the dreams and wishes they would like to attain.

You have a wonderful, promising life ahead of you. The life of a leader or a colleague, who is accepted, and respected, valued as a member of a team. Take your life in your own hands and work with all your strength and possibilities, so that you can make out of your life the masterpiece it is meant to be.

Now start immediately!

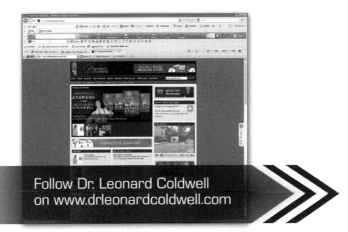

WORKSHOP FOR SETTING GOALS

Nobody can make effective, clear and quick decisions without distinct goals and values. Making decisions is, for many people, a cause of serious stress.

If you want to make quick, clear and effective decisions, decisions you can stand fully behind, you must first determine where a decision will lead you and at which goal you want to direct your energy.

You remove a serious stress-factor when you know exactly where your decisions will lead you.

It will be easier to make a decision, if you ask yourself before you make a decision: "Will this decision bring me closer or move me away from my goals?"

If you have set yourself a clear goal, it will be much easier to get back on track, when you have temporarily lost your way.

A person, who has not set any goals at all, will, of course, end nowhere. Their life will be without successful experiences, and they will miss the security of developing and moving ahead.

Because you will want to give your life a distinct direction in several areas as soon as possible, so that you will not waste time and energy by wandering around without a goal, I have prepared a workshop in goal-setting. Please follow this workshop as exactly and scrupulously as possible, because this goal-setting workshop will become the map for your future, an outline of your territory. Without a map you will flounder and lose your way.

Because you have this map for the future, you can look back and check why you made certain decisions and why you started a certain task and it will help you to return quickly to your chosen path.

While you write down your goals and plan your strategies, your subconscious will receive the messages and get the feeling of being in control. A feeling of helplessness, which is a serious stress-factor, can be diminished and even completely removed.

Our work-shop will start with a systematic conditioning of the brain in the desired direction; therefore I must ask you to follow my directions accurately, **do not skip any part or change the progression.**

Step 1: Approach this exercise when you have time to be alone. Simply go back to the time when you were still a child and you could enthusiastically write out a list of everything you wanted from Santa Claus. Put your mind in a mode of expectations. Feel confident that everything is possible.

Now make a list of all your personal wishes and dreams for the future. It does not matter whether your desires are realistic and whether you expect to realize them. Just imagine that you pop up in a fairy tale or fable and in the next few hours you can ask for anything you wish, no matter what.

It is, of course, not easy to think this way, but you should try to take life a bit lighter from now on, with a bit more humor perhaps, like the child that is till hidden in you—somewhere.

Now write down everything you would like to enjoy, if you could have it all.

Step 2: You can now put the book aside for 24 hours if you like, because you have encouraged your subconscious to contemplate your dreams, wishes and goals.

Write down any new thoughts and ideas that will come to you every day and put them all down. You will even find empty pages at the end of this book for all the information you will gather during your work.

After a 24 hour break, or when you decide to continue, write down why you want to reach and realize every single goal.

You will see which fantasy is really a goal and which one is not, because if you cannot define why you want something, it is not a real goal.

Now write down again every goal you chose, and write down at the side why you want to achieve and realize this goal.

Step 3: Now, scrutinize each goal for its effectiveness and answer the following questions for every goal you wrote down:

1. Is this really my own goal?

2. (Many goals, for which we strive, have been programmed by our environment. Frequently we do not realize that a goal is not really our own.)

3. Is this goal morally acceptable and am I willing to live with the consequences?

4. Does this goal fit in with the scope of my other goals?

5. Can I motivate myself emotionally to work on the realization of this goal?

6. Will I fulfill my wishes when I work on the realization of this goal?

Please write down all those goals that you could answer with an unambiguous "yes."

Step 4: Now, scrutinize every goal again.

Please answer the following questions:

1. Will I be happier when I reach this goal?

2. Will I be healthier when I reach this goal?

3. Will I have more friends when I reach this goal?

4. Will I be more at peace when I reach this goal?

5. Will I feel better about myself or more secure when I reach this goal?

6. Will my relationships improve when I reach this goal?

7. Will I have more self-confidence when I reach this goal?

If you cannot say yes to at least one of those questions for one or more of your goals, strike them of your list.

8. Now write down the remaining goals and leave space for a two-figure number.

Write beside every goal in parentheses the number of months or years in which you want to realize this goal. One month, three months, four years, etc.

Step 5: Consider the following concepts:

1. Many goals should be large goals, so that they will encourage you. They are needed to push you forward in your development and to help you use and exploit your full potential.

2. Other goals should be of long duration, so that a short-term set-back or failure will not lead to frustration or cause you to give up.

3. Other goals must be small in scope or should be daily accomplishments, so that you will experience success regularly; this will keep you grounded. You will receive signals that you are coming a little closer every day to the fulfillment of your long-term goals.

4. Many goals should be without end; those goals will demand perpetual development or improvement. This will prevent stagnation in your life.

5. Some goals, such as education or a training-course, which demand a certain amount of time, must of course be taken in account ahead of time.

6. Your goals must be absolutely specific. A nice car or a beautiful house is not a goal; a distinct goal demands a specific definition, for instance: "I want a white, two floor house. It must be 2400 square feet and have six rooms, two full baths and one half-bath; it must have an extended basement with four rooms, the ceilings must be seven feet high. The lot must be two acres, with 400 feet adjacent to the woods and the street must have side-walks; the house must not be further than an hour's drive from an airport or a 20 minute drive from the center of a city, where I can buy everything I need.

For a goal to be effective, it is important that you program it into your mind as exact as possible. Only when you have defined it as exactly as you want it, will you be able to make a quick decision when you go house hunting. If you, moreover, write down what you absolutely do not want, it will be easier to make a decision.

Step 6: Now identify the four most important short-term goals and write them down in order of importance:

Step 7: Please write down the important values of those goals:

1. Identify the goal.

2. Write down all advantages you, or those around you, will enjoy if you reach this goal.

Now, to give yourself an extra push in the right direction, move to:

3. Write down what it will cost you, when you do not realize this goal. What will you have to give up and what will be the social, emotional, or physical pain if you do not reach this goal?

4. Write down all the obstacles and difficulties you will have to overcome in reaching your goal.

5. Now make a list of all the knowledge and skill you will need to realize this goal.

6. Now define the people, advisers, teachers and others you will need and in which organizations, social clubs you must participate to successfully reach this goal.

7. Write a plan of action, develop a strategy of the manner on how you want to reach this goal.

Set a date for the finish of your project.

8. It is important that you deal with the corresponding tasks immediately; you will find that you will become really motivated only while you are working on, or after you set your goals— never before.

9. Be specific in every area, because your mind is now being programmed. It will be prepared to set goals, develop plans and strategies, so that it can give you directions in all corresponding areas.

My physical goals

Write down everything you are or would like to be, what you do or would like to do; and everything that has to do with your body: weight, appearance, clothing, etc.

Now follow with your physical goals the same directions you used for your life-goals. Repeat your examination in the same manner as before.

My intellectual goals

Write down everything you want to do for yourself, what you want to reach or achieve: the books you want to read, the languages you want to learn, etc.

Follow again the now familiar questions and directions.

My spiritual goals

Define your spiritual goals: peace, harmony, emotional development, etc.

Follow the same directions.

My creative goals

Write down what you want to achieve, create, invent, develop, etc.

Follow again the same directions accurately.

My family goals

What are the goals you want to achieve for and together with your spouse?

Follow the same directions.

My career-goals

This should include everything you want to achieve in your profession.

Follow again the same directions.

My social goals

What would you like to achieve for your environment, your friends, your team, your co-workers, etc? What would you like to do more often, more intensively, what would you like to create?

Follow the same directions.

My financial goals

Write down what you want to achieve financially, and what you want to own. Do not just write down what you want to earn, but what you would like to possess: house, car antiques, property, etc.

Follow the same directions.

My goals for fun and games

We all have some foolish wishes and dreams or we have some crazy ideas, things we would like to do, but that do not quite fit in our normal way of thinking. Perhaps we would like to buy something strange but we have not bought it so far. Now write down all the foolish things you would like to do or buy.

My goals for immortality

Do not be afraid to write down those things that you would like to leave behind, that would leave traces of your existence. Things you may want to do that will outlive your earthly existence, perhaps something you invent or develop, a book you may want to write or something else you want to accomplish.

Follow again the same directions.

My goals for regeneration

Please write down exactly how you want to regenerate yourself, what do you want to do to keep your balance? This will include relaxation, breathing exercises, short breaks and long vacations.

Follow again the same directions.

My activities

Congratulations, you did it. You made a map for your future. From now on you know exactly the decisions you must make in every area of your life, so that you will come closer to your desires and goals. So that you can break through the wall of indirect passivity and are able to start immediately, I would like you to write down the most important goal in every separate area.

Now write down two things under every separate goal that you could do today or tomorrow, so that you can come—if only a little—closer to your goals:

Goal 1: My life goals

Goal 2: My physical goals

Goal 3: My intellectual goals

Goal 4: My spiritual goals

Goal 5: My creative goals

Goal 6: My family goals

Goal 7: My career goals

Goal 8: My social goals

Goal 9: My financial goals

Goal 10: My fun and game goals

Goal 11: My goals for immortality

Goal 12: My goals for regeneration

YOUR INDIVIDUAL MANUAL FOR PERSONAL SUCCESS

A ll illness comes from lack of energy, and the greatest energy drainer is mental and emotional stress, which I believe to be the root cause of all illness. Stress is one of the major elements that can erode energy to such a large and permanent extent that the immune system loses all possibility of functioning at an optimum level. The fact is that 86% of all illness and doctor visits are stress related and then I just learned that the Stanford University concluded after a major study that 95% of all illness is stress related. I am referring to the mental and emotional stress that is caused by continuous and/or long-term compromises against yourself. These vary from person to person, but some examples include living in unbearable relationships and marriages, doing jobs you hate or hating your boss, or experiencing problems with family, all of which lead to you compromising your sense of self. Emotional and mental stress comes from living with feelings of constant fear, doubt, hopelessness, lack of self-esteem, worry, and, most of all, always compromising your inner feelings, instincts, and personal needs. The main component of all these energy drainers is fear. But the Bible tells us over 100 times: Not to fear and to trust in God! Your faith can heal you from fear!

The solution is to start by defining what it is in your life that keeps you from feeling happy. Can you answer the question of why you don't respect yourself enough? Or love yourself? Now identify what needs to change or happen in your life to make you feel good about yourself and your personal environment. What is it that you don't want to do, accept, or take anymore from yourself, your spouse, your children, your boss, or your coworkers? Is there someone in your life that makes you feel badly that needs to go? What are your wildest dreams and goals? Looking at your life, what is it that always takes away your energy, and where do you compromise your personal needs and feelings? Identify everything in your life that keeps you from being your true self, and start working on the development of the true you! This is the first and most important step toward achieving optimum health and happiness. And remember that happiness and hope are the most powerful healers and energy creators in your life. Pay attention to your instincts, listen to your inner voice, and start loving and respecting yourself so that you behave according to your true personality. You need to accept the statistical fact that the medical doctor or medical profession is the number one cause of death in America. That means you cannot rely solely on another person, the MD, with your health and life. What is even worse, is that I believe today that the US Government or better the different agencies of the Government like the FDA and FTC are the leading cause of death in this world because of their manipulations, suppressions, rules and regulations that prevent natural health, natural healing methods, natural cures, healing foods and supplementation and natural healers to do God's work.

If you do not live your life according to your needs, you will get or stay stressed, which will reduce your energy and eventually produce an illness. You are the only one who can change your life and improve your health. So start today by defining, creating, and living your life the way you believe is right and good for you. Create your own self-healing system—This book is my personal one for educational purposes only.

Please read the entire book first before you attempt to apply any changes for your life and health and before you do anything ask a qualified professional for help and support. You can also write to me and or licensed and practicing MD's that I have personally trained in my system (Instinct Based Medicine®—IBMS™). write to instinctbasedmedicine@gmail.com

What is IBMS™?

IBMS™ is the acronym for Instinct-Based-Medicine® -System™. It is a method by which we can use the abilities and skills of our bodies to send messages to the brain, inducing bio-electrical and neuro-chemical stimuli that correspond with our wishes, feeling and behavior.

The brain is nothing but an enormous bio-computer, which functions in the same manner as a commercial computer-system. Only, the commercial computer is a far cry from the unbelievable diversity and capacity of our brain.

Our brain responds with certain reactions to stimulation over our nerve endings, which is only possible as a result of internal and external communication; our nervous-system controls our behavior with mental and physiological stimulation.

During my years in medical research I came to the conclusion and could prove scientifically that it was possible for every human being to trigger and release helpful, healing and energy enriching neuro-chemical processes in the body, in a very short time.

Every neuro-chemical emotional condition of emotional origin in our organism, can be followed physiologically and can be measured in the circulation of our blood and the cells of our body. We therefore know that we can influence our nervous-systems significantly, and so stimulate the neurophysiology of our health, our enthusiasm, passion, contentment, harmony and love in our bodies and our lives.

The IBMS™—System I have created is a "Help to help oneself-system," which I have later enlarged into a "Teaching-method for limitless personal success and excellent health." It is nothing but a manual that tells you how to stimulate and program your brain, so that the self-help system will always be available when you need it.

A strong stimulus can, as we learned from the experience by the Russian scientist Ivan Pavlov, activate internal neuro-chemical reactions at a pre-determined time. This led me to the realization that human beings could also install stimuli in the nervous system by activating one of the five senses, which would release a neuro-chemical reaction in our body in return.

It would make it possible for every person to assume control of his energy, health and his emotional and physiological behavior.

While I developed my IBMS™-system for the conditioning of personal success and motivation, I have continually searched for new ways and possibilities to produce quicker and better results for every area of life. The most important recognition was the realization that the only true help was help to help oneself. Based on the information I wrote a concise manual for self-help. It would make it possible for every person to use his talents and skills thereby assuming control of his energy, health and his emotional and physiological behavior.

The IBMS™-system can only work if you are willing to modify the directions according to your own needs, your own imagination, dreams, wishes and goals, so that you can create your own personal success system and turn your life into the masterpiece it is meant to be.

How did IBMS™ develop?

The IBMS™-system was originally, like many other systems a hypothesis, a great dream. The need to overcome helplessness and a wish to take control, were the motivating factors.

The illness of my mother (the final stage of cirrhosis of the liver and terminal liver cancer) combined with the diagnosis of her physician that she had only two more years to live, contributed to my search for ways and opportunities to realize some better positive results for my mother. The fight for her life and my continuous search for alternative and even metaphysical ways made me realize that the solution to every human problem lies in the person himself.

Research at the University of California pointed unambiguously to the fact that the brain can be stimulated to produce a larger amount of interferon in the fight against cancer. Similar scientific results have moved me to keep searching for new and more effective ways to help people in the ability to concentrate on their own healing and regeneration.

From the successes I enjoyed and from the people, who experienced "miraculous healings" similar to my mother's, I received the self-confidence and strength to keep on searching, so that I could use this knowledge in every other area of life.

To bring this information to other people I augmented this system into a manual for self-help in every area of life.

My documentation of the conscious stimulation of bio-electric and neuro-chemical processes in the organism through desired internal and external triggers of the senses attracted attention in the medical profession, which offered me the opportunity for extensive study and research in America. I was then in a position to perfect and broaden this thought process and its application.

How does IBMS™ work?

My system works because you get in tuned with your common sense and instinct again and you will learn how to life your true life your true you the champion in you. You will learn how to define your personal true goals, your individual motivational techniques and to condition the behavioral patterns of a champion. You will learn to see your individual uniqueness and how to unleash the winner in you to become the champion you were born to be. You will develop individual action plans and strategies for total success. Total success means: Optimum happiness, health, success in every part of life, great personal and professional relationships and most of all that you find and live the true YOU.

The IBMS™ is an essential summery of every existing success and result producing system for human success, happiness and health combined with my over 30 years of experience, success and knowledge. I developed this system in a way that it is easy to understand and to apply to everybody's life. The IBMS™ is the action manual to live your true potential and experience life on its highest level.

Because we are aware of only a percentage of our skills, possibilities and strengths, we use them ineffectively and partially; the results we produce are inconsistent and random. Einstein believed we are using 10% of our brain and neurological capability but modern science proofed that we are using only 1 to 2 % of our potential.

Because, with IBMS™, you can take conscious control over your internal and external communication, as well as your visualization and the optimal stimulation of your physiology, you can control your energy and your emotions. This allows you to determine your behavior at any time.

You will learn to control your emotional, mental and physiological behavior. You will be able to determine the results you want to produce in your life. You will know your true goals for every part of your life and you will learn to produce action plans and how to put them into action and your goals into reality.

The true success of this system comes from the fact that you are enabled to uncover and live your true self and the true you. As you have read, in all my books—you have to uncover the root cause of life challenges and success production and use this knowledge to produce success in any part of life that you desire. There is no difference if it is related to health, love, success or happiness. The IBMS™ is the manual to help you find and to live the true champion in all parts of your life. If you are sick, unhappy, unsuccessful—stressed, depressed or experience anxiety then you have not found your true self and you don't live and use your full potential.

You may be controlled, brainwashed or manipulated to live a life that is not your life. That would be one possible cause of a life filled with STRESS.

To eliminate and reduce stress, to prevent or stop depression and anxiety, you need to uncover the true root cause of these symptoms of not living your full potential in every part of your life, and you need to eliminate the root cause that lead to these symptoms of an incomplete life. The IBMS™ is your manual to find your individual way for stress reduction and elimination of depression and anxiety. Always remember; your conscious and unconscious decisions and actions caused the stress, anxiety and depression. And only your own decisions and actions can change this. Only then can you be happy, healthy and successful. If you learn to understand that you were born to be a champion and that you deserve that best of the best in every part of your life you will not take anything less from life then "The Best of the Best"—never anything less than what you can be, achieve and have. There is only one way to total happiness: YOUR WAY!

IBMS™ is your personal manual to happiness, health and success
The IBMS™-system, therefore, offers you the possibility to take complete control of your life. The working of the IBMS™-system is based solely on natural bodily functions, on every person's inborn skills, talents and possibilities.

You have certainly heard or read that I have been able to help patients with chronic illnesses, including cancer, muscular dystrophy, rheumatism, gout, asthma and cirrhosis of the liver.

I have also worked with many athletes, helping them to reach the pinnacle of success in their country and even the world.

Because there are no standard solutions for every human being in the many diverse individual life stages, you must tune the knowledge and intelligence you have gained through your IBMS™-training to your own needs. You alone can change your life according to your own desires. Only a you, can create and maintain a life free of stress, a life that is effective, productive, filled with love, harmony, and success.

The methods I offer you in the IBMS™-system are luckily easily adopted in every area of life. You can modify my directions yourself, so that you can develop your own IBMS™-success–system out of mine with a short period of practice, so that you can determine and influence your own health and success.

IBMS™ is "only" the promotion of a method for an effective way to handle one's personal life. IBMS™ does work only when it is used in correspondence with your own personal desires and needs.

Defined exactly, IBMS™ is a training manual for personal development, for programming success, motivation and health, "a manual for a method" we create for ourselves, so that by using this method we can make the best use of our talents, skills and possibilities in every area of our lives. It teaches us to produce and reproduce this success, hold on to it and use it to build and broaden our potential, continuously.

You are a miracle of nature with limitless possibilities and IBMS™ is the method to realize this masterpiece—a perfect human being. Nature has given you everything to create this success and acquire this quality of life; IBMS™ will help you to recognize and use your full potential!

The IBMS™ is the world's most advanced scientifically grounded self-help training system. This system represents the culmination of 30 years of research, therapy, and experience in the development of self-help applications which are proven to target and eliminate the root causes of mental and emotional stress that can lead to illness.

When you use this system, you will be training your brain from the ground up, and you will discover that what you are experiencing is nothing less than a total rehabilitation of your brain's cognitive functions.

These applications have been scientifically proven to do the following:

- Eliminate the root causes of mental and emotional stress that inevitably lead to illness.

- Facilitate active stress reduction and regeneration of the entire nervous system.

- Enable your body to utilize oxygen, a crucial component for optimizing your health and energy, at its maximum level.

- Boost your determination, self-esteem, confidence, and power to act.

In addition, most people who use **IBMS™** report:

- A sense of calm with more energy and lucidity than before.

- Feeling well-rested and better able to cope with and solve problems.

- Improvement in the ability to sleep at night.

IBMS™ A Truly Unique Approach!

IBMS™ is a manipulation-free self-help system that uses your personality and character traits to assist you in realizing your personal dreams, goals and instincts by giving you total control over your self-conditioning and stress reduction. You will attain a state of deep relaxation during your sessions where your body is totally relaxed physically while your brain is clear and alert. This gives you total control over your sessions and its outcome, enabling you to holistically address the root cause of stress and stress related health problems.

This system is the only known system that can guarantee that there is no manipulation of any kind and that all conditioning is entirely determined by you.

The World Wellness Organization™ reviews other techniques:

Hypnotism is based on manipulation and can make people dependent, schizophrenic, mentally and emotionally weak, and can eventually lead to multiple personality disorder or delusions.

Meditation is usually only good for short term relaxation and can lead to passivity.

Positive thinking can lead to tragedy, failure or can even be life threatening because it is generally followed by inactivity and/or passivity. Positive thinking without positive actions is a guaranty for failure.

NLP is the most dangerous of all techniques as it can suppress emotions and the cause of problems; it can also hide important symptoms with very dangerous consequences. In health conflicts, it can camouflage or suppress the symptoms and root cause of illness and create or increase major health problems.

"The primary cause of illness is lack of energy; the primary cause of lack of energy is stress, mainly mental and emotional stress."
—Dr. Leonard Coldwell

The Deadly Stress Cycles Stress, Energy Loss, Illness
Overweight
Stress causes many people to overeat and gain unwanted pounds causing more stress and leading to more eating and so on. A generally unrecognized fact is that, when you are stressed, your digestive system basically shuts down so you are unable to convert food to energy...and, in the opinion of the author; lack of energy is the primary cause of illness.

Depression
Stress can lead to anxiety, which can lead to depression, which

can lead to more anxiety then more depression, and so the cycle continues. It all leads to lack of energy, and lack of energy is the primary cause of illness.

Health
Stress induced health breakdowns lead to increased stress which leads to a weaker immune system, thus resulting in greater and more dangerous health breakdowns. This cycle stems from lack of energy, and lack of energy is the primary cause of illness.

What is stress?
Stress is the body's reaction to a primary stimulus: danger. Danger is perceived by human beings as anything that threatens their mental, emotional, or physical well being. Under stress, people can experience confusion, loss of control, abnormal behavior, and irrational fear. When the body is threatened with danger, it immediately produces stress hormones.

These hormones trigger fight or flight reactions, but since people cannot run or fight in normal life situations, the hormones stay in the body and alter emotional, mental, and physical behavior. This can lead to abnormal actions and reactions such as binge eating, panic attacks, nervous or physical breakdowns, random aches and pain, depression, burnout, even suicidal tendencies.

Are mental, emotional and physical stresses different? YES
Mental stress comes from **creating** or **remembering** disturbing mental images. Examples would be imagining negative outcomes of future events—such as an irrational fear of being fired or humiliated or harmed—or recalling images of threatening situations, domineering parents, abusive caretakers or teachers or spouses, etc.

Emotional stress comes from **experiencing** threats, severe illness, worry, hopelessness, helplessness, anxiety, self-doubt, fear of failure, lack of self-esteem, or living with unfair compromises. Some

examples would be suffering in a bad relationship or oppressive work environment, being physically or emotionally abused, undergoing divorce or bankruptcy or death of a family member, or being helpless to aid or comfort a loved one.

Physical stress comes from exceeding normal physical capabilities that lead to physical exhaustion. Examples would be excessive drinking or eating, exhaustive physical exercise, constant extreme pain, sleep deprivation, unruly children, and working under deadlines. Also included are internal toxic and/or acidic reactions, some allergies, as well as nutritional deficiencies.

NOTE: All three stresses can be interdependent and interrelated.

Is one type of stress worse than another?
Continuous, uninterrupted mental and/or emotional stress often goes unrecognized and untreated. This will sap the body's energy reserves and eventually lead to a health breakdown and severe illness. Complete physical exhaustion (stress) will halt the body's ability to continue any activity at a specific point in time, but will seldom cause a health breakdown. Physical stress can be alleviated by proper rest and nutrition and/or reducing workload.

What are some of the symptoms of mental and emotional stress?
The **symptoms** of mental and emotional stress can be divided into two categories: physical symptoms and psychological signs.

Physical Symptoms:
Exhaustion, fatigue, lethargy
Headaches, migraines, vision problems
Heart palpitations, racing pulse, rapid shallow breathing
Muscle tension, aches, spasms

Dehydration

Joint and back pain

Shakiness, tremors, ticks, twitches, paralysis

Nervousness, panic attacks

Heartburn, indigestion, diarrhea, constipation, nausea, dizziness, ulcers,

Dry mouth and throat

Sexual dysfunction, lowered libido

Excessive sweating, clammy hands, cold hands and/or feet, poor circulation

Rashes, hives, itching, eczema, adult acne

Nail biting, fidgeting, hair twirling or pulling

Loss of appetite, bulimia, anorexia

Obesity, overeating

Sleep difficulties, insomnia

Teeth grinding

Asthma, allergies

Increased use of alcohol and/or drugs and medication

High blood pressure, weakened immune system

Psychological Symptoms:

Irritability, impatience, anger, hostility

Anxiety, panic, worrying, denial

Agoraphobia

Moodiness, bipolar tendencies, sadness, feeling upset

Energy swings

Emotionally exhausted, overwhelmed

Involuntarily crying, depression

Helplessness, hopelessness, lack of self-esteem

Neurotic or uncommon behavior, schizophrenia

Paranoia, claustrophobia, ADD, ADHD

Intrusive and/or racing thoughts

Memory loss, lack of concentration, indecision

Lack of motivation

Frequent absences from work, lowered productivity

Feeling overwhelmed

Loss of sense of humor

Why does stress affect our health?

All illness stems from a lack of energy! Emotional and/or mental stress is the greatest energy drainer affecting you. Continuous, uninterrupted emotional and/or mental stress will inevitably lead to an energy breakdown, which in turn will be followed by a health breakdown from a compromised immune system.

What else does stress cause?

Stress can cause dehydration, nutritional deficiencies, lack of oxygen and restful self-healing phases. Stress is also one of the main causes for diseases and symptoms such as:

Cancer, heart disease, ADD/ADHD, Parkinson's, Alzheimer's, sexual dysfunction, bulimia, pre-aging, lowered immune function, rheumatic/arthritic/fibromyalgia, joint and muscle pain, constipation, insomnia, memory loss, suicide, toxemia and acidosis.

Is dealing with stress really that important?

Untreated, constant (chronic) mental and emotional stress can shorten life expectancy, poor quality of life and result in numerous health challenges. Alleviating the stress allows you pursue a happy life on your own terms.

What is the primary physiological effect of stress?

Chronic stress leads to dehydration, one of the primary causes of physical degeneration, atrophy, and death.

Scientifically confirmed symptoms of **dehydration** are:

DNA damage

Lowered immune functions

Inability to absorb foods, vitamins and minerals

Lack of energy supply from digestion

Reduction in efficiency of red blood cells

Some emotional manifestations of **dehydration** include:

Depression

Anxiety

Feelings of inadequacy

Irritability

Dejection

Self-consciousness Cravings (caffeine, alcohol, drugs, etc.)

Agoraphobia

Scientifically recognized physical signs of **dehydration** include:

Fibromyalgia

Asthma

Bronchitis

Allergies

Indigestion/acid reflux

Chronic arthritic pain

High blood pressure

Higher cholesterol

Chronic fatigue syndrome

Angina

Strokes

Ear related symptoms, dizziness, equilibrium problems

Deafness

Visual problems

Cataract

Vitreous detachment

Uveitis

Multiple Sclerosis

Note: The main cause of dehydration (other than not drinking water) is stress!

Some facts to consider:

- Scientists at Cambridge University have evidence that the human life potential can reach 160 years.

- 112 million people take stress related medication.

- 250 million prescriptions for tranquilizers are filled annually.

- 25 million Americans suffer from high blood pressure.

- 15 million people have social anxieties.

- 14 million are alcoholics.

- 5 million people are depressed.

- 3 million people suffer from panic attacks.

- 1 million people have heart attacks each year.

- Muscles are a primary target for stress manifesting in cramping, spasms, back and jaw pain, and tremors.

- Stress can play a significant role in circulatory and heart disease, sudden cardio death and strokes.

- Stress can increase blood pressure, raise cholesterol levels and speed up blood clotting.

- Stress causes more heart disease than smoking.

- Heart disease kills more people than any other disease.

- The Harvard School for Public Health published that 65% of all cancer can be prevented by diet.

- The American Cancer Society published that at least one third of all cancer could be prevented by diet.

- Studies have shown a 66% decrease in cancer among women with a higher oxygen level.

- Mainstream medicine agrees that your body can only heal while asleep. Experts worldwide agree that a positive attitude contributes to a major part of health and wellness.

- Today 86% of all illness and physician visits are stress related.

A scientific review of the IBMS™

Every IBMS™ session provides stress reduction. However, it is important to note that while you are in a state of deep physical relaxation and total mental clarity, it is also possible to effectively and quickly condition your brain to achieve specific objectives like building self esteem, improving your golf game, conquering test anxiety, overcoming trauma, etc. Every IBMS™ session can provide an immediate benefit to everybody because with the body's enhanced ability to fully relax, it is supplied with an abundance of energy, oxygen, nutrition and optimum blood flow.

Fundamentally, the system works because the brain needs a comprehensive blueprint and the proper software to direct the nervous system to achieve a desired goal. Normally, this blueprint develops over years of trial and error decision making combined with constant repetition, which is the foundation for dendrite formation (software) that directs your mental activities. Using golf as an example, the sport requires years of practice, on-course play, the selection of proper clubs, the development of an ability to relax, focus, align, breathe, and swing in order to play well.

All of these are components of the blueprint to pull off the perfect game. By practicing you build the dendrites (software) to execute the swing and play the game. IBMS™ assists you in achieving your goal faster while bypassing all the years it would normally take because you can quickly condition your brain to perform the desired swing and play your best game while listening to IBMS™ program. Results will vary with each person.

Remember, IBMS™ program utilizes a combination of brain states and generic "I" based audio commands to effectively program the mind and nervous system so that the result you want is permanently installed as software in the brain. It is important to understand that you must be in a specific brain state at a specific time in order to achieve the proper programming. You must be in the beta state (14-30 hertz) to clearly define your objective. You then must shift to the alpha state (7-13 hertz) to be able to create a blueprint for action. Immediately thereafter you must return to the beta state (14-30 hertz) to commit to the blueprint. Then you must transfer to the theta state (3-6 hertz) so that the brain can begin building the new dendrites and install this new software throughout the nervous system.

Note: The brain has no sense of the concept of time.
With this process, you are able to produce results that might normally require years to produce. IBMS™ was created to function within the natural mechanism of the nervous system which is why the sessions are so effective. It simply allows natural neurological mechanisms to function faster and more efficiently.

Note: You can only achieve objectives that are intrinsically beneficial and derived from your personal goals and desires.
If you instinctively believe that your objective is right for you then you will achieve it. While IBMS™ facilitates your ability to achieve your objective faster and more efficiently, please be aware that any stress reduction or conditioning system that is not based on your instincts will not be permanent and can actually cause negative effects. For instance, hypnotists use the alpha state to manipulate and control

human behavior and can direct you to behave in a manner contrary to your natural instincts for a limited time (witness the ridiculous antics of hypnotized subjects on stage), but once you return from the alpha state, there is no further programming. This is because you cannot build dendrites in the alpha state; therefore, there is no software to initiate further action. This is why hypnotic suggestion has to be constantly repeated. It is, in fact, brainwashing. The person being hypnotized is required to give control of their mind to the brainwasher. We believe this can be harmful, and can even cause multiple personality disorders in some subjects. It surely creates a dependency in the subject and has the potential to lead to bipolar disorder and, in extreme cases, to paranoia and/or schizophrenia.

If you have any questions or suggestions please write to
instinctbasedmedicine@gmail.com
or go to
www.instinctbasedmedicine.com
You may also visit
www.drleonardcoldwell.com

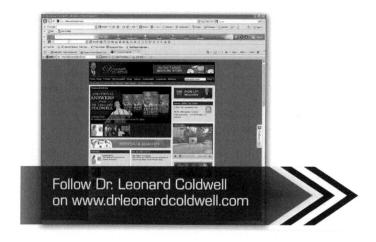

THE SUCCESS QUOTIENT

—POWER—

Success is not a thing; it is a feeling

As unique as you are in the universe, so unique is your performance; are your goals, dreams and wishes. There was never anybody in this world, who was just like you, and there will never be anybody just like you.—Yes, you are truly unique.

You should use this uniqueness to produce distinctive results and go your own way, without letting other people influence you, or by being side tracked by your surroundings, the past or by being held back by doubts or fears. You can be sure, the human being is the most perfect creation of nature, and you are not meant to suffer sorrow, failure, fear, worries, doubt or from problems with your health.

Sense and purpose in life depends on personal maturity and development. We can only be content and successful, when we have a feeling that we are on the way of knowing and using our full potential. Every day we must become more aware, so that our goals become clearer and more sharply defined. To achieve our goals we must continuously develop, in other words: change! It is not important how much you own at the end of your life, but who you have become. You will have become successful, when you have a deep feeling of contentment, harmony, happiness, freedom and love.

To be successful, you must feel successful. You can only reach this feeling, when you take care of your own needs, dreams and goals; this includes the use of your unlimited potential.

You are special and unique in this universe, and therefore you not only have the right but also the duty to walk a special path and achieve unique results.

We should feel good about our lives and ourselves. We should have the feeling that we can control our lives and enjoy continuous further development.

Cause and Effect

People were, in the past, absolutely convinced that fate was either an accident, or was predetermined by a higher authority and could not be changed.

But what would be the sense of life, if everything was predestined? Where would be the sense of honest and upright effort? Why would we want to live correct and be industrious? We would be helpless puppets of fate and our own initiative would be useless.

Every person is responsible for their own life and the development of their own future. Nobody can put the blame on the past, lack of opportunities or possibilities, set backs, physical handicaps, or their surroundings; anyone can take control of their life, and shape their own future. There is plenty of proof that people with handicaps, or people who have suffered from disastrous or adverse circumstances, and who were severely restricted or heavily burdened, have achieved great and seemingly impossible feats.

Helen Keller, who became deaf and dumb after suffering from scarlet fever very early in life, became one of our greatest writers. People, who suffered from serious physical defects have won gold medals in the Olympics, remember Wilma Rudolph, who became a gold medal winner in Rome in 1960. Wilma suffered from infantile paralysis when she was young. People, who have been abused, or grew up in the most impoverished areas of the world have achieved greatness and became examples for millions of others. Think of Neil Rudenstein; his father was a prison guard and his mother worked part-time as a waitress. He was president of Harvard University from 1991 to 2001.

To become and remain successful we must definitely not do what losers typically do: blame other people, events, circumstances or the past for their own failures or wrong behavior.

We must be big enough to take responsibility for our life, our mistakes, as well as our failures. A person has started to take control of their life and shape their future only, when they grow above themselves and takes responsibility for the development of their life according to their own desires.

As long as we make excuses for our failures and idleness, we cannot expect to live our life in agreement with our full potential.

People have the tendency to fall in a rut of convenience: "others are not doing as well as I am doing." Sure, somebody in this world suffers from hunger, or somebody is affected by war. In our immediate environment there are also people, who are not doing as well. There are people who are very ill, or people, who are living in the street.

If we focus and measure ourselves against people, who are doing worse than us, we become passive, and it will be hard to bring up the determination necessary to struggle for improvement.

We will become satisfied with our situation in life only, when we concentrate on a more beautiful, harmonious, happy and wonderful life, and believe that we can enrich our life and make it more successful, so that we can be happier and more content, create a better understanding with our partners, gain greater respect and are a better example for our children. If the pressure caused by dissatisfaction is strong enough, we will look for solutions, answers, changes and improvement, putting more effort into our work.

You can, of course, focus on fewer results, but why would you do that? You did not enter this world to vegetate in humility and modesty, live in poverty, and suffer with worries, doubts, fears and illness, while you lacked the necessities of life.

Brighten your life with the light that has been waiting to enter, since the time of your birth.

Nobody should suffer from lack of success. Nobody should be unhappy, sick or poor. To avoid fearing the future, you must take responsibility and control of your decisions and actions now. Only then, your future will no longer be an accident of fate; it will be what it is meant to be: the result of sensible goal-directed actions that correspond with your own ideas, performances and desires.

You carry the seed of success of failure within you. It has nothing to do with the circumstances in which you are living and has nothing to do with your past. What is important to your development and future is your reaction to whatever you experience in life.

Cemeteries are the most affluent places on earth; there are the people with unfulfilled dreams, with unachieved goals, with unfound inventions, unwritten poems and unused potential.

If you do not compose that song or write the book you carry within; if you don't develop the invention in your mind or be the spouse you can be; the world will be so much poorer. All of this will result because you did not contribute the unique results that were yours to give.

Many people conclude at the end of their lives that they lived for only ten percent. When they are older, they realize that they have so much more to do and that they have squandered so much of their lives.

You know those unhappy, angry people, who lived their lives in bitter loneliness, because they never reached the success that they had hoped to achieve. They were not successful and were afraid to act or too lazy to persevere, now they begrudge the success of their fellow man. Those losers even try to stop others from improving and enhancing their lives.

Losers, people who are not willing to put aside their worries, doubts, fears and limitations, and who never try to emulate happy and successful people, but rather they try to impede the success and happiness of others and try to pull them down to their lower level of life.

Losers do not believe that they can be successful; they therefore fail to try and achieve the success they observe in their successful and happy fellow man. They look for reasons for their failures: "My classmate, my sister, my brother or my neighbor were not very successful either."

Success and failure depends on how we see ourselves. It depends on the descriptions and pictures we carry in our mind of ourselves, of our abilities, talents and achievements. This image we carry in our mind is our self-image. This has nothing to do with mysticism, magic or metaphysical laws; it is merely a normal function of the brain.

Our brain is nothing but a huge biological computer that needs a distinct software program, so that we can work with it. We program our brain with self-assessments, such as: "I am a failure," "I can't do that," "I could never do that," or "Of course I can do it," "I will succeed," "I know I can do it." We also program the images we have of ourselves, of our abilities and possibilities, in our brain.

Everybody thinks in images. The language of the brain (or of the sub-conscious) is an image. When I ask you to please look into yourself; I ask: "Who do you see in your mind's eye? "Do you see somebody who is overweight, weak and helpless? "Do you see a smoker, or do you see a healthy, slim, vital and active person? "Do you see someone who is independent and free from the influence of others?" What image do you have of yourself at this time?

How would you picture yourself if you were giving a lecture in front of a group of people, or if you were in a serious discussion with others? How do you picture your abilities, and what kind of a parent do you think you are? How do you see yourself in your career and in your professional development?

Your life will proceed as you see yourself at this moment, because your brain can only use the program you entered.

In the past we had little influence on the programs that were entered in our mind. As a child we heard all too often: "That is not possible." "You won't be able to do that." "Nobody can do that." "Leave it alone, you cannot do that." "That is too much, it is too big, too heavy, too…"

By the age of twenty-five we have been programmed 204,210 times to become a failure. According to a study at Harvard University we have heard 204,210 times: "No that does not work, you can't do that; it is not possible…" In that way we were programmed to do nothing, give up and become failures.

This had, of course, a dramatic influence on our thinking, our desires, the images we have of ourselves and in our confidence of possibilities we see in our future.

Parents, grandparents, teachers, nannies and other adults meant well when they stopped us from doing the things we wanted to do. But they curtailed us and gave us a negative self-image.

Please think back a while: How many dreams, wishes and great expectations did you have as a child? What did you want to become, achieve and change? Haven't we all been robbed of our dreams and illusions over the years?

Of the information we receive from our surroundings and the media, 87 percent is negative. This is one reason that only ten percent of the people accomplish great feats. Many are simply not able to overcome the onslaught of negative information. They become convinced that it is impossible to achieve certain things in life. They may believe that only specially gifted people, blessed by fate, can make it to the top, and they do not belong there.

I know that this is not so. I want to help you with this book, so that you can learn to believe in yourself again. You will regain the ability to dream, so that you will have positive expectations again, with great goals that inspire you to work for your life and future.

Make sure that you know how very special you are.

Please concentrate for a while on how wonderful and special you are as a human being. Now take your success-journal and a large piece of paper on which you can write proudly, everything, all the special skills, talents and personality traits you possess.

Exercise 1:

Write down every single success you have achieved. This may be a test of survival, an athletic achievement, or maybe an excellent and successful conversation with one of your children. No matter what the success, write it down. Take your memories way back into your childhood.

Exercise 2:

Now, write down the personality and character traits that make you who you are. Perhaps you are very helpful, patient, caring or understanding. Write down as much as possible, because you must start to believe again how great, special and unique you really are. The signals we receive from our environment are all too often negative, and there is hardly anybody who points out our positive qualities, talents and successes. It is, therefore, very important that we remind ourselves regularly that we are special and valuable people. Your brain can only work in correspondence with the program that is in place.

Exercise 3:

Please, also write down your outstanding talents and skills; perhaps you are a good communicator, work very well with your hands, or are an excellent writer…

Exercise 4:

This book is a work-manual in the truest sense of the word, therefore I ask you to define what success means to you: "What does success mean to me? What should happen in my private and professional life? What do I expect of my health; what should be the reality, so that I can feel happy, content and successful in every area of my life?"

Once more: please do every exercise and all the tests I advice you to take, immediately. You will break through the wall of complacency, hesitation and even fear, only, when you make imme-diate use of the moment. At the same time you will develop a new pattern of behavior, of acting quickly. Do not waste time; start immediately on the improvement of the quality of your own life and that of your fellow men. You will feel better right away.

You can train yourself not to hesitate, not to look for excuses, not to push things away or avoid action. With certain exercises you can program yourself to do just the opposite and act immediately. When you are requested, or must do something, do it immediately. It will put you on the road to success, happiness and contentment.

We have become accustomed to lethargy, laziness and hesitation; we must push this type of behavior away from us. The more often we give in, the more entrenched this negative behavior becomes. We must break through this negative demeanor; then our life will change for the best.

Each behavioral move becomes a pattern through regular repeat. It becomes a computer program for the brain. If you do the same thing regularly, the frequency will increase and it will soon turn into a habit.

Why should you keep doing the wrong thing and make it a part of your regular behavior, if you can program a better habit instead?

If you give yourself either a small task, or face a big life task, you will start immediately and look for solutions. It will quickly become a conscious behavior pattern that will run on automatic. You will act instead of hesitate. You will go from somebody who has let others stand in your way, to somebody, who now goes your own way, no matter what happens.

Now identify those areas in your life in which you, knowingly, behave differently than you should, because it is simpler and easier.

Exercise 5:

Now please write down the behavior you want to change in the future. Which behavior dissatisfies you; perhaps you have outbursts of anger, because you are afraid, lazy or aggressive. Write this all down on a clean page of your success-journal.

Exercise 6:

Now, write down how you want to behave in the future in those situations. Think of a simple trick to remind you, so that your brain can easily recognize and program the desired new behavior.

Program yourself

Be aware: Our brain cannot differentiate between something that really happens, something we really experience and something we only imagine in our mind. For the brain, it is the same, whether we just imagine or actually experience a certain event. The brain will, therefore, react in the same manner, whether something happens in the mind only, or whether it is reality.

This can be proven scientifically: the bio-chemical changes and the bioelectrical processes in our organism are the same when something happens in reality or only in our imagination.

We all know that we soon feel the same as we did before, when we relate to others an exiting experience or a movie we really enjoyed.

When we tell a story of something that happened to us, we must see the picture in our mind, otherwise we cannot talk about it. The memories will trigger in the mind the same feelings we experienced before. At that time the brain will undergo the situation just as it happened in reality.

We can use this natural function of the brain to consciously program our mind, and install the physical, emotional and intellectual behavior we desire.

To introduce desired changes in your feelings or behavior, you must start by creating images in your mind of things you want, and of ideal behavior you would like to be a part of you. This means that you could experience a discussion with your spouse or partner in your mind with images of you being completely calm, factual and loving, showing understanding and eminent perseverance; just as you would like yourself to behave in the future. You will no longer see yourself as you were before, with a lack of understanding, and perhaps even angry or aggressive.

You start by picturing the future and desired behavior as clearly and emotionally as possible in your mind. You must develop a feeling that you are really in this situation and that it corresponds with your wishes. This process is difficult at first. But after five or six repetitions it will become easier, and above all clearer and a matter of course.

Repeat this process 25 to 35 times in a row. Do it until you automatically see and experience the desired behavior in your mind that you wanted to program in your brain.

From then on you will automatically behave in a similar situation, as you want to behave. Just like you deleted an old song from your mp3 player and replaced it with a new song you want to hear.

If you want this process to succeed, it is necessary that you do not see yourself as an observer of a movie in which you play the main part. It is important that you not only see it in your mind, you must experience, feel and hear it; just as you would, if it were really happening (Association). Play an active part in the pictures in your mind; don't be an observer (Disassociation).

We have all, at one time or other, picked up and often programmed incorrect behavior; the new programming may become weaker after some time and the old habits may creep back in. When we put a new program in place, we should repeat the process every day for some time. If you find yourself in a situation where an old habit creeps back in, repeat the pictures of your desired behavior in your mind and work hard on establishing and living in the way you want to behave. The old program will be destroyed in a short time. If you regularly repeat the behavior you want in your mind as well as in the real world, the old behavior pattern can never get hold of you again. If you stop a certain behavior while you are in the middle of it and do not let it take its course, the brain will discharge the behavior, because the brain cannot cope with incomplete information. You can disrupt the habit of reaching for a cigarette, first by stopping yourself before you hold and light it; by saying loudly: "no!"

or perhaps "ping." You give your brain an extra reminder.

Put your pack of cigarettes away and hum your "ping" during the day, so that it will stay in your mind.

It takes about 25-30 repeats to program a new habit effectively. Experience has shown that if you do these 21 days in a row, the new wished for behavior is fully conditioned. The more feeling, joy and enthusiasm you put into the programming, the quicker and more effective the result will be.

The Meaning of Life

Many people suffer from boredom, from a feeling of discontent or being incomplete. They often do not know what to do with their life or themselves. The reason is that they have not found a meaning for their lives and feel unfulfilled.

If you have clear ideas for your future and a purpose for your life; if you know what you want to achieve, you will neither be bored nor feel unfulfilled.

Each of us must find a personal meaning and lay the foundation for our own life. We should not allow other people to tell us how to live and what to do. What may be important, valuable and right for one person may me totally different from what is right for you and me.

We get direction in life by the goals we set and the decisions we make. Every decision we make and every action and aspiration gives our life a certain direction.

The problem is that too many people have no clue where they want to be in five, ten or twenty years, or what they would have liked to accomplish at the end of their life. Those people lack goals and direction. They are unhappy and dissatisfied, and they waste their time on meaningless pursuits.

Those people waste their life by "killing time," because they have no goals. They do not know how to use their time wisely or more effectively. It is, therefore, important to give your life direction as early as possible.

The Foundation

You will quickly become aware what your dreams, wishes and goals really are, when you skip over a large segment of your life and decide what you want to have accomplished at a certain time. It will give your life a personal and individual meaning. You will be able to develop a plan of action, so that you can reach your goal. As a positive side effect, every thing you do will go easier; it will especially be easier to make decisions. From then on you will only have to ask yourself: "Will this decision bring me closer or take me further away from my goals?" You will know immediately what decision to make.

Exercise 7:

Please write down the decisions you must make. What do you have to do and what action is needed, so that you may realize the goals you want to reach before your ninety-fifth birthday.

Self-Fulfilling Prophecies

Our expectations, no matter in what area, determine the results we enjoy. Our expectations and our believe-system will determine whether we can or cannot do something.

Our brain searches and reacts continuously for already pro-grammed and determined life situations. We cannot make a speech in front of a large group of people, if we carry in our mind a picture that we cannot do so.

The action of our brain will follow the mental images of the type of behavior we have programmed. Our behavior is no accident. It can only respond to the images we have of a certain situation, whether this is related to a discussion with our boss, with a colleague, or whether it is a difficult task we must complete; the brain will feed back what has been programmed before.

Every thought, every image we have of ourselves, of our skills and accomplishments, whether we are good parents, good friends, good workers, or good colleagues…., will determine how we behave in every area of our life. Our behavior determines the results we produce; thus our thoughts determine our behavior and our behavior determines our results.

The Sixth Sense of Success

It has nothing to do with a so-called sixth sense, when someone says: "I know I cannot take this full cup of coffee into the living-room without spilling." It will have to do with the programming of that person's brain. We all have heard ourselves or other people say: "I knew I could not do it." Those statements are not only a direct result of our thinking; they determine the outcome of our action.

Our belief-systems (our conviction over what is or is not right) determine our achievements and results in every area of our lives.

The following story appeared in USA Today: An excellent student passed a university entrance exam with 89 points. When the student read that he had been accepted with 89 points, he thought mistakenly that the score of 89 was his intelligence quotient.

The student's belief in himself was effected so negatively that although he had always been number one in his class, he now passed his exams with rather low grades.

The advisor asked to see him at the end of the semester and asked why his grades were low while he had been an excellent student before. The student answered that his grades were hardly a surprise, if he had only an I.Q. of 89.

After hearing how the young man had picked up the belief that his I.Q. was 89, his advisor explained that he had passed the entrance exam with very high points and that only two students had scored higher than he. The young man's grades immediately picked up to the level that corresponded with his abilities.

This story shows the danger of losing faith or of forming a negative opinion of our skills and talents. The following example of a scientific experiment shows the same result:

The leader of a study-group gave three groups of students a group of rats. He told group one that their rats were extremely stupid, to group two he told that their rats were of average intelligence and he informed group three that their rats were quite intelligent. Each group had to perform certain tests with their rats for six weeks and try to teach them, moreover, some tricks.

At the end of six weeks the so-called smart rats had learned some tricks, the average rats had done reasonably well and the so-called stupid rats had done very poorly.

The students were surprised to hear that all the rats had the same parents and that there were no stupid, normal and intelligent rats. In psychology, receiving results according to expectations is called; the Pygmalion effect.

The last example shows that recipients will perform according to the expectations they perceive to get. This information is especially important in the education of your children, the training of people in your work force, or in the contacts you have in your professional and private life. You will treat your children as you perceive them, whether this is incapable, very intelligent or efficient. The response from our fellow man is determined by the expectations they think we have.

Treat your spouse as the best spouse you could have. He or she will respond with a corresponding positive behavior.

Always believe that your children will be great students and that they will perform very well. Show the same conviction that you give your children to your fellow workers, your colleagues and to all other people, with whom you are regularly dealing.

"If you see people as they are, they will become less. If you see people as they could be, they will grow and become greater" (J.W. v. Goethe).

If you have negative expectations from someone, do not be surprised if you get, in the future, exactly what you expected.

This law has two sides. We will not only get what we expect from others and ourselves, but the expectations of others also have a real influence on our development and achievements.

Most of us are influenced by the expectations of our parents, grand parents, siblings and teachers. Many people can never free themselves of the influence and expectations of their early child-hood; they may still suffer, years later, from their opinions. We frequently act totally different to our parents than we behave around others. Different expectations lead to different behavior.

It is therefore important that you surround yourself with as many positive people as possible–with people, who believe in you, in your efficiency and expect you to have a successful future. You will be supported by the positive expectations of your fellow men.

I have advised and taken care of many companies, and I have always been careful that I had created a positive attitude of expectation among the workers and between the leaders and the work force. I have always encouraged the creation of a pleasant work-atmosphere, so that all the employees, and the company as a whole, would be more productive and successful.

I hear repeatedly: opposites attract one-another. This is not so. People, who have similar interests, similar hobbies, dreams, ideas and goals; who are similar in appearance and have the same political outlook are attracted to one-another.

You will conclude, when you give it some thought, that your best friends, the people you enjoy the most, and the person who is most important to you, is very much like you, or like the person you want to be.

People attract people, who have similar thoughts and ideas. You can even think that your thoughts, like a magnet, attract exactly what they emit.

If you want different people, different results, different developments and different behavior in your life, then you need only to change your thinking, so that you will, in the future, attract and achieve that which corresponds with your thoughts.

Mental pictures and our Attitude toward Life

One of the pioneers in the study of the factors that lead to success, and in the training of achieving personal success, Earl Nightingale, revealed in his best seller, *The Strangest Secret*, a simple, but unbelievable solution for success. His message was: "You will become what you think, or you will become what you believe you will become."

The results of a study at Harvard University showed that no matter in what area of life people are or were successful, 85% of their success resulted from the positive mental attitude those people had about life or of their corresponding situation in life.

No matter whether it involved their education, the development of their careers or the use of their skills and talents, 85% of success was the result of a positive attitude. Only 15% of somebody's success depended on knowledge, talent, education and other outstanding abilities.

Your mental attitude toward certain subjects or toward your total life is influenced by the outlook with which you view certain developments in your life. If you believe that you can give a successful speech in front of many people, then you will approach the occasion full of anticipation, enthusiasm and optimism. If you, on the other hand, are convinced that you will forget the text, will stutter and stumble, or that your speech will be a debacle, in other words if you have negative expectations, your speech will turn into a disaster.

It is therefore especially important that you always expect the best possible ending to a situation, performance, the use of your talents, and the execution of a certain task. Do not focus on what may go wrong. Don't paint pictures in your mind about disastrous developments, because it will diminish your ability and eagerness to persevere or make it impossible to give the full 100% to the completion of your task.

Our expectations are based on innuendos, confirmations, on our past, the present, on our thoughts and on the conversations we have with ourselves in our mind, and also on what other people think and expect of us.

Use the information I have given you before and program into your brain at least 25 times for 21 days the talents, skills and success you desire, because the brain, as we have learned, does not know the difference between what is real and what is imagined.

Even when the desired changes manifest themselves, as they often do, after the first day, you must keep up the conditioning; so that you can be sure that they are permanent. If you change what you believe, you change what you expect and therefore you will change your life.

The positive picture or the belief you have in yourself is the foundation for successful action in every area of your life.

The concept you have of your Self-Image

We carry, deep within ourselves, a mental picture of our skills, talents and possibilities. This picture determines the goals we want to reach and the output we are willing to give to achieve our dreams.

This mental picture is a form of programming (like computer software). Our actions correspond with this program. We make decisions and set our goals correspondingly. The sum of our behavior in every area of our life is controlled by this mental programming (our self-image) that we have installed.

The brain starts immediately after our birth to search who we are, what our abilities and talents are, or, to say it differently, our brain begins to determine the all-embracing life questions: "Who am I, what am I, what can I do, and where do I want to go?"

Our self-image (the computer program of our skills, talents and actions) will very early be placed by our parents, grand-parents, caretakers, teachers, educators, and the people around us, with additional underscoring by leaders and professors.

Almost everyone suffers daily from 87% negative programming by the media, (TV, radio and press) because 87% of their information is negative. We program and condition this information; it tells us that life is hard, bad, difficult, unfair, and that we have no control over the outcome.

As a result, many people fear the future instead of joyfully embracing the unlimited possibilities and opportunities that are waiting for them; opportunities that could fill their future with happiness and contentment.

We carry a concept about our clothes, our weight, our vitality, our energy and our ability to achieve, we also carry an idea in our mind whether we are or are not a good spouse, a good parent, and a good friend.

We have a self-concept for every area of our lives. We also have an overlapping general concept of the ideal mental image, a desire of who and what we really want to be. If this general concept is too modest or even negative, then we can hardly expect to achieve great results.

Reasons for a poor self-image

Reasons for a poor self-image are:

- living in a negative environment, having a pessimistic family or negative friends

- having an unusual appearance, such as a big nose, flaring ears, for some women, large or small breasts

- suffering from negative experiences within the family, such as abuse, violence or a parent, who is an alcoholic

- the feeling of not being loved, rejection or lack of acceptance by people in authority, or by people we respected or loved, disapproval by teachers, care-takers or fellow-students

- loss of a job, financial collapse, or personal setbacks

- a constant confrontation by authority, or coping with immoral behavior of others

The results of negative programming in the past can be turned positive. I will tell you later in more detail how this can be done.

We often find a negative self-image in people:
- who are very critical, arrogant, conceited or sarcastic

- who have a hard time making a compliment

- who keep trying to get center-stage; you know the class clown

- who talk too much; they believe that what they have to say is interesting; they want to be noticed by quantity instead of quality

- who want to appear wealthy (their invitations are extravagant. Those people believe that they can buy friendship.)

- who have drug problems, or who have no moral or ethical values

- who always see and stress the worst in others (Those people do not believe in their own success and therefore try to diminish the success of others, so that they can narrow the gap between themselves and people, who are more successful.)

- who dress too eye-catching and usual (They want to draw attention, although their self-esteem is low. It is of course an easier way to get attention, then by earning the respect of others through hard work and achievements.)

Pay attention to your appearance

You must have noticed that your wife acts differently, when she has had her hair done, or your husband when he wears a brand-new suit. Let your appearance be of importance; pay attention to your clothes. Dress, so that you feel good, take care that it is always appropriate and clean. Dress today, as you would dress when you have achieved your goals.

Perhaps you still remember: Did you wear something special, when you knew that they were going to take the class pictures; did you pay more attention to your hair, or to your whole appearance? A study was done that showed that on the day the class pictures were taken, students' work improved by 80%.

Exercise 8:

Please take your success journal and write down the weight you want to have, how you want to dress and speak. Write down how you want to be as a partner, parent and friend. Make a kind of blueprint for your personal development and experience that you can use as a reference. Put down your ideal self-image, so that you know exactly how you want to behave in every area of your life. This will help you to change, perfect and develop, so that you can be happy and reach your full potential.

Our self-image is an inner mirror image that spreads to the outside. You must change your self-image, if you want to change your life in a certain area.

Exercise 9:

Now write down, which areas and what behavior you want to change. What are the talents and skills that you want to acquire or use more intensively?

Your self-esteem, the feeling you have of yourself and how much you like yourself, determine your ability to succeed and the outcome in every area of your life. People, who have very low self-esteem, are arrogant and overbearing, or fearful and withdrawn. They develop these irrational patterns of behavior, because they do not like themselves.

Other people cannot like and accept you, if you do not like yourself. It is therefore important that you learn to accept and like yourself. You can look forward to liking yourself, even though you do not like yourself yet. We will now start to work on the changes that correspond with your new self-concept, so that you can begin to like yourself.

Exercise 10:

Please write down the special character and personality traits you would like to have. Start by writing: "I like myself, because I am a valuable human being." Add all the personality traits you would like to have, for instance: "I like myself, because I am a good friend and a good parent. I am loyal, honest and sincere. I have clear goals and live according to my own strong moral and ethical principles. I am a good speaker and I will never again let others stop me from facing my problems and challenges. From now on I will see every handicap as a challenge to my further development and growth. I will never again be satisfied with less than I can be, own or achieve."

Write your self-program similar to this. Go to the mirror three times each day and while you look yourself in the eyes repeat three times what you wrote down.

You will come to the conclusion that you will feel better, stronger and healthier in a short time. Always end your text with: "I like myself, because I am a wonderful person and I am always willing to accept the challenges life offers, so that I can make every day my own special day. Yes I am born to be successful."

It is a cry for help, when someone acts in an arrogant and aggressive way toward you, or when he or she rejects or dismisses you. It is a cry for attention, a cry for approval, confirmation of self-esteem and acceptance.

Be big enough to approach other people with understanding. Nobody really wants to be bad, no matter how negative his or her behavior may be sometimes. Everybody would like to be a winner, and nobody wants to be a loser. Do not let your self-image be so fragile that others can pull you down to their own lower level.

Nothing should stop you to be and stay friendly, even when others are unkind and unfriendly.

Conditioned to lose

You have probably asked yourself, just like I did, why an elephant, a great and a strong animal, can be tethered to a small block of wood with a thin rope. Why does the elephant not rip the rope or pull the tether out of the ground?

The elephant does not free itself, because as a baby it was bound with a strong chain to a heavy block of concrete. The little elephant pulled and tugged, but could not free itself. The little animal learned that it could not free itself when someone tied him by his leg; it accepted (by neurological anchoring) that he could not ever make himself free. As a result you can now tie this animal with a thin rope without risking that the animal will try to escape.

We all have been conditioned in the same way, so that we cannot reach certain things. Just as we have seen or heard that other people could not reach certain goals, we have also been conditioned, or perhaps have conditioned ourselves to believe that certain corresponding desires are beyond our scope.

By trying later on the elephant could have found out, that simply because you fail once, it does not mean that you have to fail again the next day or at another time.

You must therefore never give up trying to reach a worthwhile goal, no matter how often you have tried already, or how many others have tried without success. Give it another go and realize your dream.

An eleven-year-old girl survived a boating accident by swimming to the coast of Miami through 13 miles of turbulent water. Experienced swimmers and experts considered this impossible—but somehow she did. When a reporter asked her how she had accomplished this seemingly impossible task, the girl answered: "I did not think about the distance, I only thought about living. No matter how hard it was, I only concentrated on the next stroke and kept saying: 'You can do one more stroke, just one more!'"

Just like this young girl concentrated on doing one single stroke after another to achieve the impossible, I ask you to concentrate on one more step, and then another. Do not look at the complete mountain of tasks, obstacles and problems. Concentrate only on the final goal you want to reach; you will then be able to work step by step on the realization of the image you carry in your mind.

Remember, if you change 1% of your life a day, than you have made a 100% change after 100 days. (Mathematically, you could say that you changed more than a hundred percent, because every next day you build on the increased total of the days before.) Just so we want to work step by step on our self-image (Software for the use of our skills, talents and other potential) in the same way we wish to program ourselves.

There are no Losers

Most people are unsuccessful, because they don't take action. They don't act, because they are afraid of failure, rejection or refusal. They do not act, because they are afraid that others may laugh, or that they will botch the job.

Every person is born with unlimited potential and the road to success depends on experience—both positive and negative experience. Whenever we try to accomplish something, and it does not work, or at least does not function the way we want it to do, we collect information on how not to do it. We develop at the same time a new understanding of how we can do it better.

Every successful athlete, every successful scientist, every speaker, every executive or every successful parent is successful, because he or she has learned from experience, and yes, even from failures.

You need to see failures as steps of a ladder that will lead you to success. Every large development and every great success is a history of errors, failures, rejection and disappointments. It is perseverance that separates the people, who end up winners from the losers. Consistency, perseverance, keeping on track, no matter how many setbacks somebody experiences, that is what sets the winners apart from the losers!

Nobody is an overnight success, although it sometimes seems that way. The successful pop-singer Tina Turner had relatively little success when she sang many years in nightclubs after her divorce from Ike Turner, and "suddenly" made many millions in just a few weeks with her LP *Private Dancer*. The founders of a number of computer companies were working years in rented garages, suffering high investment costs, before they earned millions. Thomas Edison produced 10,000 documented failures before he succeeded in the invention of the light bulb; he suffered another 25,000 failures in the development of a battery. When he was asked whether he did not feel like a failure after so many unsuccessful attempts, Edison answered: "No, I now know 25,000 ways how not to make a battery." On the question whether he was ready to give up after 2 years in search of the light bulb, he answered: "I felt that I must be successful very soon, because I am running out of possibilities to fail."

He was saying: When you run out of possible failures and keep on trying, you will necessarily run into success.

There are basically two ways to fail:
- No action

- To discontinue your action

Learn from successful Failures

Albert Einstein did not talk until he was four years old. Thomas Edison was considered feeble-minded. Some that heard him, believed that Julio Iglesias could not sing, and even Enrico Caruso had to leave the school of music he attended, because his music teachers felt that he could not hold on to certain notes. Some people believed that Elvis Presley lacked a sense of rhythm; after his first television appearance a well known music critic said: "we won't hear from this Jumping Jack again."

People considered the Wright brothers crazy, if they thought that they could invent a machine which would allow people to fly. They laughed when Alexander Graham Bell expressed the desire to send the human voice through a wire. We could go on and on about people, who were not considered successful and now belong to the most famous successful people in history.

It is not the talent or special opportunities received from wealthy parents and other lucky breaks that determines a person's happiness, contentment or success; you determine your path. It is not important how you start your life; what counts is how you end it.

Don't Lament—Act

The success you achieve in life is not determined by your assumptions, your past or your circumstances. Your determination, the goals you set for yourself and your perseverance determines what you will achieve in life.

Moaning and crying that you are too large or too small, or that your skin has the wrong color does not help. We have to play the game and make the most of it with the cards we have been dealt. We must not burden our life with self-pity and cry continuously that others have what we would like to have, or complain that somebody else's life is easier than ours.

The past will no longer play a roll, when we let go of it, instead of making the mistake to belabor it. Learn from your mistakes and then let them go.

The brain functions in a very simple way. Whenever we dwell on horrible things that happened in our past, the brain experiences the same situation as if it were happening again or perhaps it seems even worse. It induces the same neuro-chemical and bioelectrical processes in our organisms as it did before, when we really experienced the unpleasant situation. We will suffer the same pain every time we dwell on the traumatic past. We waste our present, our time, strength and future every time we cry about the pain we have suffered in life, or about what others did to us. We cannot change the past, no matter how often we complain, cry, or try to do something about it. We cannot change the past, but we can change the present, and therefore the future.

Do not waste your wonderful potential and valuable time, so that negative past experiences will destroy even more of your time, energy and strength.

I call people, who keep complaining and who are always looking for excuses, energy devourers, because they bother others, and with their wining and crying they drain their energy, without ever trying to improve or change their own lives. Those people want neither solutions nor change. They just want to take center-stage and fill their senseless life with the attention of others.

Successful and happy people, on the other hand, can accept the blows of fate and keep on going. They have learned to make the best out of every situation, no matter how hard it is.

Their only choice is moving on, because this is the only life they have, like it or not. This is their body and their life, and life can only develop positively, when they are positive and act correspondingly. Leave the past for good behind you and live from now on in the present and work toward a future determined by you.

The difference between successful people and failures is that successful people act and people, who fail, talk about action.

Nobody should be a failure and nobody should be a loser. There are, however, many people, who fail. They fail:

- because they did not write down clearly defined goals and make the plans of action to reach those goals, because

- they have never been taught to motivate themselves for success.

- they have no reasons strong enough to motivate them.

- their behavior is not flexible enough. They repeat behavior even though they know from experience that it will not lead to desired goals.

- they believe that they cannot be successful. They have a negative self-image.

- they have never taken the time to consider their possibilities and how they can achieve certain goals in their lives. They become indolent, lazy, afraid, and lack the energy to start.

- they lack moral and ethical values, such as honesty, loyalty and strength of character.

- they always have an excuse that it is just not the right time: the economy is bad, it is the wrong time of the year, or it is the weather…

- they do not understand that you have to be part of a team to make it to the top and stay there.

- they do not understand that you must first give, before you will receive. They can reach everything in life, if they are willing to help others to reach what they would like to have.

- they believe that the past influences their present and future. They believe that if they did not get what they wanted in the past that they will not be able to reach it in the future. The past does not have to influence the future, because tomorrow is another day.

- they always focus on the negative instead of on the positive. They will receive the negative, because that is where they focus,

- they associate with pessimistic or even criminal people.

- they believe that somebody else, or some group, can solve their problems.

- they depend on alcohol, other people or, in the worst case, on extremist groups or sects.

- they blame other people, things or circumstances for their own mistakes, they never look into themselves for the cause of negative results. Only by recognizing that they are at this point, thanks to their own behavior, and accepting the responsibility while they find the way to success.

- they are arrogant and pretentious, and therefore display a negative self-image. They develop a dream world that has nothing to do with reality. They live a fantasy, which they keep artificially alive. Therefore they cannot change. They close their eyes to the truth and think they are great.

- they are not willing to try something new; they are inflexible and refuse to develop further. Those people will say: "We have done it like this for ten years; we can do it like this for the next ten years."

- they do not take responsibility for their own behavior, their further education and development.

- they do not have enough energy. They do not take care of their health and body.

- they concentrate on whining and self-pity instead of action.

- they believe that by thinking positive, instead of acting positive their life will change.

- they care too much what others think about them. Those people should only think about people, who are important to them. They should not care about other people's opinion. What they think of themselves is most important.

- they see themselves as helpless victims, at the mercy of life. Therefore they do not take action and simply give up.

Program a complete change

Because the brain acts as a computer, you can simply erase the program and get rid of it, as if it never existed.

Walk through a negative experience in your mind and change it into a positive event, picture it as you would have liked it to happen. You will now remember this experience as you have just re-programmed it. Change, in your mind, a situation in which you were helpless into a situation in which you are full of confidence and have great self-esteem, strength and energy. Once you can see it confidently, go back to the bad situation and shout "bang" and let it explode into a thousand little pieces. Repeat this cleansing exercise quickly, many times, until you have the feeling that the image is no longer around, and you can no longer see anything but the exploded image.

You will now see this experience as you want to see it; you were not helpless, but strong, confident and successful. You have now conditioned this situation and remember it as an event in which you were strong and confident. Repeat the exercise with the explosion until the images or the memories are completely removed from your mind. This exercise may seem simple, but it works perfectly. Try if first and then decide whether this method works.

Do not let anyone stop you

Losers often find security on the assembly line or in a permanent position, where they will receive the same salary month after month —and still do not earn enough to make it. They envy people, who are more successful. Although successful people necessarily take greater risks and make better use of opportunities, those, who do not do so well, envy their higher income and success and try to persuade them to avoid the more successful and more challenging path.

Before you consider whether somebody else's advice is right or important, ask yourself: "Should I listen to this person and accept his advice?"

- Is this person more successful than I am?

- Is this person financially independent?

- Is this person happy?

- Is this person an excellent team-player in his private and professional life?

- Has education and experience given the person the competence to have an opinion on what I do?

- What are this person's motives and what do they gain by their remarks?

It is important to know that losers never try to emulate and reproduce the success of other people; they will not compete or surpass a winner, because they believe that they cannot do so. Losers have the self-image of a loser conditioned in their brain and cannot believe that they have the skills and achieve what the winners accomplish. They do not emulate successful people, because they do not want others to see them fail, they therefore try to bring others down to their own low, loser-level.

It is always wise to consider who is talking, why this person is saying what he or she says, and whether this person is informed and knows what they are talking about; they may just be an alarmist.

People, who drain your energy, who bother you with their doubt and undermine your self-confidence with questions and remarks like: "Do you think that is possible?" "Do you think that will work?" "If that was possible, somebody else would have already done so." "There are some very smart people out there, who could not do it, and you think you can?" An energy drainer will say: "Give up, it makes no sense anyway," or "You are just reaching for the stars."

The world around us and people in our immediate environment influence our thoughts, our focus, our point of view and even our opinion. Therefore they affect our behavior. It is therefore very important that we surround ourselves with the right people. People, who are successful and strive for success; they are willing to give it 110%. These are people, who believe in their future and success; they are willing to do everything that is necessary to produce results.

Hope and believing in your own future, in yourself, your own abilities and future success, are the foundation for success. Surround yourself with people, who inspire you and encourage you to go on. They will say: "You can do it," or "it is possible; you have overcome other hurdles and you will prevail this time too, and then it will be smooth sailing."

Surround yourself with people, who are successful, even more successful than you; you can learn from them to do even better. You will also build the image that such success is possible in your mind. Once you observe the success of others, it will be easier to believe in your own.

I have learned from experience that successful people are always willing to help others with word and deed on their way to success. Successful people enjoy being part of a team; they like to help others and let them be part of their own team. Team play is a foundation of the ultimate success, happiness, contentment, harmony, balance and health.

Surround yourself continuously with success, with positive statements, successful and optimistic people, people who work hard and are willing to take responsibility and control of their success, their life and their future. Pretty soon you will accept this pattern of be-havior for yourself.

Your Decisions determine your Life

You have produced who you are, what you are and where you are, because you have determined with your actions where you are, what you have and who fulfills your life at this moment.

You will probably say: "No! I am not exactly where I would like to be." I did not say that you are where you would like to be, but that you are where you decided to be. Nothing happens in life without your participation, but do not forget that doing nothing is also a form of activity. Making no decision is always the worst decision.

You are at this point in your life because you have made, at one time, the decision that set you on this path. Every decision carries an end-result that was determined by corresponding behavior.

- If you decide to take a few drinks today, you have decided to have a hangover tomorrow.

- If you decide today to eat too much and be unhealthy, you will have gained weight by tomorrow.

- If you decide that you would rather go to a party tonight, then go to bed in time, you have decided to be tired and unmotivated tomorrow.

- If you decide to smoke a cigarette, you have decided to die 14 minutes earlier.

- If you decide to be unkind and unfair to your spouse today, you have decided to have a 99% chance to be similarly treated by your spouse in the future.

Every decision you make has a direct influence on your life, your behavior and therefore on the behavior of the people around you.

It is important that you make the decisions for your future yourself. Decide where you want to go and how you want to get there. Decide with whom, when, and for what reason you are willing to strife and act.

Either you are in control and determine your life by making your own decisions, or your life is determined by outside events or circumstances and the decisions of others. Your fate is decided in the moments you make decisions.

Who are you really? What makes you tick? What are the wishes, dreams and goals for your life, your future, your company, your peer group and your family? You must decide what you really want to achieve with your actions and strife. Do not confuse activity with the realization of success, because only goal oriented sensible action will bring you to your goal.

There is a scientific paper that describes the habit caterpillars have of following each other in a circle around a flower-pot. In the pot were pine needles, the cater-pillars favorite food. They followed each other in the circle for seven days, one after the other, and then they all died from hunger and exhaustion.

Too many people believe that if they keep doing the same thing they will necessarily develop and produce success. But that is not so. Only goal-oriented, sensible and flexible action leads to success. You can work day and night, completely exhaust yourself, but if you, like the caterpillars, confuse activity with productive action, you will be exhausted and will have wasted a full day when night falls.

You know, of course, that you will not achieve success without clear goals.

Success is never the result of luck or coincidence. Lasting result always follows logical, goal-oriented, sensible, continuous and flexible action. Print it in your mind: "You do not get luck, you make your luck." Of course it is the same for success. Zig Ziglar, in my opinion, is the best trainer of salesmen in the world, puts it this way: "Success is nothing but luck—just ask any loser."

Only losers, who have never managed to achieve any success,

think that success depends on luck. Every successful person knows that success is the end-result of a long hard road.

Over 20 years ago, several business schools (among them Harvard and Stanford) and several magazines did studies on success. They found that only 3% of the students leaving high school had clear, formulated goals and plans.

They interviewed this group of students 20 years later and came to the conclusion that these students, with clearly defined goals had achieved more than the other 97% combined.

Even though you know the margin and the examples, I would like to mention again how important it is to have goals. I observe over and over, when I take charge of the leadership of a large company that many know exactly how and why to set goals—but still do not do it.

There is always the pitfall of familiarity. We know and have heard some things so often, we recognize them so well that we take them for granted and do not put them into action.

It is the same with setting goals. I hear it often enough: "Yes, I know, I should have done it; I should have written down clear goals with the date that they should have been finished, with a plan of action and the reason why it should be done at a certain time, but I did not always have time and then it slipped my mind." When I have taught a workshop on goal-setting to future executives, the participants are always happy with the clarity they can now approach the subject. They can now be more effective and successful in every area of their business and their life.

TAKE YOUR LIFE IN YOUR OWN HANDS

Giant Strides to Success

If you really use the unlimited potential you carry within you, you will develop enormous strength that will help you and make it possible to realize your dreams. It will lead you in the right direction to a more beautiful and better life. To become really successful, you must be aware that you can only reach true success when you do a similar service to others in return—but never do a service at the cost of someone else.

- If you desire to become a generous person, then you must first do something really generous, which will, in turn, make you generous.

- If you want to become really wealthy, you must first give away something valuable.

- If you want to be healthy, you first must learn to not indulge in things that can make you or others sick.

The tools and directions that I give you in this book are merely seedlings for a successful life. You must plant them, so that you can later, after making wise decisions and doing the right things, reap the results you desire today.

I hope that you will have the right attitude and a burning desire to cultivate those seedlings. I can only wish that you will keep growing thanks to a greater creativity, enthusiasm, believe and faith in yourself, so that you will enjoy the fruit of more intense actions and activity.

It works often like a digital lock. Many of you are already successful or on the road to great success. I compare it with a number combination that will open the door to our unlimited possibilities and opportunities. You may need five digits to open the lock. Many people have the first two or three numbers and need three or two more; others may need only one more number or one idea, skill or view to open the door to greater personal achievement, to the fulfilling of their dreams, wishes, visions and requirements.

The real profit you will gain from this book does not depend on what you read and do, but of what you feel and do with those feelings. It will depend on your enthusiasm and energy and above all on the unflinching determination to follow your goals.

Many people fail, because they were unaware how close they were to success, when they threw in the towel.

Discover an unlimited strength within yourself

Look within and recognize your own uniqueness and grandeur. Take a pause and give yourself time to develop and strengthen your self-esteem and self-confidence. They are all you need to take the obstacles and hurdles in life and to overcome the lows with greater ease and speed.

I would like to show you the secrets and strategies that can conduct every area of your life to a higher level of success. I will show you ways and possibilities, so that you will have the strength that results from the effective use of your mind and body.

1. The first step to a successful change is the development of a

magnanimity to agree that nobody is perfect, and that we will not reach, own or live for one hundred percent in every area of our lives the way we would really like.

2. In the second step we must identify exactly what we really desire in every specific area.

3. In the third step we must develop a deep yearning to realize those visions and dreams in our lives.

We must learn to inspire and motivate ourselves enough, so that we are eager to start to work on the realization of our goals. We must shape our life with joy and pleasure and above all work with enthusiasm, so that we can achieve what we want for ourselves and for those around us.

It is not enough to program success, if we really want to be successful; we must do what is necessary to realize success. Nobody else will solve your lasting problems or reach your goals for you; rather they may use or exploit you.

Many people believe that the past, the expectations at their birth or the way they have lived so far determines their future success, or whether they may be successful at all. My message to them is: The past will not determine your future, if you don't let it.

We must free ourselves from the past, from the lies and self-deception, from whining and self-pity, no matter how justified this may be. We can do nothing to change the past. We can influence the present—our thinking, feeling and behavior. At this moment, when you take charge of your life, you already determine the present, and your future will be different from your past.

If we want to change our lives and no longer want to come up with the same outcome and results we did until now; if we want more in our relationships, privately and professionally, in our career and our profession, in health and financial situation, then we must do things differently than we did before.

We can expect to bring about different results from the one we made before, only, if we make the right plans and change our actions correspondingly. We must start doing things differently as before, with willingness and flexibility.

With whom do we like to spend our days? Are that not people, who are friendly, positive, full of optimism and energy? I am sure that they are not people, who are unpleasant, whining and complaining.

Seen from a psychological perspective, people, who boast have usually a poor self-esteem and little self-confidence; they have such a poor self-image that they cannot believe positive things will happen in their lives. To avoid disappointments or reaching poor results, those people never work up to their real potential. These people are in their life and actions plagued by fear of rejection, of failing or to be seen as a failure. Because they believe that they will never reach the results they desire or fulfill their hopes and dreams, they do not want to see other people reach theirs. Cynicism, envy, negative criticism and pessimism are the result.

Those people therefore like to boast and show themselves as realists. In reality they are destroyers of dreams; they kill their own visions and dreams and all too often the dreams of their fellow men. Realism is often nothing but pessimism.

Realism is being successful and making something special out of your life, the way you want and deserve. Because you are absolutely unique in the universe, you have the possibility to produce unique results and to live a life that was fashioned from your true requirements and desires.

Every insurance company in the world would be broke, if all the negative things forecasted by realists (pessimists) had actually happened. Because houses usually do not burn down and people do not die early because of an accident, insurance companies do quite well. The chance that your house burns down and you die an untimely death is only 0.4%; this means that your chance for success is 99.6% .

Many people do not use their full potential with the corresponding possibilities, because they spend their energy and strength on everyday trifles. They get bogged down in the small things, while they concentrate on paying the bills, what to do tomorrow, what they will eat and what they will watch on TV that night. Many people worry about problems that they may have to face in five years, which have usually disappeared before a year has passed and that have no influence on their future.

Not enough people develop a burning desire and a real need to work on a more beautiful and enjoyable life, to create a better and more prosperous life for their family, so that all their loved ones will be happier and more content.

The problem is this: Most people do not have a clear image of their future and therefore lack the planning for what they really want to achieve.

We will get direction only if we set goals for ourselves. Our life will get direction at the moment we set the goals for our movements. Our life changes forever at the moment we make the decision to use all the possibilities we have at our disposal and start working on the fulfillment of our goals. We decide our destiny at the moment we start making decisions.

Exercise 1:

Please, pretend that you can, as if you were in a fairy tale, change your life completely. You can reach everything you wish, and fulfill every dream and desire; a good fairy or Aladdin's lamp will grand your every wish. What would you wish? What would you change? What would you want to be, to have or to own? Close your eyes and determine the life that you think is ideal and that you would like to have. Now determine how you want your life to be in five years. Experience in your mind how your life will be, if everything you wish would be there five years from now.

Who is your partner and where are you living? In what house and town do you want to be? How did you furnish the house? What car do you drive? How do you spend your free time? How is your family life? Who are the members of your family? How are your career, your health, your fitness and vitality? How are your finances?

Please close your eyes and imagine how your life would be in five years, if you could design it today?

Now that you have the images of your needs and desires printed in your mind, I want you to write them down, so that you know how your life should be five years from now. You now have the mental images of your private, physical, financial and professional life, as well as of your health and your life with your family.

A Burning Desire

There is a considerable difference, whether we see our goals merely as wishes, or if we develop those wishes into burning desires with the determination to reach those goals under all circumstances.

There is a big difference in saying: "I really should lose ten pounds, I could lose ten pounds, I ought to enter an aerobic fitness program, I should eat differently," or " On the day of my tenth anniversary I will, no matter what it costs me, wear my favorite dress or suit." "I am determined to lose ten pounds!

The last version is successful, because you want to reach a specific goal, which will make the reaching of that goal a reality, we may really expect this to take place. We do, in our mind, not accept the reality of defeat, and we have combined the reaching of this goal with a motivation to succeed.

Once we have decided to make a change with such intensity, there is no longer a place for "Yes, "No, or "Maybe," there is only the question: How; what will be the plan and strategy to reach this goal?

Whenever you have decided to make and bring about positive changes, you must first become aware of the necessity to reach the desired result. What are the real reasons that motivate and inspire you? Reasons are stronger than obstacles, and once we know why we want to change something, we must and will find the way to do so.

Exercise 2:

Write down the reasons why you absolutely want to reach the desired results in every area of your life for everything you wrote down in the previous exercise. In order to do this exercise as effectively as possible, use the principle of "pleasure and pain."

What is the worst that can happen to me, and to all those around me, if I do not accomplish success in every area of my life? What must I give up, and what will I never experience or enjoy, if I do not use my full potential and achieve success?

Our brain tries under all circumstances to avoid negative or physical difficulties, and emotional pain. It is for this reason important to avoid thinking about negative complications and developments. If we do this it will be much easier to motivate ourselves and act with determination.

Exercise 3:

Now write down the pleasant and positive things that you will gain for yourself and others when you fulfill all the wishes and goals you have in mind. What are the pleasant and positive things you and others will get when you use your full potential and realize your visions and dreams? What will you enjoy and experience, and how much more beautiful and wonderful will your life be when you have the courage to set your goals; act, persevere and then reach them?

Exercise 4:

Now write down the reasons, why you absolutely should use your full potential, why you "must" live your inner goals, dreams and wishes. Also please write down: "I must and will be successful, because...."

The difference between successful people and others is not strength and knowledge; it is willpower.

Never Give Up!

I know that it is not easy to set great goals, if you are at this moment in a very difficult emotional or financial position or perhaps even in a poor physical situation. We have all known the feeling that our struggles and problems make clear thinking difficult, and at times it is difficult to believe in positive developments and success.

With you it will be as it is with other people; we all have problems and dilemmas. If we do not want to give up and throw our lives away, we must find a way to cope with challenges, tasks, conflicts and the lows of every day life. No matter how successful we become, there will always be ups and downs in the some areas of our lives.

Our contentment and happiness do not depend on what happens in our lives, but on our reaction to what happens. We cannot determine the direction of the wind, but we can set the sails.

We must accept the responsibility and take control of our lives; and we must work on our future development. We take control when we, while fully aware, make a clear decision to take the wheel of our ship in both hands and determine the direction in which we will move.

Do not start to doubt, when your first try does not pan out; it does not mean failure. Remember Edison and his first ten thousand failed attempts, going on and finding the solution to the light bulb. People, who are successful, are people who know from experience that you seldom succeed on the first try. They have learned that success depends on experience, and that we always gain experience from our so-called failures and mistakes.

Only when I try over and over in different ways, do I learn how something functions and how I cannot reach my goal. The better I learn how not to do something, the clearer the understanding will be how I can finally reach a successful result.

The courage of perseverance determines whether we can consider our lives a success or a failure. Every successful person will tell you that real great success is the accumulation of many so-called failures, errors, disappointments and judgments, combined with continuous perseverance. It is the willingness to get up when you are down that determines whether we can see ourselves as successes or failures.

Taking stock of our lives

Please take a personal inventory, so that you will become aware of how you are doing in different areas of your life. Only when you know where you are, can you determine which changes and developments are necessary to arrive at the different areas of your life. Because no one else is going to read this personal inventory, you should be as honest as possible and not fool yourself.

Now make a list of those different areas, and put a number from one to ten after each item corresponding with the point where you think you are at that moment in time. One would be the lowest and ten the highest point in expressing your contentment with the use of your skills, possibilities, talents and satisfaction. To get you started I have listed 9 areas to evaluate. Please, circle where you fit on a scale from one to ten.

Area 1: What are you doing for your personal development? Are you moving forward with education in your different talent and skills? Are you keeping up with your fitness and health programs, your own and those prescribed by your physician? Are you working on the development of your physical, mental and emotional skills? 1 2 3 4 5 6 7 8 9 10

Area 2: How are your relationships with your family and friends? Are you content with the situation? How would you evaluate those relationships on a scale from one to ten? One means a very poor relationship and ten a happy and contented one for everyone concerned. 1 2 3 4 5 6 7 8 9 10

Area 3: How do you feel about your career and profession? Do you go to work every day with enthusiasm and motivation? Are you working on the development of your career? Do you enjoy your work or do you dislike it thoroughly? Would that be a one or a ten on your scale? A ten would mean that you go to work every day with cheerful anticipation; you enjoy your work, your progress and your personal development on the ladder of success. You work in a

pleasant environment, have colleagues and co-workers you enjoy and you are fortunate to work with good employees and superiors.
1 2 3 4 5 6 7 8 9 10

Area 4: How are your intellectual and spiritual skills? Do you use them to your full potential, or are you suppressing your ideas, dreams, wishes and visions? Are you using your creativity and flexibility to increase and improve your intuition and standard of living or do you compromise and let others influence you? Do you let other people push your wishes and needs to the site? Or do you perhaps have not enough faith in your own ideas and opinions to share them or to work on the realization of your goals? How would you rate yourself on a scale of one to ten? 1 2 3 4 5 6 7 8 9 10

Area 5: Are you satisfied with your financial freedom and independence? Can you take care of the education, clothing, security and comfort of your family; do your finances support vacations in your favorite places? Do you perhaps deny yourself and your family small pleasures or do you have to save up a long time before you can enjoy some pleasant recreation? Must you say all too often to your spouse and children: "We cannot afford such things." Can you afford a visit to a physician, buy medicine, or engage a lawyer in a family emergency, or do you have to depend on social services?

Are you ready to live and experience your dream by realizing your own wishes and those of your team? Do you enjoy your home while you are making it more pleasant and attractive, so that you can share it in a warm atmosphere with your family? Can you enjoy going out for dinner together, or do you miss out on those pleasures for lack of enough money? Are you an example to your friends and family, because you took hold of life and are now financial secure and independent? Or do your neighbors feel sorry for you, because you have to drive your family in a dangerous jalopy and the children are dressed in castoffs? When you look at this, were do you think you fit on a scale of one to ten? 1 2 3 4 5 6 7 8 9 10

Area 6: How is your social life coming along? Do you get along with your neighbors? Are you politically active, do you enjoy it? Do you have the right contacts for the children's schools, kinder garden, and social institutions? What is happening? 1 2 3 4 5 6 7 8 9 10

Area 7: How is your private and social life? Do you have friends? Do you participate, are you a member of certain groups, do you have hobbies and do you enjoy good fellowship? 1 2 3 4 5 6 7 8 9 10

Area 8: How is your intellectual life? Do you take relaxing walks to clear your mind, so that you can think quietly and make some plans and decisions? Do you take time to relax and recharge your batteries? Do you use your creativity; do you sing, paint or draw? Do you communicate with nature; do you pay attention to the birds, the flowers and the trees? What are you doing for your mental development? 1 2 3 4 5 6 7 8 9 10

Area 9: This is the most important area, because without your health, everything falls by the wayside. Are you fit and vital; do you have strength and energy all day long? Do you sleep well, so that you can jump out of bed restored, full of enthusiasm to enjoy the new day, ready to determine your own fate and future? Or are you miserable when you get up, wishing you had gone to bed in time the night before? Do you feel tired, weak and listless all day; do you feel depressed or suffer from frustration; so that you just do not have the physical and emotional energy to face the day? Are you often sick; do you frequently have colds, the flu, regular backaches or digestive problems? Do you perhaps walk around so full of energy and vitality that others envy you? Are you enjoying every new day with a strong, pain-free, healthy and energy filled body and mind?
1 2 3 4 5 6 7 8 9 10

Exercise 5:

Write down in your success journal for every area of your life what it should be like to get a ten on your scale. Let every area be filled with contentment, harmony, balance and happiness in an optimum quality of life.

Exercise 6:

Now please write down what it should be like in every area. How should it be; how should your life be? How should you be? What must you own or have to find yourself on the ten of your scale?

Only in this way can you find out exactly what your personal goals, wishes and needs are, and how you would recognize it when you really reached your goal. Every person has of course different rules and a different belief-system. Everyone has different demands, how it should be and how we would like it to be to feel really happy, content and successful in every area of life.

Exercise 7:

What do you have to do to make full use of your potential in every area of your life? Develop a plan of action, so that you can make the necessary changes to reach your desired goals in every area. Add to this how you can make those changes, so that you can move from step five to ten.

Give your Life Direction

You will soon come to the conclusion that clarity means power. Once you reach the point where you really know what you want in your life, you can work with greater consistency, more effectively and goal oriented on the full use of your true potential.

To reach a goal or part of a goal, you must first determine what the goal really entails. Only then can you know in which direction you must go and make the changes to guide your life in the appropriate direction.

Many people fail, because they do not know what they really want.

They remain stuck in phantom goals because they say: "I want more money," or "I want a better life" or "I want to live somewhere else." The brain can do nothing with thoughts like that. It cannot develop plans or strategies; neither can those thoughts give motivation or perseverance. The brain does not know what is required.

If you would say to your employer: "I want to make more money," he may say: "sure," and give you $5.00 more at the end of the month. You got what you asked for, —more money.

This was of course not what you wanted, but because you did not phrase it correctly, this could easily happen. Always phrase correctly what you want, so that you will get exactly out of life what many others leave up in the blue. They will have to wait for what happens to fall in their laps.

Be careful that you always subdivide your plans in long, middle and short-term projects. Do not make the demands too great for unrealistic time limits. It is not important that you reach all your goals tomorrow at the same time. It is only important that you start working today and keep on working every day. Even if it looks as if you are making little progress, you can be sure that you will reach the goals you have set for yourself.

You will probably lose the needed motivation and enthusiasm to act, if you cannot review your progress until six months or perhaps even three years later. It is therefore very important that you can see some improvement every day.

Only when you can obtain and review small progress every day, can you maintain the motivation and above all the willingness that is needed to sustain the determination necessary to achieve success.

No matter how large or small you make your goals, as intermediate goals they will help you to develop as a person, a personality and as a human being. You will condition yourself to become a man of action and not as a person with a wait-and-see attitude; someone who hopes that fate will hand him a good deal.

Proceed in the following manner, when you set your goals:

- Identify your goal clear and precise. Your goal must be easy to recognize, so that you can quickly find it, if you would lose track of it.

- List all the benefits that will await you, when you reach your goal.

- List all the disadvantages that you and yours must suffer, when you do not reach your goal.

- List all the obstacles and hurdles you must overcome to reach your goal.

- Determine the knowledge and skills you need to reach your goal.

- Keep a lookout for people and institutions that you need, or who can assist you to reach your goal or to reach it faster.

- Develop a plan of action.

- Set an exact date to reach your goal.

The reason why 90% of the people have their goals not exactly defined is fear. It is the fear of failing, of not reaching their goals. The possibility is of course there. It is always possible that you will not reach your goal, (although I do not believe that will happen) but if that would happen, it would be merely a small blow to the ego. The greatest danger is not to have any goals at all and not to arrive anywhere.

Remember we spend nature's treasures by using them, but we lose our inner treasures by not using them.

You will never be successful in life, if you do not know what you really want. Success is only granted to those who draw the plans for the path they want to follow.

When we do not reach our goals, it is not because of a shortage time; we have all the same amount of minutes and hours as a billionaire. The difference is that the billionaire really uses every minute at his disposal.

You will arrive much faster where you want to go, if you have clear directions. Motivation will supply the energy you need to reach your goal.

To make decisions you need goals, so that you will know what it is that will bring you closer or take you away from your goal.

From Neglect to Initiative

Ask yourself every day: "What can I do today, so that I can come a bit closer to my goal?" Which call can give me the necessary information? What do I have to learn or do to get or improve the needed skills and talents to reach this goal? No matter how large or small the daily goal setting or action may be, it is the regularity of those actions that changes and develops your personality. If you do something every day to come closer to your goal, no matter how small, it will be only a matter of time before you reach your goal.

Here is an example: Your garage is a mess. Tools, oil cans, garden equipment; the shelves are totally cluttered. You are stumbling over the garden-hose and the box for recycling. There is hardly room to squeeze your car between the lawn mower and the trash can. When you get in and out of your car you must be careful that the paddle of your kayak does not hit your head. It needs straightening badly! You are shuddering, when you even think of starting to clean, which is making matters worse.

Why don't you plan to work on it fifteen minutes each day? Your garage will look great after a few days. If you do nothing you will just waste your time. And what is worse, the problem will still be there; you are still stuck with a cluttered garage, and it still will need cleaning.

By working fifteen minutes a day, you can see that you make a little progress by completing a part of the goal you want to reach, and you will no longer have the feeling of being at the mercy of your problem. Your self-esteem and self-confidence will improve. You will enjoy little successes every day thanks to motivation and input. You will begin to experience yourself as someone, who takes matters in hand, who solves his or her problems and completes the jobs. You will start seeing yourself as intelligent, competent and strong, someone, who finishes the jobs and reaches the goals at hand. Doing those little jobs has another wonderful effect; you will be more successful in different areas than you were before. Your self-image will have made a positive change and you will respond by acting as you now see yourself and produce results that correspond with your new self-image.

Everyone can do everything when they determine that they can do, if they convince themselves and believe strongly in their goals and their wishes. Nobody can succeed in their personal programming if they do not aspire to reach their goals by using and developing their skills and talents.

The brain is stimulated by small successes and new information. Those small daily successes contribute to the positive growth of your self-confidence and self-esteem.

What and who do you really want to be? Imagine that you had all the skills, talents and character traits with the body, looks and presence that you would really like to have, including your true potential and possibilities.

Picture in your mind a clear image, in exact detail, of your personality. Don't just see it, but feel and experience it as if it were real. You will create the same positive motivation effect of a car-dealer, when he lets you take a ride in the car of your dreams, or lets you use it for a weekend. In that way you will be able to experience and enjoy the same wonderful feeling of living the fulfillment of a great wish. You will no longer want to give up this wonderful feeling. You will probably want to buy the car and wonder how soon you will be able to buy it.

It is the same with mental images: They represent optimum self-motivation. You motivate yourself, if you can feel and experience in your mind the desired changes or goal as if they were really happening. Once you have experienced the joyful feeling of being slim, fit, healthy, full of vitality and energy, with the determination to be polite, correct, kind, successful, content and happy in your emotional world, you will want to experience this feeling in your real life for ever.

Mental pictures are for this reason, combined with feelings, especially motivating and helpful. It is important that you don't disassociate yourself from the mental film. This means that you should not look at it as an outsider, as someone who looks at a movie, but that you associate with the picture and play an active roll. Experience it, see, hear, feel, smell and taste it as you would, if you lived the situation in real life.

Exercise 8:

Now please write down the pictures you saw. Describe the colors you saw, the sounds you heard and the sensations you experienced.

Desires turn into Requirements

We all want, of course, a wonderful life, better relationships with our partners or more financial independence. Others among us would only like to lose a few pounds and be more energetic. Nothing changes, if we only want it. We must develop a passionate need, so that we have no other choice but to do everything that is needed to really want to be fit and vital, so that we will really work to reach our desired goal.

We must pay attention to what we eat, and exercise more. The yearning: "I wish that I could lose some weight," must become a strong conviction, a passionate need: "I absolutely have to lose weight, no matter what it takes."

Many people say: "I wish I had some more money, so that I could pay my bills or could afford to go on vacation or just have more financial security." But before those people can change their lifestyle and the quality of their lives in a positive way, their desire must become a passion, an absolute must. If those people really wanted to change their life and turned it in an absolute must, they would not spend so much time in front of the TV and just wish that they did do more.

To be and stay really happy, content and successful, you must live every day according to those needs. The most important part is discipline. It is necessary that you discipline yourself with small decisions, to not be satisfied with the way you are, what you own or could possess or achieve. You must, moreover, work every day and improve the quality of your life, so that you can reach your goals and fulfill your wishes.

If it were simple to lead a successful life, there would be very many successful people. You know it already: only 3% of all people have clearly defined goals and corresponding plans to realize them. When you scrutinize the successes, relationships, health, and the professional and financial situations of those people, you will determine that the 3% are happier, healthier, more successful and content than the other 97% together.

Those numbers should wake us up and frighten us. Every person carries from birth the potential to experience and enjoy a wonderful, content, happy and successful life. Everybody is basically born to be a success, not a failure. There are no mistakes in nature. We are doing something wrong, if we are not on the way to possess what we would like to have.

I am here to help you to take charge of your life. We take charge of our life, when we are willing to accept, no matter where we are today, that what we have is the result of our former decisions, thoughts and actions. We alone can determine and change our life.

Action and Perseverance

Once we have the self-confidence and self-esteem with the corresponding self-image to take the responsibility for all the battles and failures, for the hesitation, the losses, laziness and even fear, then we are on the way to success. We can no longer blame our failures on the weather, circumstances, the economy or other people.

We all have lows, stages of depression,, frustration and self-pity in our lives. But we must put and end to them some time. We must at least from the time we become aware that the life we live solely the result of our own decisions, actions and thinking; that is when a completely new life begins.

Even when we find fault with someone else; it won't change where we are and it won't help us. Not until we are big enough and ready to let go of the past, can we change our lives. Otherwise you will send your mind the message that you can not have any influence on your life. Your life will be determined by other people, the past, the weather and the ups and downs of the economy, but not by your own decisions and actions.

No matter how often you had to cope with failure, no mater how often you did not reach what you attempted; it still does not mean that you can't get good results today. Every day offers new possibilities and opportunities. Every day is a new birth with new opportunities for change.

Do not let other people discourage you. Nobody but you knows what you have to offer and what you can do. Other people may be able to hold you back for a while, but only you can hold yourself back forever!

It is, of course, not easy to change your life and turn it into the masterpiece it deserves to be. But you can be sure that the energy, the fight and the input of your time will pay off, when you do what is the most important thing: act and persevere!

Persistence is more important than Talent!

Life is neither fair nor unfair. A thunderstorm destroys the houses of the good and the bad, of lazy and active people in the same way. Active people will start rebuilding their house and restore their quality of life immediately. Honest people will rely on the correct way of doing what they can do for themselves or with the help of others.

It is more strenuous and expensive to be lazy than it is to be industrious. It is more demanding to pretend that you are busy, so that others will not notice how lazy you really are, than it is to do the work. To dispose of the necessary work and then to enjoy a feeling of success, happiness and contentment is much easier and satisfying.

Dishonest people are uptight and tense all day. They live in the constant fear of being discovered. They do not sleep well, because their guilty conscious does not let them rest.

Nobody can live relaxed, when he is dishonest or a criminal. By nature we are all programmed to be good, honest and ethical. Negative behavior is learned behavior (taught by others or acquired on our own,) which leads to actions that you do not really want to do.

Everyone, who lives different from his beliefs, convictions, rules and wishes will become at some time sickly or seriously ill.

Accept yourself as you are. No matter what others think or say; do not let others change your ideas, goals and dreams or stop you from acting the way you want. Churchill's most successful speeches were also the shortest; he told the students at the University: "The most important principle in life is: "Never, never, never give up!""

Energy Robbers

A rotten apple can spoil a bushel, and a bad person can, at a bad time in your life, be responsible for you not acting, so that you give up before you start—and that you may give up on the realization of a dream.

The world is filled with people, who are so programmed that they accept the negative as unavoidable. They are conditioned to believe that it is better not to act at all, so that they won't risk that something may go wrong.

In the first class every child wants to answer the teacher's questions. A child wants to say something, whether he or she is right or wrong and whether it does have to do something with the question or not at all. Children have at that age not yet experienced the pain of rejection or failure, but in the fifth grade some have already learned that it is better to say nothing than to say something wrong. That is when the trouble starts, these children will already fear to act and fear to fail.

Nobody is strong enough to fight windmills by themselves. With fighting energy-robbers it is the same, they always fear the worst and always spread pessimism. If you are exposed to those people long enough, you run the risk of accepting their negative outlook. Then you will stop believing in yourself and give up on your dreams. Your actions will stop, and you will no longer believe in a successful and happy future.

One example of a typical energy-robber is the person, who lives by himself and has been divorced five times. People no longer talk to him, but he will give you advice and tell you how to deal with your partner. He will tell you how to live and how to bring up your children, although he has not talked to them for 15 years. He knows and does everything better than others. If you want to write a book he will tell you what you are doing wrong and that he could do a better job than you are doing. He knows how, but he just is not interested in doing so. He will advice you on a good weight-loss program, although he is quite portly himself. He will tell you how easy it is to quit smoking, while he smokes three packs a day. No matter what others are achieving, he could do better. If you tell him about your success, he will say: "Just wait and see, you never know what will happen; the cat might just get the early bird before the day is over." His specialty is criticism, taking people down and spreading pessimism.

I think you get the idea of what I mean by energy-robbers. You know the people I am talking about; you probably have met some.

It would be only a matter of time before you will absorb their negative approach and joined them at the bottom of the barrel, if you did not avoid them. You must stay away from people like that, and surround yourself with positive, optimistic people, instead. Only then will you become a survivor, a person, who lives his life the way he chooses.

There is however, another group of energy-robbers very different from the ones mentioned before. These are people, who want the best for us: our parents or grandparents who, because they care or are afraid for us, try to talk us out of certain actions. They stop us from reaching too great a goal, because they want to spare us disappointments. You cannot solve this problem by distance. They are not the negative energy-robbers I mentioned before. You could say to those people: "Dear grandma, I know you mean well. Your point of view was fine twenty or thirty years ago, but I must live my life now; get my own experiences and make my own mistakes. I have to make my own life, so that I can be happy and content. I have to do that for my family and for others, who are important to me. I must ask you not to be negative, otherwise I have to distance myself and see you less often. I love you, but I can not waste my life, throw it away or squander it, simply because you do not believe in my goals and visions and discourage me to realize my dreams."

Exercise 9:

Please listen to all the persons with whom you come regularly in contact. Write behind every name, whether this person influences your life in a positive or negative way.

If the contact is negative, you must draw your own conclusions. Consider how you can best deal with these people in the way I suggested, if they fall in the second category.

Exercise 10:

Please write down the names of the people you should contact and of those people with whom you would like to meet more frequently, because contact with them could lead to more positive development. Look out for positive, optimistic people, who could help you to work with enthusiasm on improving the quality of your life.

Programming does not last

By now everyone is dealing with computers. We all know that a computer can only give back what we have put in before. I cannot expect a book to appear if I put the file in an English-German program. In the same way we can hardly expect numerous positive answers, if we have filled our brain (the largest bio-computer in the world) with negative programming.

If we fill our brain with poor information, we can only expect bad results. If I send positive thoughts to my bio-computer, through my actions, images and continued information, I will, of course, receive corresponding good and desired experiences and behavior.

Our brain can only act and react in agreement with the mental images it receives. If you look at life without expectations and feel at the mercy of circumstances, other people and events, you will program a negative self-image. You program: What am I worth? What can I do? What can I achieve in my life? The results will correspond with your input.

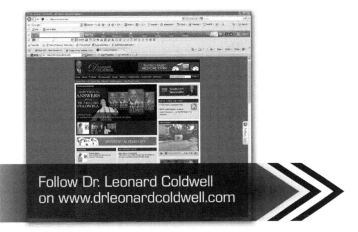

Follow Dr. Leonard Coldwell
on www.drleonardcoldwell.com

YOUR PERSONAL SUCCESS

Success will make you happy

What really is success? You could say: Success is a feeling of being successful, of being happy with what you are, with what you do and own. That is personal success.

Another definition is this: success is having the feeling that you move consistently toward the reaching of your goals.

Every person must find out for themselves what makes him or her happy and what makes them feel successful. There are directions to help us. Everyone desires:

- Freedom

- Health

- Happiness (Joy—Pleasure)

- Wealth

- Friends

- Good Relationships

- Peace

- Security

Every person desires these for their future. When those wishes are fulfilled they will become the basis for true success.

You are successful…

- When you really let go of the past, concentrate completely on the now and look with optimism to the future.

- When you no longer let your friends and acquaintances influence you negatively. When you are ready to forget and forgive those who have harmed you, when you are ready to bury quarrels and when you have gained the love and respect of those, who are close to you.

- When your life thoughts and actions are filled with hope and love, and when you live without hatred, feelings of guild, with sadness or revenge.

- When you live your life with clear moral and ethnic values and with only do those things that you believe to be good.

- When you focus on necessary actions and duties instead of only on enjoyment and instant gratification.

- When you can give hope to the hopeless, friendship to those who are without friends; love to those who need love and encouragement to people, who have hit bottom.

- When you realize that success does not make you victorious and failure does not make a loser.

- When you can look back without regret and look forward with hope; when you can look down with compassion and look up with gratitude.

- When you know exactly at what point you have arrived and behave accordingly, when you are in peace and harmony with yourself and your fellow men.

- When you realize that denial is an occurrence not a person, and that yesterday ended last night, that today is a new day with new opportunities to start and act more efficiently.

- When you acknowledge that those who give the most of themselves and who offer the greatest service and highest value, will also be the most successful.

- When you are cheerful to the disgruntled, friendly to those who are cold, and generous to people in need, because you know that it is better to give while the joy of receiving is short and the joy of sharing has duration.

- When you accept and develop all your physical, intellectual and spiritual talents with the realization that you use them for your own benefit and for the benefit of all mankind.

- When you can say with complete satisfaction at the end of your life: "Well done!"—with the feeling that you have achieved and accomplished the possible.

Exercise 1:

So that you may define exactly what success means to you and what your long-term goals are, I ask you to do the following exercise: Pretend that you are 95 years old and doing great. Your friends are throwing you a birthday party and many who are present want to commemorate your achievements and accomplishments.

Write down the speech you would like to hear or put it down, as you would like to hear it.

Do not write it down, as it would be exactly, but give some thought how this speech would really honor you. At the end of the speech you should be able to say: "I have done well, I can be proud of myself, I am and was successful."

Write this speech of recognition and appreciation just as you would like to hear it on your 95th birthday, as if you could in that way determine your future and your destiny. Watch out, do not turn this speech into an obituary or a eulogy.

This exercise will help you to determine what you must do and how you will feel successful; you will focus on your life goals with this exercise. It will make you aware of what is important to you, what you want to do, achieve and own, what success really means to you. You will then be able to set your short term, middle- and long-term goals, and make it possible to define and develop the necessary strategies.

There is no such thing as an overnight success.
Some people seem to have all the success: successful relationships, their marriage and families function very well, they have wealth and respect and their careers run smoothly. Others, on the other hand, must be satisfied with the leftovers.

This is not at all true. There are no over-night successes, just as there are no self-made millionaires. Those so-called millionaires have been helped by a lot of people on their way to the top. Nobody becomes a great success without help, and nobody remains at the top. Success depends on the ability to be a good team player.

We frequently hear about a person, who has suddenly unbelievable success. He or she sings a song and the song hits the top ten immediately. They make a tremendous amount of money overnight. Nobody ever heard of him or her and now this person is in the center of the spotlight.

It looks as if this person happened to be at the right place at he right time, had the right connections and knew the right people, or was just plain lucky. This is, of course, not so. Success is never an overnight happening. In 99% of cases like that, you will hear in interviews that this person struggled for years without success but made all the right moves. He or she had to overcome many obstacles and hurdles, and dealt with many rejections and disappointments. This person became successful with continuous motivation and perseverance, while focusing on clear goals, and following with mapped strategies and plans of action.

Never in my life have I spoken to a very successful person, who did not have to overcome numerous failures, the anger of his children, shortness of cash, fear of the future, and crisis in relationships with his partners. They even had to cope with stages, when they did everything right, but still did not reach the desired results.

The ability to dream made it possible to become successful, happy and above all content, it frequently resulted also in good health. You can dream, imagine and develop clear yearnings and absolutely believe in the fulfilling of those desired goals. You will then be willing to do everything that is needed to reach those desired goals.

The participants in an experiment at the University of Irvine, California were prevented from dreaming. Whenever a participant started to dream he was awakened. Those people were nervous and unbalanced after one day without dreams. After two days without dreams they became aggressive, had difficulty with concentration, and were dissatisfied and unhappy. After the third dreamless night they felt ill. They were extremely irritable and could not concentrate; they became aggressive, explosive and unfair. They started to suffer from depression. The experiment was quickly ended for this reason.

I told this story to explain how important dreams are. We need to dream when we sleep, but we must especially dream when we are awake! We must dream about a better and more beautiful life, about the reaching of our goals.

Your goals depend on your dreams and on believing in and realizing your dreams. Your body is guided by your conscious; if you are not convinced that you can be successful, you will lack the necessary strength you need. Why should I persist and put in so much effort, when I have programmed my mind for failure?

By concentrating on accomplishments and successful experiences, on what you can do to become a valuable person, you grow in self-esteem and self-confidence. Don't concentrate on the weaknesses and on the mistakes you have made in the past.

You develop a strong and great faith in yourself, when you nourish your mind with regular small confirmations telling your brain that you are a valuable and successful person. Tell your brain this: I set myself clear goals, plan and finish my plans and work to reach those goals regularly. I solve my own questions and take control of my own life. I am a person, who does not just hope, wish and do some positive thinking, but I also use my true potential.

With this approach you will soon concentrate on solutions and actions; you will not hesitate and focus on problems. Winners do, losers only talk about doing. Whenever you think about yourself, you must see yourself only as a person who behaves positively, ready to go and explore all his possibilities.

This regular programming will change your life in a short time, because your brain cannot see the difference between reality and imagination. It is possible to experience and program in your mind many satisfactory events. You can repeatedly imagine the way you accept and solve the tasks and demands in your life. You must repeat this until your belief in yourself and your self-image have changed positively. You can even imagine situations that never really happened. In this way you can create a better self-esteem, more self-confidence and a healthy self-image, the way you want it to be.

I would like to ask you to think about certain life patterns that are not in correspondence with your personality and are not the way you like them to be, so that you can start using your brain more intensively. Ask yourself: When do you behave differently than you would like to behave? In what situations did you act, so that you later regretted your behavior?

Exercise 2:

Write down the situations and the ways you behave that are not according to your true potential; then write down the type of behavior you prefer.

Now program in your mind, over and over, the way you want to act in the future; keep doing this until you can only see and experience the desired manner in which you want to behave. Do it as many as 25 to 30 times. Your brain now believe that you behaved

20 to 30 times in the desired manner and is now programmed to have you act that way in the future. You will now unavoidably act in similar situations, as you want to behave, thanks to the program you put in your brain.

The first step in your new life

To influence and change your life immediately in a positive way, you must start with the way you get up in the morning. You must begin to use your mind and body to your greatest advantage.

You must program tonight how you want to get up tomorrow morning. You decide at what time, exactly, you want to get up. You see in your mind that you are getting up early at the desired time, full of strength and energy, taking immediate control of your day.

Make a list of the things you want and must do and write them down in the right priority, deciding what has to be done first. Write down what you want to do tomorrow in the necessary order, so that you will reach your goal.

Now the most important part: waking up. When the clock of possibilities (no, not the "alarm"-clock!) rings, turn off the ring with a loud "yes." Get up energetically, clap your hands and say loud and clear; "This is my day and I will make the most of it."

This will already change your life. You will no longer waste away the first two or three hours and wrestle through the necessary hygienic activities. You will start this day in a positive way and take complete control from the very first second. This way of waking up puts every other time management in the shadow. You cannot save more time than with this way of waking up.

The Second Step

You should use this practical pattern of behavior at the same time to build up your feelings of self-esteem and self-confidence wisely. Walk full of self- possession and strength to the bathroom, as if you already possessed all the success in the world. Look into the mirror, clap your hands again; look yourself in the eyes and say: "Yes!"—"I am great!"

First you will feel ridiculous and laugh. But after a few days you will get used to the way you take control of your day. You will be optimistic and program optimism and purpose. You will moreover have the advantage that now all the others in the house will also be awake. You will absolutely be the center of discussion!

The Third Step

You have now started with the positive programming of your self-image. We will now start to use the images in our mind, the power of self-communication and the verbal programming in our mind.

Exercise 3:

Now please write down in your success journal the talents, skills, personal characteristics and behavior patterns that you like or want to intensify.

You could do it in this way:

I, _____, am a loving, confident, positive and optimistic person, who expects the best possible experiences for my actions in the future. I am a good team player and readily share my experiences, knowledge, talents and skills with my co-workers. I will always try to find solutions for problems and overcome any obstacles. I will persevere until I reach every goal I set. I am understanding and a good listener; I appreciate and respect my fellow humankind and myself. I will no longer be satisfied with the average in my life or be satisfied with less than I can be, with less than I can posses or less than I can reach. I know I am born to be successful. I know that renouncing the very best is nothing but a lack of self-esteem and self-confidence. I will always get up when life throws me down. I will work for 100% on the realization of my dreams. I will always be ready to go the extra mile and do what is necessary to achieve special success.

Say the last sentence self-assured and determined every morning and every evening when you stand upright and confident in front of the mirror. You will find that you have changed into a completely different person within thirty days. You will find it easier to deal with every day life and make all the needed changes quickly and efficiently.

Success is no accident, you do not get success; you earn it. And happiness is something you make yourself. The definition of happiness is: "When our inner willingness is combined with a corresponding opportunity and meets with a positive action we will experience happiness."

If somebody does not expect opportunities and possibilities in his or life, he or she will not see them when they are there and not use them as the result. Only when you are willing to look with positive expectations for opportunities and possibilities will you become and remain happy and successful.

Use the Psychology of Success.
If you do not want to avoid problems, challenges or threatening situations repeatedly, you must not only solve the problems mentally, you must also attack the obstacles with physical strength, confident of success.

You will, for instance, draw back and even shrink together in your chair when a person screams angrily and even threatens you. Your mind gets the clear signal to take flight. You will feel helpless, weak, at someone's mercy, unable to take control of the situation.

What would happen if you stood up energetically moved a few inches closer, looked that person in the eye and answered that person in a strong, perhaps slightly raised voice and gesticulating hands. You would feel strong, confident, bold and ready to go. By taking this position you would not let another person frighten or stop you.

In past times people believed that a person acted as he or she felt. We know today that this is part of a cybernetic circle. It works like this: We will breath, move, speak, mimic and gesticulate as we feel, and in response we will feel as we act.

This means that you will act quite differently when you are exhausted, sad, dejected and frustrated, from when you are enthusiastic, confident, full of optimism and eager to go.

You will say: "But that is clear and simple." However there is something else in play: many people are superstitious and believe that wisdom is power and that wisdom will change things in life.

Wisdom carries only the potential of power. Only applied wisdom; wisdom changed into action produces corresponding results. Most people know exactly what they should do to bring about desired changes and success in their lives. Only a few people use this knowledge. Instead they say the following: "I ought to... "I should... "I could..." This is the reason that so many people do not turn their life in to the masterpiece it deserves to be. Those excuses are always caused by hesitation and failure. It is better to say: "I will do it, because..." than to make excuses later and look for reasons for doing nothing.

Wake up the Winner in You.
To avoid misunderstanding, I will give you my definition of a winner: A winner is (to me) a person, who can overcome his or her worries, doubt and fears, conquering that inner voice that says: "Give up, do it tomorrow, let it be." I believe that a winner has the ability to overcome his or her own laziness and cowardice. Nobody is free of those feelings, thoughts and behavior patterns, successful people, as well as those who have little success. Successful people have learned to overcome those negative feelings, restrictions and poor situations and act anyway. I think those people are winners, who can conquer themselves.

To wake up this winner it is important to leave the past behind for good and never let past experience, programming and failure influence you negatively. Distance yourself once and for all from negative experiences. Only hold on to positive experiences and information.

This includes that you will never be willing to compromise at the cost of yourself, your life or your future. What are the things in your life that satisfy you, and in which situations do you always swallow the behavior of others? When do you compromise? When do you do things from which you know that you should not do them and do just the opposite from what you know to be right?

Exercise 4:

Now write down in your success journal those areas that leave you dissatisfied with your behavior, when you do not act, or let something negative occur. Hit the table with your hand (without hurting yourself) after you write this down and say forcefully: "Never again!"

I ask you to make use of this symbol, because rituals and symbols help the brain to portray a situation. Images are the language of the brain. Everyone thinks in images and symbols. It is therefore very important that you use symbols and rituals in the conditioning and installation of future behavior patterns.

You can install your own symbols. You will improve your ability to communicate, if you turn the following into a ritual or behavior pattern: imagine how you can become a more friendly, self-confident and focused person with every phone conversation you have. Slowly sit up straight in your chair. Sit confidently in your chair, when you pick up the phone, or stand up (what is easiest for you) and answer in a clear and friendly voice.

You will conclude within a short time that your phone partners react very well and many people will ask you why you sound so pleasant. With regular programming you will soon solve the problem of being annoyed with the ringing of the telephone.

Meet other people with a pleasant and optimistic attitude and treat them as you want to be treated yourself. Spread optimism, hope and friendliness. Always ask yourself how your help, work and actions can be of the greatest use to others. Within a short time you will be one of the happiest and most successful people around.

Friendship, team play and the willingness to give more than you expect are the foundations of continued success. You can say: "If you find more in life (help, dedication, quality) than you get in return, you will soon get rewards in abundance." Living means giving and taking. Be aware: giving comes before the taking.

No Monuments for those who are critical

Meet your fellow humankind with encouragement, optimism and friendliness, if you want to have a positive and joyful life. Some people can light up a room just by leaving. Then there are people we love to see and whose company we really enjoy. The last are never critical and never wear us down. People, who whine and are critical, aren't achievers. For this reason they try to diminish the success of others, so that the gap between their lack of success and the achievements of others does not seem so big.

Someone, who presumes to criticize or assess other people's life or work without knowing the details, is nothing but a high-handed fool. We should not judge a person by his deeds. Too often we act differently from the way we want to act. Sometimes it is caused by sadness; sometimes it is caused by despair or pain. If someone would judge our behavior at times like that, they would get a negative and false opinion of our personality.

We can get to know a person by their desires, their dreams and on what they try to achieve with positive actions. We should not evaluate a person at the basis of a one time action.

A critical person takes the liberty to judge a person and express an opinion without really being informed about situations or cir-cumstances. That person refuses to try a dish they do not know, without even giving it a try. They will form an opinion based on a look or smell without tasting it. Their taste and nutrition will never change or expand, because they never try something new. We can only find out, whether we like something or not, by trial and error.

A critical person, who never tries something new, will always move mentally, physically and emotionally in a narrow frame work, where they knows their way around. They avoid risks to experiment with something new and unknown. They will make use of only ten percent of their possibilities and opportunities. The reason for the negative remarks of a critical person is not that they are unkind, but because their self-image, the mental portrait they carry of their abilities and themselves, is so low and disastrous that they believe that they can not cope with changes or reach a desired goal. They fade in the woodwork, so that nobody will notice that they are not able to deal with certain situations.

A critical person often avoids doing something, so that those around them will not notice that they are afraid and in need of help, that living itself frightens them. They cannot show any results. They often keep others at a distance. They avoid the risk of disappointment, rejection or hurt. Those people are often quite jealous of their partner or spouse, because they have a feeling of inferiority and fear that their spouse will prefer somebody else.

You can recognize people with low self-esteem by the gaudy way they dress. They feel that others will not respect them the way they are. They will try to draw people's attention through a striking appearance, hairdo, clothing or make-up.

We all know the class clown, who makes fun of everything, makes silly remarks in serious situations, knows better, is frequently sarcastic, and does everything to draw attention to put himself in the foreground. He fears that he will not be noticed without his foolishness. This person also has a low self-esteem and tries to get everyone's attention with his absurd behavior and frequent interruptions.

I think that many of us went through this stage, when we were growing up; we were trying to find out not only who we were, but were also searching for the meaning in life. We must recognize and accept that these are behavior patterns that do not reflect our real personality. Those behavior patterns are part of our background and may have programmed negative examples in our mind. These are behavior patterns that we cannot only change; we must change them as fast as possible. We must consider how we can improve our life, how we can attain better results. Just by thinking about it we can already make a positive change. We will, on the other hand, change our own lives and that of others in a negative way, if we think and even try to diminish the success of others.

When you enjoy the new car your friend just bought as much as your friend does, you will be the first to see your friend's newest purchase and be part of his success. In this way you will frequently be a part and enjoy the success and happiness of others.

Feedback is the Breakfast of Champions

Strike! Remember, when you were bowling and someone hit a strike and threw all ten bowling pins at the same time; everyone was clapping and cheering. When somebody hits the one and last remaining pin, nobody cheers with the same enthusiasm, as if it took less skill to take the single pin, —somehow it seemed to take less of an effort.

It is the same in life, when we just work, even when it is quite right and correct. If we do not see some success, have no measurable or verifiable results, there is nothing to judge ourselves by. We do know whether we are doing well and may very well give up. We will stop trying. We have neither enjoyment nor pleasure from our actions, because we do not see any improvement. It is therefore wise to set intermediate goals, so you can judge ourselves.

To regularly program our success, motivate ourselves and persevere, we need measurable and verifiable results, no matter how small they may be.

Develop a bonus-system for yourself. Think of some rewards you deserve, when you reach a determined or intermediate goal. Take your partner to a favorite restaurant for a special dinner, or buy something you have wanted for quite a while. When you have overcome a large obstacle or reached a bigger goal, you deserve, of course, a greater reward.

Exercise 5:

Write a list of rewards in your success journal and put down when it is time for a pay-off and give yourself a bonus. Think up smaller and greater rewards.

How we create optimal Motivation

You will unavoidably be already motivated at the moment you act with enthusiasm and create the positive images that go with it in your mind. You already know that. I will teach you a new variation I developed; it will increase your motivation and perseverance.

Buy a CD or an MP3 player to record encouraging songs and music that make you feel good and that encourage you to do things. Use this recording when you feel down or have reached a low point, or just before you must finish a difficult task.

Always keep the benefits that you will enjoy when you reach your goal in mind. There are, in my opinion, two things that carry weight to reach lasting success; they are:

- the ability to build a positive self-image

- the ability to regularly motivate yourself to action with perseverance and good feelings.

We cannot regulate the direction of the wind, but we can determine the course of our ship by setting the sail.

Hesitate no more

The fear of being turned down, rejected, criticized or laughed at holds us back from trying new things. We all suffer from that now and then, and talk ourselves out of doing things.

How often have you said; I am going to do this or that? Then, when the time came, you talked yourself out of it. We might say: "Perhaps it is not such a good idea. I am not sure, if it is worth the trouble. Perhaps I will do it tomorrow. I have a whole month left to do it. It may be better to wait." Or something like that. We are held back by our inhibitions. We have self-doubt, or doubt that we cannot reach this special goal. It can also be a doubt that the work may not pay off.

We all are a bit afraid of the limelight or that others may make fun of us. We are afraid that others may ridicule or criticize us. We will never enjoy great positive changes and success, if we let those anxieties stop us. Become aware, how much better and more beautiful your life could be, if you give all you have to reach your goals and use every opportunity life offers. No matter whether you believe it or can pull it off.

Mistakes are part of success. Without mistakes and poor results we will never find out what the right ways are, and how we can reach positive results. Only when we know exactly how we can reach certain results, and what we must do, can we act more goal-oriented and effective.

Do not be afraid to try something and not get what you want the first or second time. Remember that even the best ball-player misses 70 out of 100 hits. They do not think of themselves as losers; they are confident, have fun, enjoy the game and are counted among the best players in the world, although they hit the ball only 30% of the time.

It is not the amount of the failures, but the quality of the hits, your successful tries, and the quality of your success that determines the quality of your life. Thomas E. Watson, the founder of IBM, answered the question how one could be more successful with the answer: "That's simple, just double the amount of your failures."

Watson said: "When you double your failures, you necessarily also double your work and therefore will also double your positive results." You know already that there are only two ways to fail: Giving up, or not starting at all.

Never Give Up

Imagine if Thomas Edison, who tried 25,000 times to develop the battery, had given up after 24,000 failures. He needed 10,000 failures before he found the light bulb. What if he had stopped at 9,950?

It depends on you, whether you feel like a failure, or whether you see a disappointment as nothing but a stepping-stone in the foundation of your life-success, just keep going. You have really failed, if you give up on the fulfilling of a dream or the reaching of a goal, when you let a failure or an error stop you. Being successful means that you work toward a chosen goal with regulated, measured steps.

Too many people identify themselves with the results they obtain. When they obtain a certain success, but had fifteen failures along the way, they identify and blame themselves for the failures and come to the conclusion that they are losers. Failure is an occasion and is not transferable to a person!

It is quite clear what Edison meant to say: "I am not a failure; I know 25,000 different ways how you cannot make a battery. Now I must succeed, I am running out of ways in which it cannot be done."

If you keep on going and are flexible in your approach, then one of your next tries will be successful and give you the desired result. You will also exhaust the supply of failures.

You can program your actions and perseverance. Twenty-five to thirty-five intelligent experienced repetitions of desired behavior will already lead to a programming in the nervous system. Pretty soon you will no longer be able to behave differently from the way you programmed it in your mind. The more frequently you repeat the desired behavior in your mind and the more often you act like that in reality, the stronger your behavior pattern will be conditioned. It will become an accepted part of your behavior and a natural part of your personality.

When you bolster your programming with many positive feelings, your conditioning goes much faster. Experience in your mind, how you meet and talk to people you do not know, greet them friendly, listen to what they have to say, free from restraints, be kind and friendly. You can condition all kinds of desired behaviors in your mind, (do it at least 25 to 35 times in a row,) so that every reaction, every action and all your future behavior is no longer accidental behavior stemming from circumstances, fear, anxiety, nervousness or insecurity. It is your life and it is important that you take control of it and leave nothing to chance.

You are no doubt familiar with Murphy's Law: everything that can go wrong, will go wrong at the worst time and in the worst possible way.

In situations in which you feel like withdrawing or become afraid, stand up straight, take a deep breath and incorporate your whole body, look forward, or even better a little upward, do not move, and speak in a firm voice while you are facing the solution of the problem in question.

Whenever you must do something difficult, when you hesitate and look for an excuse not to do something, clap your hands and say: "I can do this and I can do it very well." Program in your mind how you will act goal-oriented, self-confident and successful; do what is needed, and do it immediately.

You will come to the conclusion that if you overcome the hesitation, indolence, laziness and all the usual excuses for 12 days, you will have changed your behavior forever. You will no longer understand why you were so hesitant before. This happens because your new behavior has become a part of your personality. Everything you put into practice and do regularly works like a muscle. It improves and gets stronger with regular training; it increases in quality.

There is no true perfection in life. Even if the proverb says: "Practice makes perfect." Practice simply makes things better. Nobody can and will ever be perfect. It is impossible to know and do everything perfect. Whenever you have made a step forward, you will come to the conclusion that you will do it even better and more effective than before.

Exercise 6:

Please, write in your success journal in what areas you hesitate repeatedly or do not act out of indolence or even laziness or fear. Then write down how you want to behave in the future.

Exercise 7:

Now write down all your accomplishments. The things you are proud of, or of which you could be proud. Write down everything, a shot in the goal in your school soccer game, passing a difficult exam or marrying your spouse. Write down everything you can be proud of, no matter how big or small.

Cherish your own special value. It is important, so that you can motivate yourself in situations when you are alone. Write down: "I am a very valuable person, because...." The more you write down, the better.

Now we must take another step toward even greater acceptance, development and personal approval. Now please write down: "I like myself, because...." Here again write down all the things, big or small, why you like yourself. For instance the love you give to your family, because you are a doer, take yourself by the hand and persevere when you set a goal. You like yourself, because you are no longer going to be satisfied with less and will reach for the stars.

Overcome your Inhibitions and Fears.

Nothing can keep us from our most intense dreams and goals, when we learn to overcome our handicaps and fears. Program the behavior your desire in your mind, while you say vigorously and loudly: "I can do that and I will succeed."

With every form of mental programming it is essential that you always keep the final goal in front of your eyes, as if you had already achieved it. This is necessary, so that the brain has the information at its disposal and can bring it to the desired result. In this way all the action and necessary information will be directed at the desired end goal, and at the sensible action to reach this goal. If the mind does not know how and which end goal you want to realize, it cannot make use of the possibilities at its disposal.

When I was a judo trainer, I came to the conclusion that the ability to fall without becoming injured is very important. New comers, who learn in the first week of training not much more than to fall, will quickly lose interest, mostly, because they do not see the importance of those rather boring repetitions.

To let them know how painful a bad fall can be, I have slammed every new comer hard into the mat. I also told the students how dangerous a fall could be, especially when they hit a hard surface like a paved street.

Once a new student recognizes that the ability to fall without pain and danger, and to immediately get up is very important, he is ready to practice the fall exercises diligently.

You must teach the brain in the same way the sense and the necessity for sensible, goal-oriented action and perseverance. At the time, when you are willing to recognize and accept that you are the only person, who can have a lasting influence on your life and future, you have started a completely new paragraph in your life. You now know that:

- You are the only one, who is responsible for what you will do today and tomorrow, and how you will shape your future.

- Nobody else will solve your problems.

- You will only be as healthy and vital as you live.

- Your private and professional relationships will be as good as you give, or as you behave to your fellow humankind.

- You must give the full one hundred percent to every challenge in your life.

- To be successful you must always give a little extra; unsuccessful people refuse to do that.

- If somebody doubts your efforts, you must answer that person with the words: Might makes right."

- You must never be willing to be satisfied with owning, being or achieving less.

Your life will then be filled with contentment, hope, optimism, freedom, independence, unlimited success and great achievements in every area of your life.

Upwards Together

If you are repelling a mountain together with a partner, you must support and help each other; you must learn to help others and let others help you, when you are part of a team and want to reach the top.

Wild geese and wild ducks fly in a V-formation. In this way they can fly from 72 to 93% farther than a single goose or duck would be able to do. The reason is that the goose or duck that flies in front breaks the wind resistance for all the birds that fly in their wake. After some time taking the lead, the lead bird intuitively falls back to the end and the bird closest to the front takes the lead.

This also happens in team play. I am convinced that when people support and help each other they cannot only double the output of someone who is working alone, but that teams players can reach their goals in much faster time. With team-work we cannot just reach the top of the mountain; we can reach for the stars.

But consider the following: you are stranded on an island surrounded by all the wealth and luxury imaginable. You are alone; you cannot visit anybody and nobody will come to see you. What kind of success is that? You will agree with me; that is no success at all. To be successful and completely alone is not possible; it is a contradiction and therefore not possible.

On the hard road of working on a career and a profession, in the fight of financial success and financial freedom and independence, many people lose the realization how important their fellows, colleagues, friends, employees, spouse and partner are. Everything loses its meaning, when:

- There is nobody to share your success.

- There is nobody there to share your laughter.

- There is nobody to cry with you.

- There is nobody to pad you on your shoulder, encourage you, or pick you up when you are down.

- There is nobody, who understands your worries and care.

- There is nobody, who knows your dreams, wishes, and goals, and everything seems senseless.

Too many people lose contact with their surroundings on their way to the top. Once there with material and idealistic achievements, they find themselves alone and realize that this was not the success they wanted. This was too high a price to pay.

Financial Wealth, the Foundation of Freedom

Those, who maintain that money is not important, will lie also in other areas of their life. Somebody, who tells me that seriously, may have the number of my bank account, so that he can deposit the money that he values so little in there. I think money is important. A friend once told me: "I don't think money is important—it is only as important as oxygen."

But seriously; how do you intend to give your child the very best education, how do you intend to pay for good supportive shoes that are not exactly cheap? How are you going to pay a lawyer, if you must overcome problems with the judicial system and don't have the money?

One of our greatest needs, even when we have not given it much thought, is freedom. Only those who are and feel free can really be happy and content. You are only really free, when you have enough money to help and defend yourself, and do not depend on the pity and a handout of others.

When you are financially at ease, you will get older and be healthier than people, who are financially strapped. With more money you can buy healthier food. People, who run short, must feed their families with the groceries they can afford.

Do you have financial freedom? Can you go on vacations, so that you can restore your body and mind? When you enjoy financial freedom you do not have to say when your child asks you: "Mom or Dad, why do the other children have such nice clothes and such a beautiful home?" "Because we cannot afford it!"

Very many people act insincere and deceitful when it comes to financial success and freedom. The more they pretend that financial freedom and success are not important, that they do not care about material goods, the greedier those liars often are. Those people often fight the hardest for an inheritance, trying to increase what they have. They have to convince themselves that money is not important, because they have so little. They rant and rave against luxury cars until they can buy one. They look down on a big luxurious house until they live in one. Beautiful clothes are unnecessary until they can afford them.

Why are they working so hard? Do they work to waste their strength and time in order to fall in bed exhausted? Or would they like to be rewarded for their efforts and get financial compensation, so that they can enjoy a quality of life they have earned?

Everyone works for money, so that he can meet his needs and take care and give his family the security as best he can.

In twelve years NAPS, USA, has interviewed 9,038 divorced people and asked them what the main reasons and causes were of the loss of love and marriage. In 8,014 cases both partners were fully convinced that the constant lack of money was a deciding factor in the break-up. No matter how deeply they loved one-another, the constant shortage of money destroyed their strong feelings over time.

You must reach financial freedom and independence not just for yourself, but also for your family and for those, who are important to you. The more you do for your company, the more successful they will be. The more successful your company, the more secure is your working environment. The more you give to your company, the more your superiors will notice you and the sooner you will be promoted. Everybody will get more in return than he or she gives; this is so in every area of life.

Not just Financial Wealth

In 1923 the eight wealthiest men of that time met in Chicago.

- Charles Swan, president of the largest independent steel company

- Samuel Insat, president of the largest independent energy providing company.

- Howard Hopson, president of the largest gas company

- Richard Widney, president of the largest stockholders association.

- Albert Falk, a successful member of congress.

- Jesy Liebesmore, one of the most successful brokers at Wall Street.

- Erwin Kinger, president of the largest real estate associations.

- Lian Brankle, president of the largest independent mortgage bank.

After 25 years a newspaper investigated the lives of these people:

- Charles Swan was bankrupt and lived the last five years of his life on welfare.

- Samuel Insat was bankrupt and died alone in a foreign country.

- Howard Hopson ended up in jail.

- Richard Widney ended up in jail.

- Albert Falk died in jail a few days before the end of his sentence.

- Jesy Liebesmore committed suicide.

- Erwin Kinger committed suicide.

- Lian Brankle committed suicide.

I told you this story, because all those people knew how to make money. None of them knew how to create a successful life. Money is essential to freedom, but money is not everything. On the road to real great financial success, you must not forget the team that helps you to succeed. Do not forget your hobbies, your dreams and your visions, have fun and enjoy what you are doing.

Exercise 8:

To reach and increase your financial freedom, I ask you to write in your success journal what the possibilities, ideas, skills and talents are that you can use and transpose, so that you can increase your monthly income.

Develop immediately a concrete plan for what you can add, improve and do more effectively to increase your monthly salary.

Decide how much money you need to be financially free, happy and independent. I do not mean a sum with which you can survive, but a realistic amount that you will need to finance your living expenses and the quality of life you want for yourself and your family. This amount should cover everything you need and want for a happy and content life for you and your family.

Determine when you want to receive this monthly income. Develop at the same time your plans and intermediate goals, so that you can receive this income and reach this financial independence.

Build in your mind the pictures that represent your understanding of wealth, success, financial independence, happiness and contentment. Write down what you see.

Whenever you are in doubt and fear that you cannot do this, think about the story of the bee. The American Air Force did a study and found that a bee cannot fly according to mathematical and aerodynamic principles. A bee is too heavy, she does not have the correct form and her wings are too small; she should not be able to fly. The bee flies happily from flower to flower, apparently she did not read the study and nobody told her about her aerodynamic shortcomings.

To provide your belief system with the confirmation that something is possible, and that you can achieve your final goal, you must experience the desired goal in your mind as if you had already reached this goal. You will find that your motivation, your willingness to work, your will and perseverance grow steadily. Use your opportunities, talents and potential and you will earn your success in the true sense of the word.

A Happy Family

We cannot take our spouse for granted, if we want to be and stay happy with him or her. We must not consider it normal that our spouse will absolutely be there in a month, a year or ten years. If we remember that one in every two marriages ends in divorce, we should act with that in mind.

People, who love one another, do not lose those feelings overnight.

In the first days and weeks when we meet our partner, we are euphoric, passionate and full of enthusiasm; we dwell on the thoughts and ideas how we can make this relationship as beautiful and happy as possible. We concentrate on our luck to have found this person, how wonderful he or she is; why we like and love her or him. We feel like calling this person in the middle of the night just to tell him or her: "I am thinking of you."

After some time this person, whom we adored and admired, becomes someone we take for granted and we treat her or him accordingly. Once we stop idealizing our partner, we begin to focus on what we do not like or of what irritates us.

We should take nothing in our relationship for granted. Never stop telling and showing this most important person in your life what you feel and what he or she means to you.

All too often we fully appreciate what we had after we lose it. Save yourself this pain and always be aware how important and valuable this person is at your side; or what your children mean to you.

One of my colleagues wrote on 1,800 slips of paper: "Darling,

I love you, because…" while his wife was on an extended business trip. He spread the 1,800 notes, with a different reason for his love, all through his house. You can imagine what a wonderful reunion awaited his wife, and what a wonderful experience it was for the whole family.

Exercise 9:

Write in your success journal how important your partner is to you, why and how you feel about them. Imagine that your partner were no longer there tomorrow. What would your loss be like? And what this relationship means to you?

Exercise 10:

Now write down why you love this person. What is special, beautiful and favorable about him or her, and think about this often.

Exercise 11:

Now write down how you want to show this special person your feelings. Make a list and carry it out.

Before you come home the next time, experience in your mind the special things you want to do for her or him, live it in your mind. Experience the day you first met and fell in love. Meet him or her, when you come home with those feelings and show how important he or she is to you.

Speak so that your children can understand you.

One of the most important elements for a successful and happy family is the rearing of the children. I want therefore to spend a few words on effective and sensible communication with children. This will at the same time make you aware how the brain works, yours as well as mine. You will recognize the best way to communicate effectively with yourself in your own mind, and with other people.

The human mind can only work optimally in comparisons, in

analogies. It is easier to teach a child a foreign language by giving him a cup and say une tasse in French. The nervous system (with dendrite formation) connects the sound with the object. The cramming and stupid repeating of words leads often to sparse success.

You should tell a story, a fairy tale, or a cohesive story, if you want to explain something to a child. The brain needs logical building blocks and complete information, with a beginning and an end, to function effectively.

You may remind a child: "You will suffer like Aunt Joan. Remember, how she burned herself with the hot water and had to go to the hospital. She was in a lot of pain and still has a scar on her hand."

The child will paint in his mind the picture of the burning with the connection of its negative result and stay away from the stove. Never give a child the simple facts; they should be able to understand, remember and comprehend the situation.

If you have to send your child to the store for blue paint, connect the blue with something else. You may say: "Blue, like mommy's blue car." Your child will not come home with red paint.

The brain does not understand a negative. It is dangerous to say: "Do not do that." The brain will hear: "Do that."

Pretend that you are in the park in front of a beautifully manicured lawn. A sign says: "Do not walk on the grass. Your mind will tell you to go ahead, and you feel like stepping on the grass immediately.

In your mind you see yourself walking in the grass, or feel the need to do so. The brain did not register the word "no." It recognizes the message; walk on the grass. First you see yourself walking on the grass until you think rationally and know that is just what you should not do. It would have been better, if the sign said: "Use the paths please." In that way your thoughts would be send in the right direction.

Warnings: "Do not fall out of the tree," directs a child's mind to an image of falling out of the tree. The images we carry in our mind strive for realization in the real world; the possibility of the child falling out of the tree is greatly increased. A better message would be: "Hold on tight and move carefully in the tree."

A driver, whose car is in a skid, frequently hits a tree or a lamp-post, the only obstacle around. This happens because he concentrates strongly on avoiding just that obstacle. He drives exactly where he does not want to go.

Now please do not think about a little white mouse with a red hat on a green bike. You will find that although I told you not think of the little white mouse on the green bike, that is exactly what you are seeing.

Always give children and other people clear, positive directions what they should do; never tell them what you do not want them to do.

Follow Dr. Leonard Coldwell
on www.drleonardcoldwell.com

HEALTH FOR WINNERS

Successful People are healthier than those, who are not successful.
You cannot enjoy success, no matter how great, if a lack of health does not allow it.

Do you have now and then, or even regularly, a feeling of being washed out, burned, tired, depressed, or frustrated? Do you feel physically weak or listless? Have you lost your imagination and creativity? Do you not sleep well or are you plagued by nightmares? Do you have difficulty concentrating; do you have headaches, back-pain, and intestinal or other problems like so many other people? Those problems may be the result of poor nutrition, incorrect breathing, and lack of exercise or to much work.

Which life situations really bother you? When do those tensions and problems with your health crop up? When do you regularly feel physically taxed, get outbursts of anger? Do you sometimes feel dizzy get the feeling, or are you ready to give up?

Exercise 1:

Normally we do not focus on the negative, but I want to make an exception. Please make a list and write down in your success journal, of the medical problems, complaints, aches, emotional and nervous problems (hysterical outbreaks, anger) you notice. Which problems do you notice repeatedly?

Exercise 2:
List the situations that seem to be connected with these symptoms.

The reason I ask you to focus on those weaknesses and negative developments in your health is to make you aware of the regular and irregular medical limitations, cramps, little aches and pains, feelings of dizziness and unbalance or even sexual problems you may have. You may have become used to them or hardly even noticed them. You can only deal successfully with a problem (in serious situations of course under the guidance of your physician), when you have pinpointed the problem area. We must be big enough to admit that something is wrong, either in our life or in our body.

We must realize that being healthy is normal and that we all to often accept small aches and pains. We do not notice that our vitality, health and energy diminish day by day.

Let go of the past and learn to forgive.
I observed in my stress clinic in Canada that most people, who fall apart or have a nervous breakdown as a result of stress, suffer from added burdens of the past. They are full of anger, feelings of guilt, hatred and revenge. These feelings lead to tension and cramps, obstruct the regular flow of blood, including the optimal administration of cells. Those negative feelings produce stress hormones; these hormones cannot be broken down, instead they poison the body or lead to panic attacks.

Nobody is important enough for you to lose your temper; impair your health and risk your future. The people, who affect you emotionally and cause you the most problems, are often those that enjoy causing you difficulties.

Don't get angry and think about revenge, when somebody annoys you. Do you feel continuously tired and feel that you lost all energy? You will lose a lot of energy and will not have the physical and emotional energy to be happy and prepare for your future. Those negative feelings rob you from a lot of energy.

Therefore, no matter what somebody has done to you, I beg you; forgive them. To do this also symbolically and give your brain the corresponding information, use this simple trick: Write a letter to anyone who has hurt you. Write those people what they have done to you, how you feel and how angry it still makes you.

End the letter with the words: But, I do forgive you, because I will not allow myself any feelings of anger, hatred and revenge. I refuse to waste my emotional energy and strength or even my time to become ill because of you. You take others people's energy, because you cannot get your own life straight and try to ruin other people's life. I forgive you and let go of you and my past. I will no longer think about you, and should I run into you somewhere, I will think of you in a completely neutral way, because you do not deserve that I ruin my health, life, time, present and future over you.

Then take the letter and tear it in a hundred little pieces and burn them. Imagine, while you are burning the letter that the fire destroys your feeling of the past, and that you are deciding to have nothing but neutral feelings where this person is concerned.

People, who cannot forgive, destroys the bridge they may have to cross some day!

Improve your physical health.
Energy, health, strength and vitality are the foundation for success, happiness and contentment. You give yourself physical energy, when you move in a stronger, straighter, more self assured and confident way. Your brain will continuously receive the message and inducement to provide the needed hormones. You will be supported regularly with helpful neuro-chemical processes and your own natural energy. Vigorous exercises improve our blood flow and therefore you will also give more energy.

Your breathing is the most deciding factor in your health and well being. Oxygen brings energy to the cells in the human body, and only cells well supplied with oxygen are healthy cells. You know your body is only as healthy as its cells.

Your lymph system is essential to your immune system. We have four times as much lymph fluid as blood in our body. Every cell is surrounded by lymph fluid; it takes care of the detoxification of the cells. Lymph fluid is not pumped through the body as our blood is, but through the pressure on cells as a result of exercise. Aerobic exercises and very deep breathing stimulate this process. People, who breathe shallowly and incorrectly are often sick and get colds or flu's, because they have a weak immune system.

A simple breathing exercise can do much for our immune system, by pressing the lymph fluid through our body. Inhale 4 seconds through your nose, hold the air for 16 seconds and slowly exhale for 8 seconds through your mouth. Repeat this ten times.

By doing this exercise three times each day and taking a twenty minute walk in the fresh air, you have done more to support and improve your immune system than 70% of the people.

As in other areas it is important that you do those exercises regularly. Only when you do this frequently will you achieve the desired result. It is not extravagant to do those exercises every day as described. It would be best if you did these exercises every day at the same time.

Be energy conscience in your nutrition

Another important health, strength and vitality factor is your nutrition. Did you ever feel tired and exhausted after a heavy Christmas dinner with appetizer, main course and dessert? Do you feel like going to sleep after a heavy meal? I think that we all would have to say yes.

The reason is, that although the body receives many nutritional elements, the composition of the menu was wrong or contained difficult to digest food. Hard to digest food robs us of more energy than it contributes.

We can avoid these stuffed and tired stages that may stay with us most of the day, by being better informed and watch what we eat.

The body needs alkaline juices to digest carbohydrates (potatoes, rice, pasta and bread) and it needs acids to break down the proteins. (meat, fish and fowl)

When the acid and alkaline juices come together, they will neutralize each other, so that the necessary digestion cannot take place. The food remains in the digestive system. The result is flatulence, headaches, stomach and intestinal pain, partially as a result of toxins that stay in the digestive track.) You will feel bad; the body tries to fight the toxins and needs a large amount of energy to tackle the food in the digestive track.

You can avoid this and still eat enough to satisfy your appetite. You can do something to reduce weight at the same time. You have to follow, in the future, some basic rules to eat and enjoy healthy and energy giving nutrients.

Advice for energy rich nutrition

Start the morning with fruit and stay away from coffee till 12 o'clock. Eat your fruit only on an empty stomach and never combine it with other nutrients, because fruit starts to ferment immediately. Fruit combined with other food causes immediate decay, and you will achieve just the opposite from the energy rich digestion you want.

By eating fruit on an empty stomach, you will break your nightly fast and supply your body energy, vitamins and minerals. You can eat as much fruit as you want. At this point you are in the stage of detoxification and elimination.

By sticking to this rule, you will already, after 12 days, experience a drastic positive change in your health and energy supply.

It is important that your food is rich in liquids, such as vegetables and fruit. Try to eat fowl and fish when you hunger for meat.

Abide by the 70/30 rule.

According to the 70/30 rule you must eat more than twice food rich in fluids (vegetables and salads) than you eat dry food, (such as potatoes, rice, pasta, meat, fish or fowl.) Your body will have an easier time to digest the food and turn it into energy. You will feel better and healthier.

Always eat at least twice (70%) as much vegetables and salad than you eat fish or fowl. Eat the vegetables and meat at the same meal-not before or after.

This, of course, also holds true for supper. If you have to eat meat, do it in the evening. At this time you do not need as much energy for your work and you can use it for digestion. You must add one more rule: no more food in the last three hours before you go to bed. You will be surprised how much easier it will be to influence your weight in a positive way.

Pay more attention to your health and body. Without a healthy body, enough energy, vitality and strength, you cannot generate the enthusiasm and quality of life that you need on your path of success. Start eating healthy today. Start to breathe deeper all day, into your abdomen and up under your shoulders, not just shallowly in your upper chest, so that you may choke.

Drink only soda free water and fresh pressed fruit juices. Cut out milk and dairy products. Although you have been told since childhood how important milk is, there is plenty of proof that this is not the case. Milk is often responsible for allergies and ailments of the digestive organs.

We are frequently told that milk supplies the necessary calcium. This is absurd, because the body needs calcium to digest the milk.

To recognize the part milk plays try the following: Pour some milk in a cup of tea to which you have added some lemon; the milk will curdle and clump. You see what the acid does to the milk. Now think what will happen, when you pour 8 oz. of milk in the far more acid environment of your stomach. The milk will curdle immediately and your intestinal tract will be covered with a sticky mass. The milk of cows is meant for little calves, so that they can grow big and strong; it is not meant for human consumption.

Mother's milk has a completely different composition and has nothing to do with cow's milk.

Most milk products carry, moreover, anti-biotic products and chemicals that have been added, so that the animals will produce more milk and grow more meat.

Many people are allergic to antibiotics or become resistant against this life preserving medicine through the use of too much milk. Give the use of milk and milk products some serious thought.

Stages of Regeneration—
the foundation for a long energy filled life

It is not the every day burden that hurts or destroys us; we have been trained to cope with it. Too much stress and a lack of regeneration are responsible for the damage.

Compare your body with a battery, when it is used wisely and continually recharged it will last a very long time. This same battery will start having problems, when it is run completely empty or when it is not regularly charged.

It is not the ordinary stress, but too much stress, or the abuse of our body that damages our health and diminishes our energy. If we do not take enough time for regeneration, we will suffer from failing health and medical problems.

It is important to learn and train to do breathing and relaxation techniques, but I have observed in my work that doing things you enjoy is more effective than spending an hour meditating on a couch.

I, personally, prefer sensible and optimal meditation by spending an hour by myself and going for a walk, or contemplating nature outdoors on a bench, so that my thoughts can wander. It helps me to organize my day, make decisions, relax and regenerate. It is in my view the best way to unwind. Make it a habit to go regularly to a place you enjoy and spend some time there.

There are, of course, exceptions, when somebody is already sick.

In that case you need therapy. Your relaxation and regeneration must be adjusted to your therapy.

To destroy the stress hormones in a sensible way you can spend 10 minutes walking stairs. We can destroy stress hormones in the quickest way with physical exertion. They must absolutely be destroyed because they originate for a fight and flight response in the brain, which was originally needed for our survival. If the stress hormones are not wasted through physical activity, they can cause emotional or physical malfunction.

I believed originally in therapy through hypnosis, but I am now quite opposed to its use. Hypnosis leads in many cases to dependence, instability or schizophrenia (Split personality).

By observing the successful changes in many patients, I have come to the conclusion that a healthy walk, a hobby you enjoy, or doing something else that satisfies you, gives more strength and restoration. Do only those things you enjoy and can do responsibly. It is especially important that you do things you want to do. The need for meditation usually disappears. The body does need physical exercise, but in moderation. The best way to relax and regenerate is sleep.

If we force relaxation for hyperactive people or for those, who are seriously stressed, hypnosis offers frequently just the opposite. It often leads to a complete breakdown of nerves and body, not to relaxation and regeneration. It often leads to suppression of emotions, denial of conflicts and problems and as a result to serious illness. We can compare the patient with a boiling kettle of water on which we close the valve—it leads to an explosion.

There is only one way to enjoy the quality of life you desire, feel happy, successful and healthy; listen to your inner voice and live according to your own wishes, needs, dreams and visions. Develop your own talents, skills and potential. Do what is right for you and stick to your moral and ethical believes. Watch your health and vitality and take time for regeneration. You will not only reach the top; you will reach for the stars.

Individual People need Individual Solutions.

You cannot have lasting success with all-inclusive concepts. Every person has a different potential, different needs, wishes and possibilities. The reasons for failure or illness are completely different for every individual. The only possibility to be and stay healthy is to find and go your own individual way.

Therefore, I cannot give you all-inclusive prescriptions. I would not want to put you all in the same straight jacket with rigid techniques and solutions. I want to help you think on each page of this book, so that you can find your own goals, conflicts, problems and the solutions to solve them. I would like to give you directions, tools, training and possibilities, so that you can develop your own individual success-concept.

I want to offer you directions, so that you can develop your own individual directions to attain your own personal achievements and success. Only when you see the connection and develop your own way, will you experience and reach those repeatedly. In this way you will never become a victim of destiny, of other people and the world around you.

My most important concern is that nobody will manipulate you, so that you will never become a victim of a person or a group, of those who want to use and abuse you. I am completely convinced that if there are more people, who are strong, more confident, capable and successful, the better the future will be for us all.

Only weak people follow sects and say yes and amen to what others say. Only weak people are easily manipulated and gladly have others make all the decisions, set goals and take responsibility for them.

I therefore want to use all my strength and opportunities to help as many people as possible to become independent and resistant to manipulation. I want to contribute and help them to think and act for themselves, so that we all will build a better world.

MOTIVATION: THE FUEL FOR SUCCESS

Nobody can solve your problems. You are the only person who can have a lasting influence on your life. You are the only person that can use your potential wisely. Only you can use the possibilities to develop your life with enthusiasm and passion. Use that true potential and turn your life into the masterpiece it is meant to be.

I would like to give you information and training techniques to motivate you for action and perseverance. But every form of motivation can be nothing than a way of helping you to find your own lasting motivation; this is what I intend to do.

Motivation does not last, just as a shower, a bath, or eating and drinking do not last. Just as you have to eat every day, so you must inspire your mind every day. You must motivate yourself over and over again. To motivate yourself you must keep your eyes on your goals. Visualize the wonderful success you already have obtained. This is not only important for you, but for your team and others, who are close to you.

You will be strongly motivated, when you think about the wonderful things you can do for others. People are often willing to do

THE ONLY ANSWER TO SUCCESS

things for others, (their children, spouse or parents) and for themselves.

Motivation means that you show what you have to offer. You can do this best, when you constantly keep yourself aware and make use of the qualities, skills and talents you possess.

The most effective motivation is the motivation of growth. When people feel that they will grow, get better, and develop through their actions and achievements! or that they will improve the quality of life for their team or family, their motivation will be at its best. People will stay on a course, when they observe progress, can grow and develop.

Find validation for your success, so that you can believe in a successful future. You will stabilize this believe system repeatedly, when you concentrate on your success, even when it is small. Success whets your appetite for more, and you will find that not only the quantity, but also the quality increases.

Positive thinking does not change things, but it is better than the negative thinking that keeps you from doing anything altogether. Negative thinking, cramps your style, holds you back and ages you before your time. Think positive; become positive, because positive people look for a reason to believe in success.

This is how you Motivate Yourself

During an interview on TV I was asked: "Mr. Coldwell what really is motivation?" After a moment of thought, I drew a square on the table. I asked the interviewer: "How many squares do you see?" He answered: "Sixteen." I told him that the total square should also be counted; that would make seventeen; and if you looked for other squares, added them together there were numerous squares. If you kept looking and adding all the squares you would find thirty squares.

I want to show with this drawing and this demonstration what motivation really means. I asked the interviewer: "How many squares did I add?" "Fourteen," He responded.

"No, that is wrong!" I said, "I have not added any squares after

I finished my original drawing. I have only displayed how many squares there were all along."

That is motivation: Showing and getting what is already there, to become aware of it and use it. Motivation does not mean to give or get something that is not available. Motivation points at potential, talents, opportunities and possibilities and expedites their effect and sensible use,

We may believe, if we have sufficient information to think that something is true or not. Belief has nothing to do with reality. For this reason motivation and the willingness to do something do not depend on how others evaluate a situation or opportunity, or how it can be judged. It only depends on how you see a situation related to your possibilities, skills and the reaching of a certain goal.

You can create or bolster any belief-system, if you find enough validation to support it. In that way you give yourself enough motivation to act and persevere. Motivation gives you the desire to achieve. Motivation makes it possible to take the training and gain the knowledge to acquire experience. Motivation supports your strength, your personality and inner resolve to persevere, when the going gets tough.

When you decide to treat others friendly and positive, you will decide at the same time how you want to be treated by the people around you.

Regular negative input into our mind leads to de-motivation and frustration. You will get negative input into your bio-computer (brain), if you start the morning listening to news about death, war, poverty, hunger, unemployment and a bear market. Of course this leads to feelings of frustration, depression, anger and hate, or at the least to helplessness. That is de-motivation.

Start every day positive. Welcome the new day, because it is your day. Concentrate on opportunities and possibilities, not on adversity and obstacles. Concentrate only on solutions and action, no longer on difficulties and problems. Your brain will only do what you tell it. Your input decides your behavior and your feelings and therefore your quality of life.

See a problem only as a challenge, as an opportunity to grow. Mental attitude is a real foundation for quality of life and success. Use every opportunity to work with real enthusiasm on the solution of a task. Once you begin to see difficult situations, setbacks and aggravation as opportunities to show what you can do, you will grow from overcoming every task; you will develop and grow stronger, more self-confident and successful.

You get orange juice, if you squeeze an orange, and lemonade from a lemon. You can show who you really are, when life hits you hard. You can give what you have put in your mind with self-suggestion in talks with yourself, and also with what you have absorbed from your environment.

From now on give yourself only positive information. Program: "I can do it. "Now is the time. "This is my day. "I am born to be successful. "I will never again be satisfied with less than I can accomplish." Program yourself continuously for flexible action and perseverance. No matter what happens; believe in yourself!

It has been proven that inspiring and motivating information you absorb enthusiastically is responsible for the production of several neuron-transmissions; they improve your energy, creativity, and the ability to perform.

Many people suffer from what I call: "The poor me syndrome." If a person concentrates, in every situation, at the negative and the bad; if he or she always looks at the terrible things that may happen, than you can expect that his or her pessimism and half-hearted actions will lead to a lack of purpose and failure.

There are people who camouflage their pessimism with the word realism. They consider themselves realists, but are really nothing but pessimists. On every desk in all my offices stands a reminder: "We are all realists! We expect a miracle every day!"

It is not what happens in your life, but how you react to what happens that makes the difference.

It is always good to hope

Hope is our greatest motivation. I learned early that very ill patients, whose physicians gave up hope, would lose all motivation to fight thanks to the negative doubt, questions and statements of others. Those patients had nothing more to lose, because the great "medicine men" were ready to throw in the towel. The verdict of death was pronounced. They, moreover, objected when somebody else tried something new. Usually they said: "Do not give the patient false hope, it can only lead to disappointment."

There is no false hope. Hope is always good; it encourages people to do something. Giving up is bad. Without hope people will always give up. When there is no hope for the future, people will act in the past.

When you have nothing more to lose, only hope will inspire you to try something new. To give yourself a new opportunity and bring about a change; you have to have hope. Even if it does not work, it at least encouraged someone to try something new. People with hope treat their body with positive neuro-chemical and bioelectric stimulants. People with hope could often live through their time of trial with a better quality of life. They could set goals and experience some happy moments.

There is no disappointing hope; hope is always positive. When we expect that something good is going to happen, it leads to excitement and fills us with energy. We lose vitality and energy, when we have a feeling of loss and fear. Our energy diminishes, when we fear negative results, even when we are only a little afraid.

Motivation is not only important in trying times, but also when we feel good. You can be very creative especially when you feel really good and flexible; you will perform well. Use those stages for exceptional success. Just at those times you should increase your motivation with motivating tapes, enjoyable music or something else that is uplifting. In this way you will hold on longer to new attitudes, and this way of living will become your permanent behavior.

You will perform and learn quicker, better and more effectively when you feel good. You know that from every day experience. When you start with three great deals in the morning or do something else that goes well, everything else will go well during the rest of the day. The reason everything goes so well is that this day becomes magical, because you started it positive and well motivated.

When I advised vice master Marc Mazur in his golf training some time ago, he would say after a few poor hits: "I knew that I would miss."

After that I started with a new conditioning. I told him that he would never succeed, if he had the feeling that he would not hit the ball on the right trajectory, or that the ball would not go far enough. He should take a step back and get off his negative track. He had to concentrate so long on the wished for result and play this result in his mind, until he could see and feel it. Then he had to transfer this feeling from his mind into his body and hit the ball with the conviction of hitting it.

Everything that happens is the result of programming. If the programming is different from the experience you want, you will proceed in the true sense of the word with this negative and emotional attitude. Reprogram yourself, before you act again.

Everybody would like to feel like a real winner at least once in their life. Many people agree that the fear of failure or a fear of laboring in vain has hurt them or even destroyed their life. The fear of failure can hit us in any area of our life, long before we do something. Fear of what others might think or say may lead to a real fear of failure, including the ability to act.

But give it some thought: every scientific breakthrough, every successful enterprise or every successful marriage is fraud with many mistakes. Every mistake or a result we were not looking for enlarges our experience, and that is something positive. After all, a mistake usually does not last very long. It is only a moment in the total reality of life, not an experience, but an unpleasant happening, a step on the ladder in the path to the top. It is your reaction to a mistake that determines how helpful this mistake can be to you.

Today is a new day, and this is the moment to prepare for success. This attitude is motivation.

Edward E. Jones, a psychologist at Princeton University writes: "Our experiences do not only have an influence on the reality we see but also on the reality itself. "We can observe this in medical students; most of them suffer from symptoms of the illnesses they are studying at the time."

Dr. Harvey Cushings, one of our most outstanding neurosurgeons, is a classic example. He said one time at the beginning of his career that he was convinced he would die of a brain tumor. He did die of a brain tumor; his expectations became a reality.

To succeed in life we must act and persevere. When we connect confident motivating images with effective professional skills, our career situation will improve immediately. We often must open just that first door, so that other doors will open by themselves. Negative thinking is the grip that keeps us down. Once we have overcome this negative force, we need rather little expenditure to move forward.

We can justly say that motivation gets us going, but our conditioning and learned behavior will help us to reach our goal. Make motivation a part of your natural behavior; it will bring you quicker to your goal and you will have far more fun getting there.

Dr. Forest Tennant, a leading pharmaceutical specialist took blood samples from five volunteers in one of my four-hour motivation seminars. After the seminar was over he took another blood sample of the same participants. He concluded that the endorphin- and cortisone levels were increased more than 300%. He writes: "There is a bio-chemical reason that people feel better after listening to motivational CD's or by following such seminars. Listening to opportunities for success stimulates us emotionally; this releases chemicals in the blood stream, which helps the body to function considerably better."

Dr. Tennant believes that regular doses of motivation lead to better health, greater happiness and above all to more successful behavior. He says: "When it comes to good health I believe that motivational tapes and seminars fit in the same category as aerobic exercises, a good night rest and three nutritious meals a day."

Messages of hope and success, given in an enthusiastic way, lead to anticipation. This causes the brain to produce endorphins, dopamine, serotonin, nor epinephrine and other neuron-transmitters.

Negative Thinking causes Injury

Young people feel better, when they listen to Rock Music, because the brain releases dopamine, nor epinephrine, endorphins and stimulates other neuron-transmitters.

Loud rock music, especially hard rock, disorganizes the central nervous system, so that it leads the listeners to negative, self-destructive behavior. According to pianist Steffen Nilson, "Heavy metal or Acid-Rock music disturbs brain functions and the nerve paths. This sound leads to disharmony in our organisms. It causes anti-social thoughts and leads to corresponding behavior. The rapture this music creates obstructs productive brain activity and produces neuron-transmitters that can lead to dumb and idiotic behavior."

Dr. Louis B. Candy, a well known Psychiatrist writes the following: "There is growing and unequivocal proof that listening to hard rock leads to poor moral, antisocial and self-destructive behavior... I would like to emphasize that the rock music of the sixties has nothing to do with the racket that is what we now call hard rock or rap music."

Some good News

In a recent edition of *Psychology Today* we read that scientists of the University of California found that if babies or little children listened to harmonious music they developed faster emotionally, indicating a stronger brain development.

Dr. Frances Rauscher, a biologist, tested the skills of three year olds and found that children, who listen for three months to harmonious music, could do puzzles and other skills demanding logical thinking in an optimal fashion. She considers music the first intelligent language for newborn babies.

Dr. Klara Kokas from the conservatory in Hungary found that regular music lessons improved the learning ability from pupils usually by at least 30 percent.

Many therapists agree that music is nature's tranquilizer. Many people feel the same, when they want to relax they turn on their favorite music—for many this is music that is calm and harmonious.

You can improve your emotional state by listening regularly to motivational tapes, especially when your energy level is low. This motivation is a solution for physical improvement, the increase of energy and good health.

Going for a twenty-minute walk in the evening or doing some physical exercises burns a surplus of calories and lowers our appetite. The brain increases the production of endorphins, dopamine, nor-epinephrine and other neuron-transmitters to keep the body in balance. Please remember, we must cultivate not only our minds, but also our bodies. Those, who do not take the time for physical activities will later need that time to take care of their illnesses.

Positive Thinking

As mentioned before, to introduce new desired changes, positive thinking should be followed by positive action. Positive thinking alone will do little for you, although it is still better than negative thinking. Positive thinking makes it possible to use the possibilities and experiences we have in an effective way. It is dangerous though to believe that positive thinking alone can change our life for the better. This presumption leads to unrealistic expectations and keeps people from positive action. Unrealistic expectations are seedlings for depression.

Thinking has a direct influence on performance; therefore our thinking must be a foundation for positive action. Negative expressions such as: I have never been able to do that before, this is a hopeless situation, or, we can do nothing against it, create negative energy in the brain that interferes with your creativity. It makes us see problems bigger than they are.

Positive thinking alone, without the necessary skills, knowledge and sensible behavior has lead many people to do reckless things in life leading to threatening and dangerous situations.

We need inspiration, perseverance, security and enthusiasm. We also need the right and sound training to deal effectively with all the work in our lives.

You do not make electricity, when you throw a light switch. The power is already there. You let the necessary electricity that is already there do what you want it to do by throwing the switch. Motivation is the light switch to our energy source.

When you throw the switch of positive thinking and acting, you let the necessary knowledge you have already stored, and the experience you have gained do their positive work, or you make yourself do the necessary work. Positive thinking won't work, if a student does not study to know the material. But the "I can do it" attitude of positive thinking, can, together with positive action, improve performance greatly. Whether you are looking for a new job, are trying to get a promotion or hope to make a sale; positive thinking will help you.

Many people are unemployed, because they believe that the right job for them is not there; someone else told them so. Or they believe that they just won't be so lucky to find a job. This attitude will, of course, get you what you do not want. You know it; this type of behavior is often described as pessimistic intend. It is accepting the worst, in the hope of being pleasantly surprised.

When unemployed people suddenly get a job, it is often because they have changed their attitude from negative to positive. When the focus changes mentally, people undergo an adjustment from the outside as well as from the inside and are therefore open to new leadership. Their life focus, their mental pictures and enthusiasm, combined with the application of their personal qualities, make these people suddenly useful in the labor market.

Dr. Albert Schweitzer said once: "Only those among us, who will be really happy, are those who have found a way to help and serve their fellow men." Positive action creates a positive attitude, and a positive attitude creates outstanding performance.

When people, despite disastrous circumstances, achieve suddenly unusual success, it is because they have changed their personal attitude and with that have improved the quality of their actions and performance, not because of changed circumstances.

Actions are always followed by feelings. If you do not like to do something that you really must do, start by putting some enthusiasm into it; you will find that you start to enjoy it and have fun doing it.

A study at Harvard University showed that 85% of professional success is a result of personal attitude and only 15% depends on skill and knowledge. Mental attitude is for 85% responsible for obtaining and keeping a good job.

The Florida magazine Trend recently carried an article stating that a four-year-old child laughs on average about four hundred times a day; adults laugh only about fifteen to sixteen times a day. We must learn to laugh again. Laughing is good for business, releases stress, is good for the immune system and increases creativity. Of course I am not talking about trivial jokes, but about a sense of humor, so that you can laugh about the little things.

A study at the University of Michigan phrases it this way: "Good humor helps a person to develop greater creativity, emotional stability, positive realism and self confidence. We can show medically that laughing releases endorphins, which fill us with energy, increasing in our mind as well as in our body the ability to perform; it also alleviates pain."

Dr. John Maxwell states: "Someone, who can laugh about life and about himself, will be less plagued by stress. If you have a good sense of humor, you will climb the ladder of success faster than others and enjoy it more. Humor improves your ability to communicate with others, who also know how to laugh. It encourages team spirit and the productivity will rise." Humor improves our ability to persuade, humor helps us relax; it is good for our health and creates miracles for our attitude.

Point to Remember

Remember that positive thinking and enthusiasm alone do not work. When you inspire and motivate a fool you have nothing but an enthusiastic and motivated fool. Positive action is the foundation for success.

Keep working on the development of the requirements and qualifications for success; build a strong and stable foundation on which you can build for your life and future. You can build a high structure, if the foundation is strong enough, usually three parts of the concrete foundation of a house is below ground. Could it be that you are not yet aware that you already have all the requirements?

Remember the example of the computer. You can only expect correct accounting, if you put in a good program to do your calculations. You cannot get the benefits of calculations, if you put in a game. By putting bad stuff in your bio-computer, bad stuff will come out; put good things in your bio-computer and you will get a good return. If you bear in mind that you carry in you the ability to turn the input into an output that lies considerable higher, than you will understand that only positive thought and images can lead to outstanding positive experiences.

It is important that you motivate yourself daily, because life itself wears your motivation down. Motivational training is potentiality training.

If you make motivational training part of your behavior pattern, you will be able to overcome your deepest lows.

Be never critical of a person's behavior in your dealings with them, just their accomplishments. Say for instance to your child: "You did not do this job too well; you can do much better. "I expect more of you than I do of others, because you are my child and I know you can do better." In this way you praised the child while you criticized the performance. Only that will lead to optimal results.

Always Look for the Good in Life

I point out the good, pleasant and beautiful things in life, when I try to help depressed and frustrated people. I ask them to put down the things they enjoy about their job, their spouse or partner, their children or about the town in which they live. Then I demand that they repeat those loud, with enthusiasm standing upright, if possible in front of a mirror. You can see the results immediately.

The more you carry on, complain and whine, the more problems you will have to complain about. The constant complainer destroys all hope and every relation with his or her spouse and children. People, who always complain, whine and moan, have seldom many friends, because everyone avoids them. The result: They are lonely, bitter and alone.

If somebody asks you whether you enjoy your work, you will become aware what you like and enjoy and you will tell him or her in an enthusiastic way. Try to speak in an enthusiastic way about your company, your colleagues and fellow workers.

I have seen it over and over again with the people, who work for me, when they stop complaining and enjoy the beautiful things in life more, they will soon experience great changes in their career and enjoy greater professional success. By watching your language, words and statements, you give yourself a positive attitude and thereby better opportunities for complete success. The languages we use have a suggestive influence on others and ourselves. When you talk about your skills, profession, family, friends or children, you do it usually with enthusiasm, passion and conviction. This behavior influences our development strongly. If you on the other hand foster negative words and thoughts, it will have a lasting influence on your attitude.

By saying something good about other people you include yourself. When you start to recognize good things in other people, you will soon find the good in yourself. When you have nothing good to say about other people, it would be better to say nothing at all.

No matter what others tell you, there is enough room on the summit of success, but there is not enough room if you want to be idle or rest on your laurels. You must keep on working, if you want to stay on the top. It is not important where you are coming from, but what counts is where you are going.

The Characteristics of Success

"What are in your opinion the features that characterize very successful people, and what are the qualities an ideal employee should have to be seen as perfect?" I always ask these questions in my seminars and from managers in charge of large companies. I will summarize the data I collected.

Friendly, even-tempered, honest, ambitious, confident, caring, reliable, pleasant, considerate, self assured, steadfast and convincing, helpful, courageous, creative, decisive, dependable, disciplined, educated, effective, encouraging, energetic, enthusiastic, fair, positive, family oriented, flexible, focused, forgiving, generous, goal oriented, a good listener, grateful, a hard worker, health conscious, sincere, hopeful, witty, pride with humility, intelligent, informed, loyal, motivated, orderly, willingness to work and learn, objective, optimistic, explicit, attentive, well organized, patient, persistent, a positive attitude, punctual, rich in ideas, responsible, sensible, straightforward, keeps on learning, decent, sympathetic, a good teacher as well as a good pupil, a team player, frugal with his endurance, someone with visions, wise, industrious and passionate.

They described these characteristics for exceptional successful people. Usually we consider these character traits as something personal, we can acquire those traits and we can teach them to our children.

The good news is that we all poses those qualities needed for success, perhaps not for hundred percent, but in a large measure. It is now your job to recognize these qualities, to use and develop them.

COMPANIONS ALONG
THE WAY

You are not alone on the road to success. Be aware that other people are also looking forward to happiness and fulfillment. Do not look at those people as competition, but rather as companions. Make contact with those who walk the same path. It is like a journey, if you sit by yourself the trip seems to last a long time. When you sit with someone on a plane you usually end up talking. When you are going to the same place, you end up talking about it. Perhaps you exchange information. Conversation about shared goals will always motivate and bring people together.

Successful Communication
The key to effective communication is to know and use the technique of rhetoric and verbal exchange. Once you have mastered this information, you must start using and expanding it immediately, so that it agrees with your personality. When you are not natural, it disturbs your listener and others; this destroys the possibility of effective communication.

Real communication comes from within; it stems from conviction, honesty, openness and friendliness. There is no technique that can improve on it. Nothing is better than the ability to speak openly and friendly from the heart with optimism and the right attitude.

If you want people to really understand what you are going to say, you must make a short and clear statement that you have some important directions. Your listeners can prepare themselves mentally for this message. They will listen more attentive. Then make your statements clearly, or give your instructions. Then summarize the important points one more time. To avoid misunderstandings, let a listener repeat what you said in his or her own words.

Be yourself. Show them that you are human and have feelings too, but do not burden the others with complaints, self-pity, or with a show of problems and suffering. Be honest, do not lie, give the facts and let them know how you really feel, and how you must act under the circumstances.

Everyone is basically good, endowed with all the talents and possibilities to make something successful out of their life. Therefore you should not build your character or behavior following the suggestions of some trainer or perhaps questionable advisor. Something that changes your personality or does not correspond with your true image, will not work for you. It may lead to confusion, dissatisfaction and a feeling of not being true. This will hurt your self-image and leads often to serious consequences.

Do not pretend to be happy and successful. You must show yourself to others as you really are. Keep improving yourself, take classes, follow seminars, but fit what you learn always to your own personality and your own psychological abilities.

People in your surrounding will notice every rigid concept and all fake behavior; they will reject it with scorn and rebuke. And remember above all: The best approach and the best philosophy will not work, if you don't function.

Whenever you work on a project, you must be willing to do everything that is needed to get results. You must even be willing to go the extra mile that is necessary to gain success. You must always be willing to give 110%. You must always be willing to get up one more time, when life puts you down. You must persevere; keep on going, no matter how strong the wind is in your face. It is very important that you live and act according to your wishes, dreams, needs, talents and skills. The people around you will perceive and be convinced by your determination. They will trust you, because when somebody works with such determination will foster confidence. Such behavior works contagious. Nobody can resist an inspired example. Those, who fall back from the path of success, often did not earn to reach the summit of success with you.

If you bear the following suggestions in your communication with others in mind, you will not suffer from lack of companions on your way to the top:

- Talk with many people and encourage others in your surroundings, urge them to action. Fill your life and surroundings with optimism. There is nothing more beautiful than an optimistic, encouraging and friendly greeting.

- Smile as much as you can. You need 72 muscles to look angry and only 14 to smile.

- Use people's name as much as possible. The sweetest music is the sound of your name.

- Be friendly and helpful. Be a friend, a real team player, and you will enjoy the deepest happiness; you will find love and friendship.

- Be personal and speak from the heart. Talk and act as if everything you do and say gave you much joy.

- Be interested in people. Try to get to know as many people as possible. Build yourself a social network of friends and acquaintances that will catch you when things get rough; then you will not be alone. You will need somebody sometime to cheer you up, when you do not see a way out. It can safe your life, literally.

- Be generous with praise and careful with criticism.

- Always consider the feelings of others. Remember every issue has three sides: yours, theirs and the right side.

- Be willing to give, to offer your services. Frequently what goes around comes around.

- Use some humor and add to that the gift of patience, a pinch of humility, but also a little pride. You will always be rewarded.

It is not easy to make apologies or admit a mistake. Nevertheless try always to accept advice, in that way you can avoid errors. Learn from the mistakes you recognize. Suppress temperamental outbreaks and look for a silver lining. Accept honest criticism—take care it pays off.

Enthusiasm is Contagious

Give your thoughts free range. Practice patience. Smile often. Enjoy those special moments in life. Keep making new friends and remember your old ones. Let them know how important they are and what they mean to you. Don't be annoyed; forgive the person, who perhaps unknowingly offended you.

Be hopeful. Grow up. Do something crazy now and then. Remind yourself over and over of the lucky and beautiful things in life. Try to see the miracles during the day that can also happen to you. Stop worrying, and do not doubt yourself. Become generous and take time to relax.

Trust people, so that you are not afraid to rely on them. Pick the flowers and share them with others. Keep your promises, and always look for rainbows. Look for the stars and enjoy the beauty around you.

Work diligently and honestly, and give it all you have. Try to understand life and the people around you; above all know yourself. Take time for people, who are important to you. Take time for yourself, and try something new. Be open, laugh often and spread joy.

Let other people be close to you, even if you must take the risk of getting hurt. Try to become calmer and more even-tempered. It is okay to be self-indulgent and weak now and then. Celebrate life and believe in yourself. Get up early and see the sun rise sometime. Listen to the rain. Cry when you need to. Trust life, the miracle of nature. Support a friend. Develop new ideas. Learn; make mistakes. Search for the unknown. Hug a child, in short: embrace life!

Let your enthusiasm run free; all those possibilities are there. You will find that others will feel drawn to you and your enthusiasm will be catching. The germ of enthusiasm is very infectious and there are no antidotes. Who wants to find one?

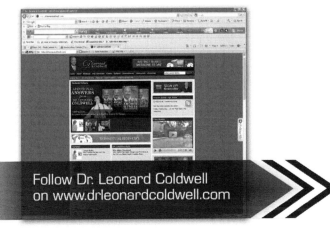

Follow Dr. Leonard Coldwell
on www.drleonardcoldwell.com

STORIES WRITTEN BY LIFE ITSELF

How your start is not important.

A study of 300 leaders, including Franklin D. Roosevelt, Winston Churchill, Helen Keller, Mahatma Gandhi, Mother Theresa, Dr. Albert Schweitzer, Martin Luther King jr. shows that 25% of them were born either with a serious physical handicap, or that 50% of them were abused or grew up in dyer poverty.

Neil Rudenstein's father was a prison guard; his mother worked part time as a waitress. Dr. Neil Rudenstein, the former president of Harvard University said: "I have learned that there is a direct connection between performance and reward; your start is immaterial, what matters most is how you arrive."

You can probably not change the world. But if you change your own world and yourself, you have made a big step in giving the world a new face.

Two Great Men

Charley Wedemeyer (Wide-eyed), the former coach from the Los Gatos High School football team suffered from Lou Gehrig's Disease. He could no longer speak or utter a sound. The only parts

307

of his body that he could still use were his eyes and his mouth. He was probably the only coach in the world, who could not speak. His wife read his lips and spoke for him and could mediate his powerful messages of hope, love and his spirit of perseverance. For his team Charley Wide-eyed was a successful and beloved coach. Charley did not let his illness stop him from fulfilling his wishes and achieving success. He passed away June 05, 2010 after battling the disease for more than 30 years. He was 64.

John Foppe is one of the most successful motivational speakers today. He speaks regularly to thousands of people. He travels alone to his seminars, dresses and cooks for himself, drives his car and lives a completely independent life- even though he was born without arms. He learned to walk although his equilibrium is unstable and could not use his arms for balance. He learned to do everything other people do with their hands with his feet, even though he could not brace himself. He says: "I have decided not to allow my physical condition to become a problem."

The real winners in life accept a problem and look for a solution. They are absolutely convinced that overcoming this problem will lead to great reward. If a problem surfaces they look for an immediate solution.

When you ask John Foppe, how he managed to become so successful despite his handicap; he answers: "I stopped feeling sorry for myself when my mother showed me a picture in the paper of a little girl who was born without both arms and legs." I knew then that there are people with worse handicaps than I. From then on I concentrated on what I have and can do, not on what I do not have and cannot do."

The message Foppes wants to give during his seminars: "No matter how many people tell you that you cannot do something; it does not make a difference. You can do everything you really decide to do." Do not look at a mountain of your combined problems; take one step at the time, so that you will gradually reach success.

A Very Special Lady

Dr. Jan Mc Barron is one of only six women who specialize in Bariatrics, a medical specialty that focuses on weight gain. She was at one time overweight, an alcoholic and she smoked like a chimney. One day she decided that she wanted no longer to live like that. She started to study medicine while she worked full time as a nurse. She finished her study successfully; she stopped smoking, quit drinking, and she now eats healthy and is fit and slim.

If you ask her how she accomplished this, she answers: "One day I had a good look at my life and I was suddenly no longer willing to accept my life as it was. I realized it did not reflect the person I was; I decided to accept the responsibility and take control of my behavior. I changed the mental picture of myself according to my wishes and achieved everything I programmed mentally."

Who's Child are You

Years ago, when people scorned children born out of wedlock, little Ben Hooper was born so, as if he were to blame for not knowing his father. People avoided him. It affected Ben badly; his self-esteem, self-confidence and performance were bottom low.

One day he heard about a priest gave very positive sermons. He gave people reason to hope, have confidence act positively. Ben decided to go to church.

He was so fascinated and enthusiastic about the speech that he forgot to leave early, as he usually did to avoid people.

When leaving in the crowd he felt a hand on his shoulder and heard the words: "tell me, whose child are you?" Everybody was quiet for a moment, because that was the question they all wanted answered, who is the father of this child?

Little Ben turned confused around and looked in the friendly eyes of the priest. The priest said: "OH, I know who you are, the similarity can't be unmistaken. You are a child of God and should live like one."

Little Ben says that is the day he had the courage to decide to go into politics. Ben Hooper became the governor of Tennessee. When the image he carried of himself was changed, so changed his goals and his visions; he developed the willingness to stand up for his goals.

Linda has learning problems

Linda had problems at birth and the doctors diagnosed that she had learning problems. Linda was delightful and became the mascot of the school she entered. To avoid that Linda should adjust every year to new class mates they let her move up every year, although she had learned little and could not pass the tests. Everyone said: "Why bother her, if she cannot learn, let us not make her life difficult.'

One day her mother took her to New York to visit her older sister. Her sister took her to an organization for the learning handicapped. The leader tested the now eighteen-year-old Linda. She took the test and the results were amazing. It turned out that Linda could pass some easy tests.

They gave her something easy to do; she mastered the work very well. They gave her work that was a little more challenging, and then more challenging again. Within twelve months Linda could take phone messages, and three years later she could do balance sheets. Pretty soon she became a full-fledged secretary.

When the image Linda had of herself changed, so did her performance. "Linda can't learn" changed to "Linda can learn."

Closed Doors

The great Houdini, the greatest escape artist, was supposed to escape from an English prison. The man, who could escape from every confinement, was told he would not be able to escape from the cells of this newly built prison. Therefore they had invited Houdini to show that it was really impossible.

Houdini had to accept to keep his reputation. The press and many people were gathered for the occasion. He explained to the wardens that he just wanted to be put in the cell in his normal every day clothes. They put him in the cell, closed the door and left him inside.

Houdini took a piece of steel wire, very thin, flexible, but solid from his waistband and started to work on the lock. After an hour of fruitless trying he was desperate, the sweat was pouring down his face. He was almost ready to give up, and when he gave the door a desperate kick the door flew open. In the excitement they had forgotten to turn the lock.

Houdini had not been able to open the door, because he was convinced that the door was locked. How many doors do we expect to be locked and because we think they are locked we do not even try to open them.

We often do not know what we have within

The singer in a bar became ill and the pianist did not think he could sing. But the customers wanted to listen to a vocalist and the bar owner said to the pianist: "You either sing or you are fired." That night Nat King Cole sang for the first time and moved the listeners to tears. That night a great singer was born.

Sometimes we first must do something, before we acknowledge that we can do it.

Come and take a walk with me

Peter Stoodweek had run many marathons in his life. He never came in first, but finished every one. The amazing thing is that Peter was born without feet. He runs on prostheses, often with bleeding stumps. Never has Peter allowed his physical handicap to stand in his way and curb the quality of his life.

Things, circumstances and other people can temporarily stop you —but you are the only one, who can paralyze yourself.

There sticks a winner in you

Vince Lombardi, the most successful football coach of all time once said to a football player in the dressing room: "You are a disaster, your training is over for today, change out of your uniform and go home."

When Lombardi came back into the dressing room after an hour, the player was still there. He sat with his head in his hands, obviously completely disillusioned. Lombardi was his hero and he wanted nothing better than play excellent football.

Lombardi, who treated his players with great humanity sat down beside the man and said: "What you did out there today was terrible, you were the worst player today. But I know there sticks a great player in you and I will be with you, until you have succeeded to get him out of there and let him play."

When Lombardi accepted Sonny Jorgenson, one of the most well-known querulous players in football, he told the press: "I present you the best football player in the world; he is the greatest team-player, Sonny Jorgensen, a member of our team." It changed the image Jorgensen had of himself and his behavior and he turned into the player Lombardi had predicted.

Treat people as if they were already "perfect'—your expectations will determine the outcome.

Follow Dr. Leonard Coldwell
on www.drleonardcoldwell.com

I WELCOME YOU ON THE SUCCESSFUL SIDE OF LIFE

O n one of many airplane flights I learned from a four-year-old girl what can make us special.

The little girl went, in what seemed to be her first flight, in front of me in the plane. The doors of the jumbo-jet to the pilot cabinet were open. She first looked to the right into the long hallway, the many seats and people; then she turned around, looked with fascination at all the instrument of the flight board, put her hands on her knees and said loudly: "Wow!"

That is the attitude we should have in life. We must stop worrying about problems, difficulties and conflicts. We must recognize again what the little girl showed us; we should be completely ecstatic about life and all the wonderful opportunities.

We must concentrate only on the limitless possibilities and opportunities of our life and shout full of enthusiasm and positive expectations and unlimited optimism and gratitude for so many challenges and opportunities: "Wow!"

Hello Champion!

I am saying goodbye for now but I am sure I will see you at one of my live seminars and winner workshops. And one thing is sure I will see you—In the Winners Circle—the Home of a Champion! Please be so kind and write me about your experiences and successes or if you have any questions write to instinctbasedmedicine@gmail.com and watch www.drleonardcoldwell.com for news, free videos, radio shows and information about a fulfilled life and happiness.

And please sign up for my Newsletter and live feeds so that I am able to provide you with the latest and important News and Information as soon as they are available. If you want to attend my Seminars for free go to www.globalinformationnetwork.com use referral code: Coldwell and sign up as a member and you have access to my live seminars on that website and also to attend my live GIN seminars in person free of charge.

"Be yourself—This is the only guarantee for success!"™
Your coach, friend and fellow Champion
Dr. C. (Dr. Leonard Coldwell)

Skeptics will laugh

Dear reader, when you start to put the ideas and thoughts that have become clear to you while working this book, into reality, when you solidify your dream by realizing it; many people may laugh and make fun of you. When this happens you must keep this in mind:

Skeptics laughed when a man said: "I will invent a light bulb." But all people applauded when Thomas Edison Lighted up a city by throwing a switch.

Skeptics laughed when Robert Fulton told them that he would build a boat that would be powered by steam. But everyone applauded when he directed his steamboat through the Hudson River.

The skeptics laughed when a man told them: " I can send a voice through a cable." But the world applauded when Alexander Graham Bell made his first famous telephone call that united the world.

The skeptics laughed when Wilbur and Orville Wright told them that they could build a machine in which they could fly. But the world applauded when the Kitty Hawk ascended into the wild blue yonder.

Skeptics may laugh when you are trying to realize your dreams. You may have to cope with foolish remarks, ironic laughter, ignorance and disbelieve. But don't let it stop you from living and using your true potential to the fullest. Turn your life into the masterpiece it is meant to be.

I will be waiting at the finish line with like-minded, successful people: we will applaud and welcome you on the successful side of life. The victorious meet each other over and over again. Where? On the successful side of life!

Get Coldwellized!

IBMS® Seminars, workshops and self help education for Personal Empowerment, Health, Happiness and Success. Millions of lives have been touched! Lives have been saved! Millionaires have been created. Experience the greatest single force for positive life change in the world—Dr. Leonard Coldwell, or as the world knows him as Dr. C.

Over 2.3 million people in live seminars, 17 million via teleclasses and internet workshops experienced Dr. C live, and over 54 million people have watched his videos, listened to his radio shows as well as radio and TV appearances and CDs.

In 2009 The Dr. Coldwell Report Radio show was the most downloaded new radio show of its kind!

Dr. Coldwell has fascinated and empowered so many millions of people with his 19 bestselling books and his Instinct Based Medicine system—CDs, DVDs and live workshops that it is impossible by now to even track the lives Dr. C has touched.

The IBMS™ audio self help, self healing and stress reduction and success conditioning system is the most endorsed and most sold system in the world. Dr. Leonard Coldwell is the most endorsed holistic doctor of our time—nearly every major expert in the field of health—works with, is friends with or endorses Dr. Coldwell and —like nothing before, consumer Advocate and NY Times # 1 Best Selling Author Kevin Trudeau says:

"Dr. Leonard Coldwell—Dr. C—cannot be measured against anybody else! He is in a league of his own!"

Dr. Rima E Laibow, the president of the largest Health Freedom Organization "http://www.healthfreedomusa.org/" www.healthfreedomusa.org calls Dr Coldwell: A Genius who is producing unmatched results.

And Prof. Dr Peter Lange, the head of the European version of the NIH calls Dr Coldwell: " The David Copperfield of his field."

Here are some of the typical comments from one of Dr C's Seminars:

(Denver 2010) First of all I want to say that I love Dr C and all that he is doing for Mankind. He is a very colorful speaker! I was so impressed with what I heard about his life and how he struggled at such a young age. I like when the speaker let's us in on some of their personal life. Because we are all intrigued by you guys and it helps us to put the pieces together as to what made you the person you are today. I have seen Dr. C a couple of times now and talked to the "newbies" about him and what they thought, and they were blown away by his presentation. Everyone was feeling great, just like a Champion!!

GIN is everything that they say they are. You can talk to these guys and learn from them. I know that if I ask a question and get an answer from Dr C that it is TRUTH. I like the fact that I can get the "inside" information. It gives me a sense of security and I can sleep better at night (because let's face it, there's a lot of scary stuff going down these days). It's good to know the Good Guys!

We live in a world full of phoney, mean spirited and dishonest people and it is so refreshing to attend one of these events. You find yourself surrounded by like-minded souls. I make new friends at each and every event (as did Dr. C encourage us to exchange emails, etc.). See You At The Top, GIN Council!

Margie
(Margaret Duffy)

Hello Dr. C! This is GIN member Frank Modesto and I had an absolutely spectacular time at your event! You're not going to believe this but I actually missed my cousins wedding to be there! It was definitely worth it. I didn't get to meet and greet you (and hug you) until the very end because you were in such high demand. You are a wonderful human being who has done more for the world than every single conventional doctor combined. I am going to try my best to make all of your seminars, or as many as possible. I am a level 1 GIN member who will upgrading to level 2 very shortly. June 19th 2010 is a day I will never forget. You made me feel like a champion! When I make my first million I will approach you (as well as Kevin) and thank from the bottom of my heart. I was not able to purchase your products that day because I did not have the money, but when I do I will get all of your books and cd's. Thank you, God bless, and can't wait to see you again!

Sincerely Yours,
Frank M

WOW! Talk about feeling like a CHAMPION! Dr. C is the most awesome speaker ever! He was amazing—absolutely phenomenal…I mean really —he was funny, interesting, and oh so spot on with everything he said.

I will never forget the wonderful day he created for me and I will never miss another event he is coming to. By the way, he's pretty easy on the eyes, too!!

Thank You Dr. C!

Dr. C,

Thank you so much for coming out of retirement . If you had not done so I would not have had the opportunity to spend time in NJ this past Saturday learning from you. It was a Fantastic experience and I am looking forward to seeing you again in Munich, Charlotte and Columbus. I'm already registered and on the lookout for more opportunities in the future to learn from you. My belief level went way up at the end of the day (and it is still there). We listened to Your Wish Is Your Command on the drive home and it just reinforced what you taught us.

I already sent a note to GIN Events but wanted to express my thanks to you personally.

Have a Fantastic Day!
Sharyn H

Dr. C's June 19th event at the Hilton/Newark NJ was an absolute SMASH! This has got to be one of his best performances since the last Kickoff event in Cancun. Dr. C has pulled me up and I think everyone else who attended to a whole new level. Three thumbs up and a big Toe for Dr. C (Dr. Champion) I can hardly wait to attend his next seminar.

He truly is a Champion!
—Royd Garcia
Nutley NJ

Hello,
The day was June 19th. The stage was set for Dr.C, and I was waiting anxiously to have my first experience at a global information network summit.

Not too long, Dr. C stepped on the stage and immediately, the room was lit up. It was amazing to see how contagious a happy mood could be— Thank you Dr. C

Everyone became alert; the ruminant of the morning sleep were cleared off the eyes, the adrenalin was abundantly released, the energy in the room overflows and I knew right away that I belong to a winning group—Thank you Dr. C

My gosh! The day went so fast but the message lasts forever. "I'm a champion," "I'm Somebody,", "Of course, I can," "I'm a winner." —are now embedded in my both nervous, cognitive and circulatory systems—Thank you Dr. C

My million is already on the way; I'm getting ready to receive it with my happy feelings and my "go out and get it attitude;" after all, Dr. C has made two things clear to me:

1. That "the quality of communication with my life and my environment would determine the quality of my life", so keeping a positive attitude, letting the past be past and feeling good at all time are the bedrocks of my success—Thank you Dr. C

2. That "we are all born to be millionaires, we just have to go out and get it," therefore, acting upon our instinct (Instinct Base Medicine System) and believe that if I can make $1, then I can make $2 and by putting a little bit more effort I'll eventually increase the dollars and within short time, I can make my first millions—Thank you Dr. C

I would like to say that this seminar was a total delight to attend. Dr. C. makes a powerful speaker and really gets to the heart of his message. I Love attending his seminars.

Dr. C. truly takes the time to speak to each and every one of us during breaks and after the seminar is finished.

Dr. C. touches my heart like no other, well with the exception of Kevin....lol. He went out of his way to discuss with me ways to heal my broken back and reduce my pain naturally. I am a champion and I will make my millions because I believe in Me!!! Thanks Dr. C.

With Much Love to you and all of G.I.N.
Teresa N

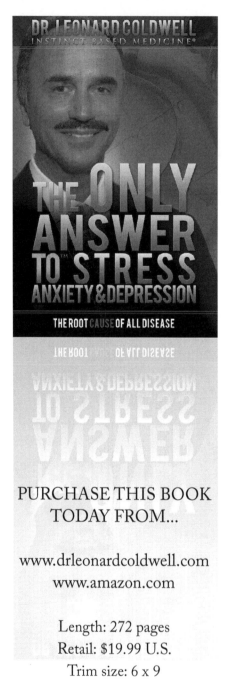

PURCHASE THIS BOOK TODAY FROM...

www.drleonardcoldwell.com

www.amazon.com

Length: 272 pages

Retail: $19.99 U.S.

Trim size: 6 x 9

www.21stcenturypress.com

All illness comes from lack of energy, and the greatest energy drainer is mental and emotional stress, which I believe to be the root cause of all illness. Stress is one of the major elements that can erode energy to such a large and permanent extent that the immune system loses all possibility of functioning at an optimum level. *The Only Answer to Stress, Anxiety and Depression* is a book of hope, and Dr. Coldwell wants the reader to understand that there is always hope, no matter how bad Their health situation is right now. The journey to ultimate health can begin today!

In his lifetime, Dr. Leonard Coldwell has:

- seen over 35,000 patients

- had a 92.3% success rate with cancer and other illnesses

- had over 2.2 million seminar attendees that wrote to him, sending in their comments and life stories.

"I have seen many patients that Dr. Coldwell cured from cancer and other diseases like Multiple Sclerosis and Lupus and Parkinson's and even muscular dystrophy and many more, and I am still in constant awe of Dr. Coldwell's talent and results."

—Dr. Thomas Hohn MD NMD Licensed IBMS Therapist™